A war was ragi

A war between guardian and man. His entire adult life had belonged to the guardian. Tonight, the man was fighting for life. He wanted these few minutes with Sedona. Wanted to relax and enjoy the peace she seemed to bring into every room she entered. Into every space she occupied—even outdoors.

He matched his pace to her more sedate one, listening to the waves. "So why are you telling me this?" he asked. *She'd said she liked him.*

"Honestly?" She kicked at the sand, sending it shooting in front of them. "I'm not sure."

"Guess."

"I like you." She repeated what she'd said earlier, but with a deeper note in her voice.

"And that's a problem?"

"It is if it gets in the way of my professional judgment."

"So don't let it."

"I'm trying not to. But..."

Another surge of emotion hit him at that *but* and he waited for it to dissipate before saying, "What are you afraid of?"

She shrugged again. Her shoulders, accentuated by the thin cotton straps of her dress, seemed so feminine to him. So...in need of protection. "I guess I'm afraid you'll like me, too."

He bent his head. The move wasn't premeditated. He touched his lips to Sedona's and just...felt.

Dear Reader,

Life, in all its messiness, is a miracle. We have to be willing to stay on the ride, sometimes just holding on, when the road gets bumpy, in order to avail ourselves of the perfect moments.

And sometimes we need a safe place in which to take a time out.

The Lemonade Stand, *Where Secrets Are Safe,* is one of those places. The Stand is going to be around for a long time. You'll have many opportunities to stay here with me. And to experience some perfect moments while you do—you know the kind, where you escape into a story, experience a whole other world, maybe find some meaningful tidbits that somehow apply to your life, all without leaving your chair.

I hope you'll also see the perfection in the messiness. The value in the struggle. Families are tough. Maybe more than anyone else, we trust our family members to have our backs. To love us no matter what. And with that trust comes the capacity for great pain—if our trust is broken. If family members aren't who we think they are. We can misunderstand each other. And we understand, too. We know that family is heart. And heart is the one thing we can't ever completely walk away from.

So we run to a place like the Lemonade Stand, *Where Secrets Are Safe* and pain can be healed. Come on in. Get comfortable. And be prepared to find family and love!

I'm a spokesperson for the National Domestic Violence Hotline (www.thehotline.org. 1-800-799-7233), and I also work with an organization called Chrysalis (www.noabuse.org). Chrysalis has several shelters and they offer certified counseling for victims *and* for abusers, as well as legal aid and financial aid for those starting over.

I love to hear from readers. You can reach me at www.TaraTaylorQuinn.com.

Tara Taylor Quinn

P.S. Watch for my new women's fiction title, *The Friendship Pact,* coming from MIRA as an ebook this month.

TARA TAYLOR QUINN

Once a Family

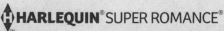

Recycling programs
for this product may
not exist in your area.

ISBN-13: 978-0-373-60854-6

ONCE A FAMILY

Printed in U.S.A.

HARLEQUIN®
www.Harlequin.com

ABOUT THE AUTHOR

With sixty-six original novels, published in more than twenty languages, Tara Taylor Quinn is also a *USA TODAY* bestselling author. She is a winner of the 2008 National Reader's Choice Award, four-time finalist for the RWA RITA® Award, a finalist for the Reviewer's Choice Award, the Bookseller's Best Award, the Holt Medallion and appears regularly on Amazon bestsellers lists. Tara Taylor Quinn is a past president of the Romance Writers of America and served for eight years on its Board of Directors. She is in demand as a public speaker and has appeared on television and radio shows across the country, including CBS *Sunday Morning*. Tara is a spokesperson for the National Domestic Violence Hotline, and she and her husband, Tim, sponsor an annual inline skating race in Phoenix to benefit the fight against domestic violence. When she's not at home in Arizona with Tim and their canine owners, Jerry Lee and Taylor Marie, or fulfilling speaking engagements, Tara spends her time traveling and inline skating.

Books by Tara Taylor Quinn

HARLEQUIN SUPERROMANCE

1309—THE PROMISE OF CHRISTMAS
1350—A CHILD'S WISH
1381—MERRY CHRISTMAS, BABIES
1428—SARA'S SON
1446—THE BABY GAMBLE
1465—THE VALENTINE GIFT
      "Valentine's Daughters"
1500—TRUSTING RYAN
1527—THE HOLIDAY VISITOR
1550—SOPHIE'S SECRET*
1584—A DAUGHTER'S TRUST
1656—THE FIRST WIFE‡
1726—FULL CONTACT*
1793—A SON'S TALE§
1811—A DAUGHTER'S STORY§
1829—THE TRUTH ABOUT
      COMFORT COVE§
1853—IT'S NEVER TOO LATE*
1877—SECOND TIME'S THE CHARM*
1889—THE MOMENT OF TRUTH*
1906—WIFE BY DESIGN+

SINGLE TITLE

SHELTERED IN HIS ARMS*

EVERLASTING LOVE

THE NIGHT WE MET

MIRA BOOKS

WHERE THE ROAD ENDS
STREET SMART
HIDDEN
IN PLAIN SIGHT
BEHIND CLOSED DOORS
AT CLOSE RANGE
THE SECOND LIE‡
THE THIRD SECRET‡
THE FOURTH VICTIM‡

*Shelter Valley Stories
‡Chapman Files
§It Happened in Comfort Cove
+Where Secrets Are Safe

Other titles by this author available in ebook format.

For Rachel Marie Stoddard.
Let your spirit soar, sweetie.
Always listen to your heart. Be happy.

CHAPTER ONE

"How old are you, Talia?"

The tanned teenager, straight from the mold of California-model gorgeousness, looked Sedona Campbell in the eye. "Fifteen."

Sedona believed her. "You told Lila McDaniels that you're ninctccn."

The five-foot-five-inch blonde, with a perfect figure, perfect makeup and skin, wearing all black, looked about twenty-five.

And, at fifteen, on a Tuesday in the second week of April, she should have been in school.

"I didn't want her to call the police. I'm not pressing charges."

"You're a juvenile. You claim you've been hit. The staff here have to notify the police. It's the law."

"Not if they think I'm nineteen and I say I don't want the cops called. I checked. They don't have to call for adults who don't want the police notified, especially if they're not getting medical attention."

The law didn't read quite like that. But the girl wasn't wrong, either.

"They'd have to prove they had no way of knowing that you're underage."

The girl said nothing.

"They know you lied about your identity."

Talia Malone, aka the juvenile sitting in front of her, slid down into the plastic chair on one side of the table in the small but private card room Sedona used as a makeshift office during her volunteer hours at The Lemonade Stand. Her gaze darted from the floor toward the edge of the table, and back again.

Sedona was not a psychiatrist, but as an attorney specializing in family law, specifically in representing women going through divorce or in need of protection orders, she was well versed in reading people.

"I'm here to help, Talia. You can trust me." And here in the middle of a workday because Lila McDaniels, managing director of The Lemonade Stand—a one-of-a-kind, privately funded women's shelter on the California coast—had phoned asking that she drop everything to tend to this situation.

Talia curled a strand of hair around her little finger. With a covert glance, she met Sedona's gaze, but only for a second.

Sitting next to the troubled girl at the table, Sedona touched her hand. "I believe you were hurt," she said, her tone compassionate, but professional, too. By the time she got to the victims, they needed help, not drama. "But I can't do anything for you, no one here can, if you aren't honest with us."

Talia's eyes were blue. Intensely gray-blue. They were trained on Sedona now.

And that emotional crack that opened sometimes,

the one she'd never quite managed to close within her professional armor—an armor that hid a natural instinct to nurture—made itself felt.

"Why wouldn't you agree to see the nurse?" Sedona tried another way in.

Talia shrugged.

"Do you have any injuries that need to be tended to?" Lila had already told her that Talia had refused to be examined by Lynn Duncan, the on-site nurse practitioner, saying she didn't have anything wrong with her.

If Talia saw the health professional, and Lynn determined that there were injuries due to domestic abuse, California law would require them to report to the police or risk a fine at the very least. Lynn could risk her license.

And still, only about ten percent of California's health professionals actually reported. For various reasons. Talia's lower lip pouted. "There's nothing right now."

"Have you had injuries in the recent past?"

She nodded but didn't elaborate.

And Sedona's mind riffled through possibilities like cards on the old Rolodex her father used to keep on his desk when she was a kid.

Was this young woman on the run?

From one or both of her parents?

Another family member?

Or a nonrelative? A teacher at school?

Was the abuse sexual in nature?

Hiding information was classic behavior for someone being abused. With her near-perfect features, Talia didn't look as if she'd taken any blows to the face. But that was more typical than not, too. A lot of abusers kept their blows to parts of the body that could be covered. Hidden.

"Has anyone touched you…sexually?" An officer would ask more bluntly. And with Talia's age, if they didn't find her family, the police were going to be called in. That was a given.

"No." Talia met her gaze fully on that one.

Satisfied that the teenager was telling the truth, Sedona asked, "How long ago was the abuse?"

Another shrug was her only response.

"A week? Two weeks? A year?"

"A month. Maybe. And then last week."

Okay. So… "What brought you here today?"

According to Lila, Talia had called from a public phone that morning and been picked up by a staff member not far from a nearby bus stop. "I was talking to…someone…who told me about this place and this morning I had a chance to get on a bus without anyone knowing."

"On a bus from where?"

"Where I live."

"Where do you live?"

The girl frowned. "I thought this was a safe place. Where people who had to hide wouldn't be found."

"It is," Sedona assured her. "But the people here have to know who you are, they have to know the particulars of your situation, or they can't help you. This isn't a runaway haven, Talia. It's a shelter for victims of domestic violence."

The girl's chin was nearly on her chest, but she looked up at Sedona. "I know." The words were soft. And not the least belligerent or defensive.

And nothing like the tone one might expect from someone as fashionably perfect and seemingly confident as Talia's appearance implied.

"Are you a victim of domestic violence?" If not, Sedona would still see to it that the girl got help. Just not at The Lemonade Stand.

"Yes."

The answer was unequivocal. Which satisfied Sedona's first concern. Between her, Lila and Sara Havens, one of the shelter's full-time counselors, chances were they'd get the rest of the information they needed to be able to help their mystery child.

To be most effective, to represent the girl's best interests and to see that all of her rights were properly respected, Sedona needed answers before the police were called.

"Then we'll help you, but we have to know who hurt you, Talia. We have to know where you live and what you're running from. We have to know your real name."

"I don't want you to tell the police."

"Why not?"

Talia looked at the floor again, where her sandaled feet sported perfectly manicured toes. "Because."

"That's not good enough. Are you afraid that if we

go to the police whoever's abusing you is going to know where you are? Because you don't have to worry about that. I promise you. The police are our friends here. They will protect your location as vigorously as we do."

"What happens to me if I don't answer your questions? What if I don't tell you who I am?"

"We still call the police. You're a juvenile on the run. We can't let you just leave here on your own."

"Maybe I lied about my age."

"Did you?"

Talia gave her a hard look. A determined one. And then her entire demeanor changed. Her chin dropped and she shook her head. "But I need a little time to think," she said. "If you call the police they'll take me away, won't they?"

"It depends," she said. "Child protective services could be called. Someone would be assigned to you. Once everyone figures out what's going on and what's in your best interest, decisions will be made."

"And what about you? Do you have anything to do with this?"

Sedona was careful about the cases she took. Because, based on her clients' emotional states, she had to be able and willing to stay with them for the long haul. Her assistance was needed when a woman's deepest trust had been abused. In a big way. Her clients were victims. Injured. Vulnerable. She had to be able to go the distance....

"I'm willing to represent you, free of charge," she

said, already aware that Talia, while well dressed and expensively groomed, had less than a hundred dollars on her person. "Whatever happens, I'll be by your side, making certain that, legally, you will get the best care."

"What are my chances of getting to stay here?"

"It's a possibility, depending on the facts." She wasn't telling what those were. Or giving any hint. The troubled teen was in survival mode and clearly not above lying to save herself if she knew the right things to say. Lila had asked Talia if she had a cell phone. The question was common practice at The Lemonade Stand after one resident's abuser found her through a downloadable tracking app he'd placed on her phone.

In response to her question, Talia had produced an old flip phone that was out of battery charge and couldn't be turned on. The phone was so old Lila didn't even have a charger that would fit.

"They said you're a lawyer." Talia's gaze was solemn—and searching.

"That's right."

"And you deal with this kind of thing all the time."

"I do."

"Will the people here get in trouble if they let me stay just one night? Until I figure out what to do?"

There were rules. And there were circumstances.

"I might be able to get you one night. But only because it's late in the day and we know that the chances of getting you to social services are slim. We could determine that it's better for you to stay here than to spend the night in jail, which is where, as a runaway, you could end up."

Because Talia didn't display any overt signs of abuse. No broken bones. No bruises or scars—at least of a physical nature.

"But you won't be free to leave," she added.

"I don't want to leave." Talia sat up. "I just want to make certain that my… That no one can make me leave here."

The girl's desperation to stay at the shelter—clearly not a cool hangout for kids her age—helped convince Sedona to fight for her.

"I'll see what I can do," she said. "But only with your understanding that if by tomorrow morning you haven't told me who you are and what this is about, I will have you turned over to the police."

Talia didn't flinch. "I understand."

And for now, that was that.

CHAPTER TWO

WHOEVER SAID WINE grape growing was easy had obviously never cane-pruned twenty acres of pinot vines. The pruning had to be done in its own time, not by a calendar man had planned, during the dormant season, when the dead leaves had fallen and just as buds were beginning to grow. In the winter. Or early spring. Depending on the vines. Sometimes it had to happen in April, too.

And it had to be done by hand. With clippers. One vine at a time.

For some vintners this meant having someone on staff, maybe a farm or winery manager, who would keep close watch and disperse employees out to the arduous but artful task, as needed.

For Tanner Malone, it meant that even though his little sister had a day off school on Tuesday for teacher in-service meetings, he had to be out in the groves all day—leaving her to get into whatever trouble she could manage with too much time on her hands and the house all to herself.

He hired a couple of seasonal helpers during harvest, but the rest of the work he did himself to save money for Tatum's college expenses.

Letting himself in the back door of their sizable but very old farmhouse, as the early April sun was setting, Tanner prepared himself for make-up, tight jeans and blonde hair styled to perfection. There'd be attitude for sure.

But maybe there'd be some dinner on the table. Even boxed macaroni and cheese would be welcome to his empty stomach.

"Tatum?" he called as, walking through the spotless untouched kitchen, he headed into the equally undisturbed living room.

His sister was good about picking up after herself, but the couch pillows were just as he'd tossed them that morning on his way out the door. He knew because one had fallen sideways and it still lay there, cock-eyed.

With a hand on the banister leading upstairs, he leaned over to see the landing at the top and called, "Sis?"

Could it be that she was in her room studying? Getting ready for the intensive college entrance exams she had coming up the following fall? Tanner and Tatum's brother, Thomas, had spent a good six months in preparation for his SATs, resulting in a full scholarship to an Ivy League school back east.

And he hadn't come back to California since he left. That was ten years ago. Tatum had been five. Talia sixteen. And Tanner? The big brother who'd managed somehow to keep his family together after their mother, Tammy, had finally done them a favor and skipped out on them, had been a mere twenty-three.

Was he only thirty-three now? He'd felt forty ten years ago.

But then he'd been the unofficial guardian and sole supporter of his younger siblings for a couple of years by then.

Thankfully there'd been enough money left from his father's life insurance policy to buy this farm with an ancient house that still needed a lot of work, but enough land to grow grapes that partially supplied a couple of California's premier wineries.

He was a moderate vintner himself now, too. Which was another reason why getting the pruning done was so important. He had a shipment of recoopered oak barrels arriving in a couple of days and had to prepare the framework upon which they were going to sit.

Tatum wasn't answering his calls.

Which wasn't all that unusual these days.

But she wasn't on her phone, either. He hadn't heard that sweet laugh of hers. Or the irritated tone she took on when someone said or did something that she deemed stupid.

Del Harcourt…

If the asshole was here…

Taking the steps two at a time, Tanner was upstairs, bursting through his sister's bedroom door before he'd finished the thought.

He stopped short. Tatum's bed was made. Her desk neat. The books he'd brought her, study guides for the big test, lay neatly stacked in front of her computer screen.

The room had one purple wall while the others were painted off white, just as his sister had wanted. The quilted bedspread covering her queen-size bed was bedecked with butterflies. The furniture was old, but she'd had her pick of anything she wanted in the barn filled with who knew how many decades of discarded antiques they'd inherited when he bought the place.

One of the jobs on Tatum's list for the summer, other than preparing for her October test, was to look up the pieces in the barn on the internet, catalog what they had and see if they could make some money on them. Which meant he'd have to get an entire barn's worth of furniture unstacked so she could begin going through it....

"Tatum?" He couldn't hold the panic at bay any longer. Tatum's bedroom, like the rest of the house, was empty.

In one stride he was at her closet, hand on the antique glass doorknob, pulling with such force the knob came off in his hand. It had been loose for a while.

Another jerk on the door, with his fingers through the hole left by the fallen knob, and the small, wood-floored space where Tatum's relatively meager but expensive wardrobe hung came into view.

He'd been fearing emptiness. Empty hangers at least. Instead, his sister's clothes hung in order, just as they'd been the last time he'd seen them. Shirts with shirts. Pants with pants. And dresses on the far right.

What happened to the days when she was a little sprite too busy exploring anything she could get into to pick her clothes up off the floor? Too busy even to put them in the laundry hamper he'd placed right in the middle of her floor to make it easy for her?

Spinning, he took in the rest of the room. Opened some drawers to satisfy him that they weren't empty, and then moved on to the bathroom he shared with her.

The drawers, split three to one in her favor, were neatly filled, and the bathroom with its pedestal sink and claw-footed iron tub looked just as it had that morning. Tatum's wire rack hanging from the shower head was still filled with her salon-purchased shampoo, conditioners and lotion-dispensing razor.

Back downstairs, he checked every room. The little library, the formal dining room he used as an office, the mudroom that doubled as a laundry room. The huge kitchen. The only thing missing, other than his recalcitrant fifteen-year-old sister, seemed to be the tie-dyed hippie bag she called a purse.

Tatum wasn't old enough to drive. For the past three months, he'd been keeping all vehicle keys on his person, in any case.

But she had friends with mothers who drove—who'd been known to help him out when he couldn't be two places at once.

Grabbing his cell phone off the holster on his belt, Tanner dialed his sister's cell number. Not surprisingly, it went straight to voice mail. And then he dialed first one and then another of the girls Tatum hung out with.

Only to find that she hadn't been hanging out with them.

Not since Harcourt. The girls didn't sound any happier about the asshole's advent into his sister's life than he was.

Taking deep steady breaths, Tanner walked, very deliberately, out to the far barn—the one that they never used because half of it was missing. In the standing half was a small tack room—the only room inside, enclosed with drywall, as though someone had once used the place as a getaway. A hideout. Maybe yesterday's version of a man cave.

An old round wooden table, with one rotted leg, stood in the middle of the room. On the walls hung several framed photos—or a rendition thereof. The frames were falling apart at the seams. The glass was broken.

And there was one unframed poster hanging there. A newer poster. One he'd hung as a reminder of why he worked and sacrificed every day. The anti-drug poster depicted a meth addict. A woman with stringy, dirt-blond hair and black gaps where her teeth should be. There were sores all over her face, so much so that you couldn't tell if the woman had ever been beautiful, or just plain. Her eyes held no light, but he still saw *something* there. He didn't know the woman, but every time he looked at that poster, he felt as if he did. He saw a woman he knew.

A woman his siblings knew, as well. She'd given birth to them.

Anytime he was feeling overwhelmed all it took

was a look at that poster, a reminder of what they'd escaped, and he found the strength to climb one more mountain.

Every problem had a solution. He just had to find it.

Tanner took a step back, feeling calmer.

Until he thought of finding Tatum with that big-spending rich daddy's boy...

Very carefully, he removed the top two tacks holding the poster in place, exposing a piece of drywall with a couple of fist-size holes in it.

With one powerful thrust he added a third. Pinned the poster back in place. And, ignoring his red, throbbing knuckles, went out to his truck, started the ignition and tore out the circular drive, his tires spitting rocks and dust behind him.

He wasn't going to touch Del Harcourt, but he was going to bring his little sister home.

Period.

"WE'VE GOT A bed for you for tonight, Talia." Lila Mc-Daniels's steady presence seemed to calm the girl as they sat on a leather sofa in her office Tuesday just before dinner. Sedona, sitting on the other side of the girl, took note. With her gray hair and no-nonsense slacks and blouse, Lila didn't draw attention to herself. But while some people might overlook her, think they could ignore her, they'd soon find that she was always there. Always everywhere.

"Thank you." Talia's tremulous smile was clearly genuine.

"I'll take you to dinner in a few minutes," Lila continued. "You'll be staying in Maddie Estes's bungalow tonight. She has an extra room."

Sedona knew a female Lemonade Stand staff member would also be in the bungalow alongside Maddie and Talia, just as she was every night in case Maddie, who had special needs, woke up and was frightened or confused. Talia wouldn't be unsupervised for a moment.

"Maddie's going to be getting married soon," Lila said. "I'm sure you'll hear all about it."

Talia's glance showed interest. "You help people get married here? Like they can stay until they get married and move in with their husbands?"

"Some women leave here to marry, but not many," Lila explained. "The Lemonade Stand is a place where women come to heal when they've been mistreated. It's a place where, hopefully, they can live with respect while being exposed to healthy relationships and learning how to love well. It's also a safe house. Those who don't treat our residents well are kept away from them."

When Talia's shoulders visibly relaxed, Sedona exchanged a glance with Lila. The older woman nodded.

"Tell us what happened to you, Talia."

The girl looked from one to the other of them. Her lips were trembling.

"You told Ms. Campbell that you were hit."

Talia nodded, her eyes brimming with tears.

"More than once?" Lila conducted the interview like the professional she was, and once again Sedona was filled with admiration for this woman who'd given up any chance of a life of her own, a family of her own, to run this wonderful, beach-front shelter and to give abused women a chance to know how it felt to be treated well. To give hundreds of women and children the chance to have happy families of their own.

"Maybe I was hit a couple of times."

"Maybe?"

Talia stared downward. "Okay, a couple of times."

"Recently?"

The girl shook her head. Shrugged. And then nodded.

"We need to know who you are, Talia."

"I'm Talia Malone."

"The ID you showed me bearing the name Talia Malone said that you live in an apartment in Los Angeles."

"That's right." Talia picked at the side of her finger with a perfectly manicured purple nail.

"That apartment complex was torn down a couple of years ago. After a fire. The address is an empty lot."

The slender shoulders between the two women shrugged again. "I moved."

"The ID also says you're nineteen, but you told Ms. Campbell you're only fifteen."

With her head bowed, the girl looked right, then left, and didn't look up at either of them.

Sedona ached to help her.

Did the girl have family who would report her missing? Anyone who would care about her absence that night?

The same person who'd hurt her?

Right now, Sedona's only concern was the girl.

"Talia?"

Those gray-blue eyes trained on her, and the wealth of hurt—and confusion—pooling in their depths grabbed at Sedona.

"You said I could have until tomorrow morning."

"You can. We won't call anyone until then. But at least tell us your name."

The girl shook her head. "I told you, I'm Talia Malone."

"Tell us who hurt you. Who are you afraid of? Who are you running from?"

Talia picked at her nails some more, around the edge of the nails, not touching the glossy purple paint.

"What if the person you're afraid of followed you?"

"He didn't."

So it was a "he."

"How do you know?" Lila's quiet concern continued to flow around them, holding them all in a sacred place. For the moment.

"Because."

"He could have had someone else follow you. Or someone might have seen you and told him they saw you get on a bus."

Talia's hands shook. She continued to pick. And if she kept it up, she'd soon draw blood.

Sedona covered the girl's hands with her own. Holding on. She had no idea how it felt to have a trusted loved one turn on you with hate in his eyes, or violence in his words or hands.

But she knew, instinctively, that this young girl did. And knew she had to do something about it.

"Tell, me, Talia, please. I can't help you until I know the problem. Who are we protecting you from?"

Talia's fingers stilled and Sedona held her breath.

"My brother."

The words fell into the room like a ton of bricks.

CHAPTER THREE

HE'D NEVER BEEN to the house, but Tanner knew right where it was. Behind the massive wrought-iron gate that might intimidate some.

But not him.

Stopping in front of the entrance, he searched for an admittance button. Had to get out of his truck to push it. And waited for a response.

"Tanner Malone here to see Del Harcourt," he told the female voice on the other end of the speaker.

"Tanner? Tatum's brother?" The female on the other end sounded delighted—and surprised.

"Yes."

A click sounded, followed by whirring as the gates opened from the middle. "Come on in, Mr. Malone," the woman said.

Hopping in his truck, Tanner did just that. Whether the voice on the other end belonged to a lenient house-keeper or a family member, he didn't know.

And frankly, he didn't care. He was on a mission.

The front door opened as Tanner pulled around the fountain in the driveway and parked in what would have been, at a hotel, valet parking: a triple-wide, paved area, beautifully landscaped with colorful blooms even in midMarch—completely unlike the single-lane dirt path that circled in front of his house.

"Mr. Malone?" A slender, blonde woman in her late thirties, dressed expensively in pants made from the same type of silken fabric Tatum had picked out for her honor society induction the previous month, came down the steps toward him, her hand outstretched.

He noticed her nails were painted red. Tatum wouldn't wear red. She said it was for old ladies.

"I'm Callie Harcourt," the woman said. Del's mom. "Please come in. I've been anxious to meet you, but every time I asked, Tatum said you were working. You're a very busy man."

Any invitations to this home were news to him. "I'm a farmer," he said, which, to him, explained everything. "But I usually make time to attend Tatum's functions," he added. He wasn't perfect. But he tried.

"We've had a couple of barbecues," the woman said, ushering him into a bright hallway with cathedral ceilings before leading the way to a great room with tile floors and voluptuous plush beige furniture that looked as if a guy could relax back into it and drink a beer if he had a mind to.

The art on the walls and various tables reminded him of some of the pieces out in his barn. Except these were in exquisite condition, hardly resembling his dusty and scarred versions.

"Tatum says you're in the old Beacham place," Callie Malone said, crossing over to what appeared to be a wet bar on the far side of the room.

"That's right." Tanner stood his ground about mid-room. Ready to take on whatever came his way over the next few minutes.

He wasn't made of money, but he was as powerful as the next guy when it came to protecting his own.

Callie stood with one arm on the bar. "The Beachams were friends of my parents. I can remember attending summer parties there as a kid. Those barns were fascinating."

"I'm told they raised horses."

"Arabians." Callie nodded. "So sad, the way he died. She just let the place fall into disrepair after that. I'm told she's in a home someplace up north."

As Tanner understood it, Walter Beacham had died at the hands of a drunk driver. And his wife had given up on life. They'd never had any children. She had no other family to help out.

Tanner had picked up the property when it went into foreclosure. Just happened to get a bid in during the fifteen-day period that had been restricted to owner-occupied bids before the place was offered to investors.

That had been eight years ago and he and Tatum had been occupying it ever since.

Another two years and his vineyards would finally start to show enough profit for them to start fixing up the property the way he'd envisioned when he'd first seen it.

And his winery would stand in place of those old barns....

"Can I get you a drink?" Callie asked, stepping behind the bar. "Whiskey? Or some wine?"

"No, thank you," he said. Alcohol was the furthest thing from his mind at the moment.

And other than wine, he didn't drink, anyway. None of the Malone children did.

"I've come for my sister," he said now. "It's time for dinner and she has homework to finish before school tomorrow."

They could do this the easy way. If everyone cooperated.

Tanner realized that it was possible the Harcourt adults didn't know that Del had been warned to stay away from Tanner's little sister. Didn't know that their son was not only dealing and doing drugs, but was trying to pressure Tatum into doing the same. And into sleeping with him, too.

Callie's frown was his first warning that things weren't going to be easy. "Tatum? But…she's not here, Mr. Malone—"

"The name's Tanner," he interrupted, more curtly than was called for. If the Harcourts thought their friends in high places were going to intimidate him— as Del had asserted when Tanner had thrown the punk out of his house two days before—if they thought their money was going to make it possible for them to take his sister away from him, they had another think coming.

He'd been raising Tatum on his own for ten years. He wasn't about to lose her now. Another three years and they'd be there. Just three more years. She'd be eighteen. Legal age of consent.

Then he could set her free—a healthy, well-adjusted, well-educated adult Malone.

A well-loved Malone.

He swallowed. "I don't mean to be disrespectful, Mrs. Harcourt," he started again, his hands at his sides as he stood tall and straightened his shoulders. He couldn't do anything about the stained jeans he'd had on in the vineyard all day, or the equally stained button-up white-and-blue-striped shirt turned up at the cuffs. "But I assume your son is at home?"

Tatum had rattled on and on about the perfect Harcourt home, the normal, perfect family Del had. Including the way they ate dinner together every night, at the same time, with no television on. Just Del and his parents, talking about their day....

"Yes, Del's upstairs doing his homework," Callie said, coming out from behind the bar, her pretty, perfectly made-up features marred with a frown.

Looking at the woman he saw more of his little sister than he liked. It was as though Tatum was modeling herself after this woman. As if he was not only dealing with puppy love, but a case of heroine worship thrown in, as well.

Distracted for a second at the realization, he wasn't about to let on.

"Can you call him down here, please?" he asked, as though he was the president of the United States addressing Congress.

"Of course."

The soft click of Callie's pumps on the shiny wood floor as she left the room was followed by her voice in the distance, calling for her son.

Tanner waited for the second call. For the sound of the woman's footsteps on the stairs as she made a climb similar to the one Tanner had made a mere half hour before. Waited for her to realize that her son wasn't home, either. The punk had taken Tanner's youngest sister someplace and he wanted her back.

"Yeah?" The male voice that sounded at the top of the stairs held none of the respect Tanner had heard two mornings before when the asshole had tried to convince him that he loved his sister and would never do anything to hurt her. It was Del. He recognized the voice. Not the tone.

It was as if the kid was speaking to someone beneath him. A servant.

Or a woman?

"I'd like you to come down, please."

"I'm busy."

Did he talk to Tatum that way, too?

"Del, do I have to call your father?"

A door slammed. Tanner heard tennis shoes on the stairs. "I'm here, now what?"

"Come into the living room, please." Callie's voice lowered, as though she didn't want Tanner to hear what she was saying. Or how she was saying it?

"What for?"

Just then another door opened, somewhere deeper

in the house. "Your father's home." Callie's voice took on strength.

And before anything else could happen, Del, dressed in tight-fitting jeans, a surfer shirt and expensive-looking rubber-soled sports shoes, entered the room.

"Mr. Malone? What are you doing here?" The boy's tone of voice changed again. Back to two mornings before. Like the asshole didn't know Tanner had heard him addressing his mother?

"He's looking for Tatum, Del. Do you know where she is?"

"No." The boy's chin lifted.

"I don't believe you." Tanner didn't bother with niceties.

Callie glanced from Tanner to her son. "Del? Do you know something you aren't telling us?"

"I'm telling you, I don't know where she is," Del insisted. Shrugging his shoulders he shoved his hands in his pockets, the blue ends of his blond hair giving him an air of otherworldliness that set Tanner's already stressed nerve endings on edge.

"Where who is?" The quiet, deep voice belonged to the tall guy in the suit who just entered the room.

"Mr. Harcourt?" Tanner assumed the financier's identity.

"That's right."

"I'm looking for my sister. I have good reason to believe that your son knows where she is. She's only fifteen, it's a school night and she belongs at home."

"I'm sorry, I don't believe I've made your acquaintance." Stepping past his son as though the boy didn't exist, Harcourt glanced at his wife.

"This is Tanner Malone, Kenny. Tatum's brother."

"Tatum's missing?" The concern on the other man's face appeared genuine as he swung toward his son. "What do you know about this, Del?" The voice was still low, but with a growling note. "If you know where that girl is, you tell us. Now." Harcourt was almost gritting his teeth.

Del shrugged again, but his head bowed a bit as he looked at his mother. "Mom, I'm telling you, I don't know where she is."

Harcourt's hand snapped out and formed a vise around his son's arm, squeezing with obvious force. "I'm warning you, son, if you're hiding something…"

The threat was left unsaid, but Del seemed to hear it loud and clear.

"I don't know where she is." Del looked his father in the eye, but backed half a step away, so that they weren't directly facing each other.

Something was going on there. Something bad. Unhealthy.

But Tanner didn't have the time or wherewithal to care. If Tatum's friends didn't know where she was… and Del didn't have her…then…

"When was the last time you spoke to her?" Tanner asked, holding his teeth together to keep himself calm. To prevent the panic that was raging inside him from taking control.

"She's not allowed to speak to me, remember? You said you'd take her cell phone away if she did."

In unison, the elder Harcourts looked at each other, then at their son.

"What about on the internet?" Callie asked.

"Answer your mother," Harcourt demanded, more loudly than his wife, before Del even had a chance to respond.

Del stared at the floor. Harcourt grabbed his son's arm a second time. "Delaney?"

"She private messaged me on Facebook this morning."

"And?"

"I don't know." The boy, pulling out of his father's grip, backed up. "I didn't answer her, okay? I knew *he'd* be watching." He practically spit the word *he'd* as he looked at Tanner.

"What did she say?" Tanner asked, still the calmest one in the room. If you didn't count the frustration— the fear—raging inside him.

"I can't remember…" Del's reply ended abruptly as his father took a step forward. "She said that she loved me."

"And?"

"And, nothing."

Harcourt slapped the back of his kid's head. Not enough to be considered violent or even cause Del's neck to snap back, but harder than a love tap.

Instead of cowing the boy, the slap seemed to have the opposite effect. Del straightened. He looked at all three adults in the room and said, "She told me she loved me. That's all." His tone told them he'd take any beating they wanted to hand out but they weren't going to get another answer from him.

Because it was the truth?

Or because the punk was that determined to have Tatum all for himself?

So he could knock his little sister around like his father did him?

Looking at Callie Harcourt, Tanner wondered where she played into the "normal" Harcourt household. Did her husband intimidate her, too? With a little physical persuasion now and then?

Or did they both just think that rough parenting was the only way to keep their far too rich and spoiled brat in line?

If it was the latter, Tanner wasn't sure he faulted them. He *was* sure he wasn't going to get any closer to Tatum in that living room right then.

"I'm going to the police," he stated unequivocally to the room at large. "If you have anything to do with this, Del, you will pay."

"I'm telling you—"

"Save it," Harcourt said to his son, walking behind Tanner to the vestibule. "If the boy knows something, I'll get it out of him."

Even though he could guess what Harcourt's tactics would probably be, Tanner wasn't altogether sorry to hear it. "I'm sure the police will want to talk to him."

"We'll be here all night."

Asking Tanner to keep them posted, the Harcourts showed him out.

Tanner, already on his cell with 9-1-1, barely noticed.

CHAPTER FOUR

SANTA RAQUEL, CALIFORNIA, had to be heaven on earth. Sedona, who'd been born and raised in the quaint coastal town, sat on her deck Tuesday evening, sipping a glass of wine, munching on Havarti, grape jelly and French bread, while she watched the waves come in. Again and again. Washing to shore. Going back out to sea. Only to return again.

They were steady. Assured. Reliable. Sometimes they were angry and plowed onto the beach with the force of a minibulldozer. Other times they were calm, almost sleepy, sliding quietly up on the sand and dissipating with hardly a trace left behind. But, always, they were there.

Like the love her parents shared. With each other. And with her and her brother, Grady, a pediatrician in Scottsdale, Arizona.

She didn't know what she'd do without her older brother in the background of her life. He was her best friend. Her confidant.

She couldn't imagine being afraid of him....

Sedona sipped. Bit off a piece of cheese and then breathed, pulling the salty tang of air deep into her lungs. Washing away the day's impurities from her bloodstream as the ocean's energy erased twelve hours' worth of tension, blanketing her in peace. When she felt a little more relaxed, she'd go in and change out of the navy suit she'd worn to work that day. Slide into some workout clothes and take a walk on the beach.

Grady had called the night before. Her older brother's wife was expecting their second child. A man who'd dedicated his life to caring for children, Grady had clearly found his own piece of heaven when his son, two-year-old Cameron, had been born. And now he'd have heaven times two.

Sedona was happy for him. She liked to hope that he'd found a bit of heaven in his wife, Brooke, as well. She just didn't see it.

The flap of the doggy door sounded behind her, and Sedona waited for Ellie—short for Elizabeth Bennet from the Jane Austen novel—to appear. The rescued, seven-pound poochin had to knock a few times before she trusted the entry and exit way Sedona had had installed for her. Every time she went in or out. Heavy plastic whooshed against metal framing again. And then Ellie made her appearance on the wooden decked balcony, stopping about a foot short of Sedona and staring at her. The little miss didn't make a sound. Didn't scratch at her or jump up. She just stared.

"You could just take yourself, you know," Sedona told her, setting her glass of wine down on the round glass-topped wicker table next to her as she scooped up her apricot-colored family member and carried her down the three steps to the small patch of fenced-in grass she'd had planted the week after she'd adopted her Japanese Chin/poodle mix.

Ellie had been a couple of months old then. Sedona had been visiting Grady and had attended a barbecue with him and Brooke in a little town called Shelter Valley, Arizona. She'd heard about the animal rescue organization being run out of the local vet's office and had asked to see the current rescues.

And had fallen in love with Ellie on sight. The little girl held herself with dignity even after spending the first eight weeks of her life locked in a windowless shed with so many other puppies there hadn't been enough floor space for them to live without lying on top of one another.

Even now, three years later, Ellie didn't travel far alone. She completed her business a short distance away and came right back, jumping a couple of feet off the ground to bounce off Sedona's hip.

Catching her in midair, Sedona thought about a walk on the beach. And noticed the Richardsons outside with their four-year-old son. The private stretch of beach behind her small house was shared by four other homes. And tonight she felt more like finishing her glass of wine than socializing.

Besides, Joshua, the Richardsons' son, liked to run after Ellie. His parents thought he was playing with the little dog. To Sedona, who admittedly coddled her little girl, the activity seemed more like torment.

Margie Richardson saw her and waved. Still holding Ellie, Sedona knew she was going to have to go say hello. And could feel the tension beginning to seep back into her bones.

She took one step and her phone rang.

From the table. On her deck. Next to her glass of wine.

"Saved by the bell," she said softly to Ellie as she waved once more in the Richardsons' general direction and hurried up the stairs to grab her phone.

"I hate to disturb you again, Sedona, but you said to call immediately if there was any break in the Talia Malone situation." Lila McDaniels did not sound calm.

"I did and I meant it. What's up?" Switching mental gears in a blink, Sedona set Ellie inside the French doors leading to her living area and, with her phone held between her shoulder and her ear, grabbed the glass of wine and plate of cheese and headed indoors.

"Lynn Duncan just left Maddie's. She called right afterward to tell me that Talia looks like a girl she'd seen a picture of on the news a little while ago. She's a missing person. And if it's the same girl, her name's not Talia. It's Tatum."

"Can you wait for me to get there before you do anything?"

"Of course."

Wine down the drain, Sedona dumped the remainder of the cheese and bread into the trash and, making certain that Ellie was in her bed, grabbed her keys and was out the door.

"She's safe here."

"Exactly." The old Ford Thunderbird started up first

try and Sedona was on her way. "If she's been reported missing, the police might return her to her family. With no bruising, no reports or evidence of previous abuse it might be that the most we can hope for is the assignation of a caseworker for follow-up...."

Her mind was racing. With the laws. And the ways to use those laws to protect her young client.

"I can't not report her. Not now that I know who she is. She might be just what they suspect, a runaway. I can't risk the lives of my residents if I get embroiled in a lawsuit."

"I know. I'm not suggesting that you should. Just let me talk to Tatum. And then I'll call the police myself."

Good thing she'd only had a couple of sips of wine. It was going to be a long night.

TANNER WASN'T ABOUT to just go home and wait. He wasn't a sit-by-the-phone type of guy. But the law enforcement representative he'd spoken with, a no-nonsense dispatcher who'd taken his report immediately at the neighborhood station when he'd stopped in, said an officer would meet him at his house.

While the calm and efficient manner of the phone representative had reassured him, the urgency with which the department was acting set his anxiety levels soaring again.

He'd pulled Tatum's recent school photo out of his wallet and handed it over. He'd emailed some photos from his phone while he'd been standing in the station. He'd already given a list of the social media sites she used, complete with usernames and passwords, explaining that he'd made her share them with him as a condition of her right to go on the sites.

And while he'd nodded, expressing his thanks for the officers' help, they'd scared the shit out of him.

They'd assured him that an Endangered Missing Advisory would be issued immediately.

Endangered missing?

The words conjured up all kinds of horrible images. He couldn't allow them to take root.

He wasn't going to lose Tatum. He couldn't lose her. He'd loved the others—Talia and Thomas—still loved them. He'd taken good care of them. He'd give his life for any of his siblings.

But Tatum...she was more daughter than sibling to him. He'd sacrificed everything for her.

And she was going to be okay. They'd find her. There'd be some reasonable explanation for her absence. Just because he couldn't come up with it didn't mean it wasn't there.

She'd be home, sleeping in her own bed that night, or, at the very latest, tomorrow. And life would go on. Just like normal. Things would be fine.

She'd take her SAT test in October. Outscore her older brother. And the sky would be her only limit.

Because she was sweet baby Tatum....

A tan-colored four-door sedan was parked in his driveway as Tanner pulled in, barely getting the truck into park before jumping from the seat. He didn't recognize the car, but if someone had brought Tatum home to him…

A couple got out of the car—one male, one female, both in dark suits. Both pulled badges from their pockets as they approached.

Detectives Morris and Brown, they introduced themselves.

"We'd like to take a look around your sister's room," the older of the two, the female, Morris, said. "According to our report this is the last place she was seen, is that correct?"

"Yes."

They entered the house. Tanner stood in front of the cockeyed pillow in the living room, finding it incredible that it was only that morning that he'd tossed the stupid thing. Unbelievable that something so horrific could have occurred while the pillow just sat there as if nothing had happened all day.

"We'll need the names of everyone she knows or has had anything to do with now or in the past."

Calmly standing, while the detectives sat down uninvited, disturbing his pillow, Tanner listed every name he could remember. A total of nine.

There should have been more. A lot more.

But he'd been busy growing grapes and couldn't remember.

"You can check her Facebook page," he said, relieved when he came up with the idea. "Everyone she knows or has ever known is on there."

"We've already got someone doing that," Brown

said. Tanner nodded. What else did a guy do when everything that mattered to him was on the line and he stood there completely helpless?

"Does she have any enemies?"

"Not that I know of." Did Morris just frown at him? Okay, so maybe he'd been a bit preoccupied lately, but it was only so that he could make enough money to send Tatum to college if she didn't get the scholarship she was hoping for.

He'd had to spend a sizable chunk of savings the previous year to buy Talia out of her marriage to a man who'd been pimping her out to powerful acquaintances for profit. In fact, Tanner had bought her "services" from the man for an extended vacation, which had actually been time she'd spent in a safe house while she got help to divorce the man.

After which she'd returned to exotic dancing.

But the detectives didn't need to hear any of that.

"What about family?" Morris asked. She wasn't writing any of this down.

"No one in our family would hurt Tatum. We all adore her. She's the baby." He and Thomas and Talia fought sometimes. They didn't always agree on life choices. But they'd never once disagreed about Tatum. That baby girl had been their only joy when they should all have been having the time of their lives.

So could Tatum be with Talia?

"Who is 'we all'?" One of Morris's very thin brows rose. Her tone of voice had changed. And for the first time Tanner realized that he might be a suspect.

The detectives weren't just there to help him find Tatum. They were there to investigate him.

Here he was ready to piss himself or puke he was so worried, and they thought *he'd* done something to Tatum?

"I'M SORRY, MR. MALONE, I know this is difficult, but we have to ask, were you and Tatum having problems?"

Brown had stayed with Tanner in the living room while Morris went up to Tatum's room to look around. And now she'd returned to grill him some more. No telling what she'd found in his sister's things.

Lord knew he wasn't her favorite person anymore.

"Yes, we were," he said now, hands in his pockets as he stood in his living room facing the two detectives sitting side by side on his couch. "But I didn't hurt her. I was out in the vineyard all day. I can show you the fresh-cut clippings to prove it."

"But you don't have an alibi?"

"No, I do not." He wasn't going to lie. There was no point. But… "Put someone on me, look into every aspect of my life. But please, don't stop looking for my sister while you do so. I am not your man and if you waste time focusing solely on me, God knows what will…"

No. He couldn't go there. He'd had enough heartache to last him a lifetime and could not borrow more.

"You said you two had trouble…." Morris's tone had softened, though not perceptibly.

"About two months ago Tatum met this rich kid, Del Harcourt, at a party. He's spoiled and selfish and I'm pretty sure he hit her. She had a bruise on her arm, a bad one."

"You saw the bruise?" Brown's eyes widened.

"Not at first. She kept her arm covered. But I grabbed her once—" which sounded bad "—and she flinched. I made her show me her arm. The bruise was faded, almost gone, but it was from a fist, I'm sure of it. She insists she walked into an old furniture spindle in the barn."

"And that's the trouble you've had? You didn't believe her about a bruise?"

Tanner didn't like the way Morris was studying him. But he wanted Tatum found. At whatever risk to him.

"Two days ago I threw the punk out of my house and told Tatum she was not to see or speak with him again. And I took away her smartphone."

He felt a cold knot of fear as something else occurred to him. It should have been his first thought. Would have been if Tatum hadn't been so crazy about the asshole.

"There is someone," he said, his mind coldly calculating. "The woman who gave birth to us…" He couldn't bring himself to say *mother.* "Last we knew, her name was Tammy Malone, but it changed frequently. She's usually high, homeless and spreading her legs, and once tried to sell my other sister for a fix. Usually I wouldn't expect Tatum to have anything to do with her, but now that she's mad at me… Anyway, if Tammy sees money for herself in having Tatum, she might try to work her."

"Is she in the area?"

"I have no idea. Not recently that I know of."

"How long has it been since you've heard from her?"

Last time she'd come begging for money. "A year, maybe two." He didn't mark his calendar with things he preferred to forget.

"Has she been in touch with Tatum in the past?"

"Not since she was five." It couldn't be Tammy. Pray God it wasn't Tammy. Tatum was at a vulnerable age. And partially because of him, Talia was out of her life and…

"Did you sue her for custody of Tatum?"

"No. She signed her and my other two siblings over willingly." To avoid a jail sentence.

It was a long shot. In ten years, Tammy had never contacted Tatum. There was no reason to panic.

"I see here that Tatum has an old flip phone with no texting capability." Morris looked down at the clipboard on her lap.

"That's right. It was an old one of mine. I called my provider and changed her line over temporarily. She has no data plan at all. For a month. She lied to me. I can't tolerate that." Tatum had too much free time, too much lack of supervision, to allow for lying. He had to be able to trust her. "But I couldn't just take her phone away," he added. "It's not safe for a young girl to be at school without a phone these days."

"Smartphones have tracking apps on them." Brown

looked apologetic as he explained the dilemma Tanner had unknowingly caused.

"Her number goes immediately to voice mail," Tanner told them.

Morris pulled a charger from the black leather satchel she wore on her shoulder. "I found this in her room," she said as Tanner recognized the charger for his old phone. And took hope.

Until another thought chased that one.

"She wasn't planning to be gone long." He voiced his first thought. And then, more slowly, his second. "Which makes her disappearance look more like she didn't leave of her own accord."

"You said her purse is missing."

"Yes."

"Was there anything else missing?"

"No. Not even her retainer case." Tatum was always careful to store the expensive mouthpiece carefully. Her straight teeth meant a lot to her.

Obviously she'd been planning to return home that evening. So…he just had to be patient. Wait. She'd show up.

And have one hell of a lot of explaining to do.

"We're going to need to take something personal of hers," Brown said as the two detectives stood. "A toothbrush. Or hairbrush…"

For DNA. Tanner watched television on occasion. He knew why they were asking.

And handed over a couple of items from Tatum's bathroom drawer without saying another word.

CHAPTER FIVE

"I CAN'T TELL you what to do, Lila, you know that. I represent Tatum Malone, not The Lemonade Stand, on this one."

That was the funny thing about volunteer service—lines blurred when there wasn't someone paying the bill. When there wasn't someone with whom the buck stopped.

"I have to call the police." Lila spoke softly, walking with Sedona toward Maddie Estes's bungalow. The special-needs woman had no idea what was going on, and Tatum hadn't been alerted yet, either. "She's a minor and I can't keep her here without guardian permission."

"That's a fact of law, yes."

"But who's to say when I found out that she's an official missing person?"

"Lynn Duncan." The live-in nurse practitioner who was not only Maddie Estes's friend and protector, but soon to be her sister-in-law, too.

"Lynn's not going to say anything to anyone."

The Lemonade Stand was a place where secrets were safe. For good reason.

And sometimes, for that good reason, law enforcement looked the other way when they couldn't conform to the letter.

"I'll take her to the Garden," Sedona said. "It's almost dark. We should be alone there. I'll do my best to find out what's going on and then figure out a legal way to keep her from being sucked up into a system that might or might not be able to help her."

Lila's footsteps were soft whispers on the meandering sidewalk. Floral scents wafted from the gardens on both sides of the path.

"If there's no proof of wrongdoing, no viable reason to remove Tatum from her home, to take away custody from a family member, a judge could determine that it's in Tatum's best interest to go home. A judge can order her home," she said.

"I know." Lila sounded less than satisfied.

"But you'd like it if I could get temporary placement here. At least until we get this figured out."

"Yes."

"I'll see what I can do."

"Thank you."

"I NEED TO speak with Talia Malone, please."

"Yes, sir, can I say who's calling?"

With his back to the room, Tanner stared out the kitchen window. His vines were out there. Sucking water and nutrients out of the earth. Growing. A testimony to the resilience of life. And to its fragility, as well.

"Tanner," he said into the cell phone he was holding so tightly his knuckles shone white. Unless she was onstage, in the middle of…well…what she did up there, they'd call her to the phone.

"Tanner? What's wrong?"

He didn't have to wait long. And she was out of breath. He didn't want to know why.

"I tried your cell, first. When you didn't answer…"

"It's fine, Tanner, what's wrong?"

He'd shown up at Talia's place of business one time. It hadn't been pretty. But he'd been assured any future calls would be answered.

This was the first time he'd tested the theory.

"Have you heard from Tatum?" Why was he doing this? It wasn't like Talia would be able to help. The sisters hadn't spoken in more than a year.

"Of course not. Even if I had, I wouldn't have broken my word to you. No contact, just like we agreed. She'll be eighteen soon enough and free to make her own choices. And I don't want her making mine. You were right about that. I don't want her future on my shoulders."

"She mimicked your every move."

"And that's why you're checking up on her? Because you think she's like me and will go behind your back and get into trouble?"

Wincing at the sarcasm in his twenty-six-year-old sister's voice, Tanner pinched the bridge of his nose, right between his eyes, in an effort to make the pain stop. The pain in his heart…

"I shouldn't have humiliated you at your place of

business, Talia, I'm sorry." The irony in the words choked him. His hauling her away from a client on the way to a lap dance was humiliating to her, and undressing onstage was not?

"You say you love me, Tanner, but you don't accept that I've made a choice I can live with."

"You're a…" He wasn't going to do this.

"What? A hooker? Go ahead and say it, big brother. It won't kill you."

Talia was beautiful. Had so much going for her…

He loved her. But not enough, apparently. Or maybe it was their mother, and her father, who'd failed to give her the validation she'd needed—driving her to find it in the eager paws of men who were so hot for her they'd pay her for privileges.

Or pay just to see her swing around a bar and take her clothes off.

"Tatum's missing."

"What does that mean, missing?" She sounded sharp, but he heard a note of concern, too.

Because, deep down, they were family. They loved each other.

And that was why he'd made the call.

"I don't know, sis." In one long breath Tanner summarized the hellish couple of hours he'd just spent. "They've put out a bulletin and now we wait. I just… They took some things…for her DNA…and I… You should know."

"They think someone snatched her?"

"They don't have any evidence of that. They've

searched all around the house, outside and in, and around the area, too, and so far there's no sign of struggle and no one saw anything."

"Have they considered the possibility that she ran away?"

"Yes."

"It's what you think, isn't it?"

Part of him wanted to believe she had, because it meant there was more of a chance that she was safe. But Tatum had been angry with him before and stayed put. You couldn't parent a child without pissing her off sometimes. Tatum's anger always passed.

"What did you do to her, Tanner?"

"I threw her punk boyfriend out of the house and forbid her from seeing him."

"That's the first place I'd look for her, then."

"I did. She wasn't there."

"Sounds like she learned from my example, after all." Talia's words brought back more memories than he needed at the moment. "I ran straight to Rex, making it far too easy for you to find me."

He'd brought Talia home that first time. The next time, she'd been eighteen, legally allowed to go, and determined that he wouldn't find her.

He'd been just as determined that he would. And hadn't stopped looking. Not for years.

She'd already been working in Vegas when he finally had.

"You were only sixteen." He stood by his long-ago choice. "Besides, this guy's a real jerk."

"Rex wasn't. He was a college graduate with a good job and he wanted to marry me. It was three months before my seventeenth birthday and we'd already set a date."

But Rex had lost his job and gone to jail for statutory rape. Because at twenty-three Tanner had been Talia's legal guardian and he'd pressed charges against the twenty-seven-year-old high school teacher he'd caught bedding his sister.

Talia had been pregnant, too. She'd given up the baby for adoption—her choice. But she'd never forgiven Tanner for any of it. If he hadn't put Rex away, she would've been able to keep her son, to give him a good, stable secure life. Or so she'd believed. He'd told her that if he hadn't pressed charges, Rex would still have been charged and lost his job. She hadn't wanted to hear a word of it. She'd said Rex had been willing to lose his job, but that he wouldn't have done jail time. With the certainty of youth, she'd believed that no one else would've filed charges against the man.

Whether, deep down, she'd realized the truth or not, she'd blamed him for her broken heart and broken life.

And no good would come of reopening the old wound.

"Harcourt's into drugs." Tanner shoved his free hand into the pocket of his jeans and wondered if Tatum could be out there in the vineyard someplace. Close by. Safe. And just making him suffer.

"Selling or taking?"

"Taking, for sure. And I think selling."

"Tatum knows better than to get involved with drugs."

Their mother had been an addict. A couple of her baby daddies had been dealers. And not one of the Malone children had ever touched illegal substances. It was like an oath with them.

"He was smoking a pipe out in the barn. There was more than just marijuana in it."

Like Pavlov's dogs, they'd all been trained from the womb to know what certain smells meant. And the consequences that would result.

"I'm guessing Tatum didn't know?"

He'd have guessed the same.

He'd have been wrong.

But there was no good to come from bad-mouthing one sister to another. Or disillusioning Talia any further, either.

"I asked her if she's ever used drugs. She said no. I believed her," he said. "I still do."

For the time being. Too much time with the punk kid who seemed to have more influence over Tatum than Tanner did, and chances were, Tatum would succumb eventually. He'd heard Harcourt pressuring Tatum to "try it" Sunday, when he'd passed the barn on his way back out to the vineyard. Hell, if he hadn't broken his clippers, he wouldn't even have known the two were home.

"She used to write to me about some girl named Amy. They told each other everything. Girls do that. Call her."

Talia's "Amy," Melissa Winchell, had helped Tanner find his sister in Vegas because she'd been worried sick about the choices Talia was making. As far as he knew, the two of them hadn't spoken since.

But then he hadn't known that Talia and Tatum had talked to each other during the years he'd been searching for Talia, either. So maybe Melissa and Talia talked, too.

Melissa used to stop by the farm now and then. Just to keep in touch.

"According to Amy, Tatum ditched all her friends when she met Harcourt."

"This guy's got a real hold on her."

"I know."

"I'm guessing the police know about him?"

"They do. The Harcourts like Tatum. They cooperated. I got the idea that this kid's a problem for them, too. If he knows anything, his father will get it out of him."

"So I can expect a call from the cops, too?"

"They asked about her family."

"I'm guessing you couldn't wait to tell them what I do for a living. How I'm such a horrible influence on my baby sister that we can't be in the same room together?"

Okay, so maybe his stance had been a bit harsh on that one. He was willing to rethink it if she would. As soon as they got Tatum home.

"No, sis. I told them Tatum idolizes you and gave them your cell number."

A long silence followed. "And you're giving me a heads-up that if the cops call, it's not me they're after."

"Something like that." He loved her. "And to tell you that Tatum's missing."

"In case she comes calling."

"In case she comes to harm. You have a right to know that she might be in danger." At the moment, he'd give his vineyards, his house and the rest of the money he had in the bank if Tatum would show up on her sister's doorstep.

Show up anywhere. Alive.

"It's not like her to just leave. She didn't take her retainer or any of her things, which indicates that she didn't intend to be gone long, and Harcourt's at home with his folks."

And Morris and Brown had asked for her DNA.

"Do I have your permission to call her?"

Instincts honed by Talia's proven lack of trustworthiness almost choked him as he said, "Yes. But I'm pretty sure her battery's dead. Her phone goes immediately to voice mail and the charger was here."

"She can get another charger." Talia's dry response made him feel a little better. For no apparent reason. "And it's also possible that she's sending the line to voice mail when she sees who's calling. Or maybe she has the phone off to conserve the battery. I'll keep trying, just in case."

"Thanks, sis."

"How much cash does she have on her?"

When Talia had left at eighteen, she'd taken all of

his money that she could get her hands on. Close to five hundred dollars.

"I gave her fifty on Saturday, as I do every week. I don't know if she spends it all every week, or if she's saved up. She hasn't accessed our joint account."

"You're still keeping your name on everyone else's accounts, huh?"

"She's fifteen, Talia. And I also put money in that account for her. Anyway, the punk could have spotted her a thousand easy."

"I'm sure the cops will find out from his parents if he did. Surely they'd know if he suddenly withdrew a thousand bucks."

"Unless he got it selling drugs and then they won't know."

"You're telling me she could be anywhere."

"Yeah."

"You need me to come home?"

Tanner had a flash of memory—Talia, back when her hair was still long and blond, sitting at the kitchen table with him and Thomas, laughing so hard she spit mashed potatoes on a bowl of peas....

"Not yet," he said. "Hopefully she'll be home tonight and I can tan her hide for putting us all through this."

"Tanner?"

"Yeah?"

"I suggest you don't touch a hair on her head. If you want her to speak to you once she turns eighteen, that is."

He'd never hit Tatum. Ever. He'd used the words figuratively. But he'd slapped Talia once. He was seventeen at the time and she'd been ten and had been using words he'd only ever heard come out of his mother's mouth when the woman was high on something and chasing her next lay.

Talia's eyes had opened wide, filled with tears, but even then she'd been too tough to let them fall. He'd been more appalled at his action than she had. Had apologized over and over.

Clearly she'd never forgiven him.

CHAPTER SIX

"WE KNOW WHO you are, Tatum." Sedona waited until they were seated in the Garden of Renewal, a professionally planted utopia on the grounds of The Lemonade Stand, designed with aesthetics, sound and scent in mind. The rock waterfall in the middle of the garden offered a comforting white noise that tuned out sounds from the world beyond.

"My brother found me and told you, didn't he? And now you're going to make me go home."

"No. Someone reported you missing to the police. You're all over the news."

"Oh."

"You didn't think anyone would miss you?"

The girl's head was bent as she leaned over, her elbows on her knees, hands on her arms, and rocked.

A defensive posture that was far too familiar to Sedona. She saw it a lot in her line of work.

"I didn't think," Tatum said. "At least, not about that part."

"So tell me what you did think about."

Tatum sat upright, her eyes glistening with tears. "I had to get away from him, Ms. Campbell. I was online this morning and read about The Lemonade Stand on someone's Facebook page. I knew I'd probably only have one chance to get here, so I grabbed my purse and left. I didn't even bring my retainer."

She was watching and listening for the "tells" because she didn't have much time.

"Had to get away from whom?"

"My brother. I was off school today and he was going to be out working so I thought it was my chance."

"What about your parents? Have you talked to them about your brother? Won't they help you?"

"Tanner's my guardian. He's my brother. Our mother took off when I was five. She gave Tanner custody of all three of us kids. He always said that was the one decent thing she did for us before she left. Otherwise, we'd have been split up."

Okay. Unexpected. Sedona slowed her mind down, reassessing.

"What about your dad?"

"I have no idea who he is. My older sister, Talia, said he was a drug dealer, just like hers and our other brother, Thomas's. Tanner wouldn't say. I just know that we all four have different dads and none of them hung around. Tanner's was pretty decent, I guess. He died when Tanner was little."

"You have three older siblings?"

"Yeah."

"And this Tanner, he's the oldest?"

"Yeah."

"You have a sister named Talia and that was the name on the ID you gave Lila when you first arrived."

"Yeah. It was hers. I found it in some stuff she left behind."

"So she's gone, too?"

"She's a stripper in Vegas and Tanner won't let me see her. Like he's afraid I'm going to get stripper cooties or something."

A picture of a drowning man began to form in Sedona's mind. A man desperate enough to use force to keep his youngest sibling in line as she tried to take control of her own life?

Right alongside that vision was a depiction of a young woman who was more alone than Sedona had ever been.

"So there's you, Tanner and Talia. What about the fourth sibling?"

"Thomas. He's in New York. Has some fancy job to do with money but I wouldn't even recognize him if I saw him. He headed for college the fall after mom left and never came back. He had a scholarship to an Ivy League school back east."

"How old were you then?"

The gorgeous teenager shrugged her slumped shoulders. "Maybe five."

"Do you and Thomas ever talk?" Just how isolated was this girl?

"Sometimes. When Tanner makes me. I mean, I don't really know the guy, you know? We had a druggie mother in common and that's about it."

"But Thomas calls?"

"Maybe like on Christmas or something. Mostly

Tanner calls him. Sometimes he answers and some-times he doesn't. Tanner leaves messages. Thomas doesn't return them."

No hope of support there.

"Are any of your siblings married?"

Was there any family that could take this girl? To keep her out of the system?

"Nope. And if Tanner has his way, I won't ever be married, either."

Not liking the sound of that, Sedona made a men-tal note.

"So what makes Tanner angry with you?"

Tatum shrugged again.

"Tatum?" She waited for the girl to look at her. "I can't help you if you aren't honest with me."

"That makes Tanner mad," Tatum said. "When he thinks people are lying to him. But he lies all the time, you know? He says that he's there for me, but he's not. He's always out in that precious vineyard of his, leav-ing me alone in that big old house. And when I try to find my own life, my own friends, and to be a part of their families, he gets mad and ruins everything."

"Like what? Can you give me an example?"

"Like…I have a boyfriend." Tatum's entire counte-nance changed. The girl's eyes brightened, her cheeks softened. "He loves me, Ms. Campbell. Me. He doesn't care that I have druggie parents who took off. He doesn't think I'm any less because of that."

"And other kids do?"

Tatum's eyes grew shadowed again. "Some do. They

say things when they think I don't know or can't hear them. They did that to Thomas and Talia, too."

"How do you know? I thought you and Thomas seldom speak?"

Maybe she spoke with her siblings more than she realized. Maybe they cared enough to step forward. Maybe Thomas had a significant other. Was part of a family Tatum could join.

"Talia told me. She said that I wasn't supposed to listen to them. And that I wasn't to let Tanner suffocate the life out of me, either."

"She said that."

"Yes." Tatum nodded. "Exactly those words—not to suffocate the life out of me."

It was tough to form a picture of a family, to get a realistic sense of the dynamics, in a half-hour conversation with a distressed teenager. And yet…she was hearing enough to know that Tatum's problems were real.

"When did Talia tell you that?"

"The last time I spoke to her."

"Was she living in Vegas then?"

"Yes."

A stripper feeling she'd been suffocated? Because the older brother had tried to save his sister from a dangerous and potentially unhappy life choice?

For a second, Sedona pitied the man. A seemingly young man who'd had the well-being of three younger siblings thrust upon him.

He could be forgiven for making some mistakes.

Sitting solemnly on the bench beside her, Tatum

shuddered and Sedona could only imagine what the girl was remembering.

Mistakes were forgivable. Hitting a defenseless fifteen-year-old girl was not.

"I asked you why you thought that if your brother had his way, you'd never get married."

"Because he hates Del," the girl said, her voice impassioned. "That's my boyfriend," she offered as an aside. "He went off on him on Sunday, and there was this huge fight. He says Del can't ever come back, I can't ever see him again and I'm not allowed to talk to him, either. He took my phone and left me with this flip thing with no data plan so I can't even text."

"Why doesn't he like Del?"

Hands clasped tightly, Tatum shook her head. "Because he thinks we're gonna sleep together, I guess. He caught us out in the barn."

"Are you sleeping together?"

"No." A new note entered the girl's voice.

"Tatum, I'm not your judge. I'm the one who has to know the truth so I can best defend you."

"We haven't had sex," Tatum said. "I've never… But he wants to. He was trying to talk me into trying it when Tanner suddenly showed up."

"Do you want to?"

The darkening night was cool, but she and Tatum both had sweaters and were enclosed in a thick circle of trees surrounding the several-acre garden. The orange-and-golden California poppies on the outskirts of the garden hadn't yet closed for the night.

"Yeah, I want to. Sorta. I mean, I want to be…you know…together and all. I just, I mean, Tanner'd kill me and…"

Sedona wasn't a juvenile counselor. But being a family lawyer specializing in divorce and family arbitration meant that she often found herself in the role of counselor. She'd had some training.

She also remembered being fifteen….

And she had decisions to make. Every hour that law enforcement personnel were searching for Tatum, an endangered missing child who wasn't missing at all, they were being taken away from other important work.

The scent from the flowering plants in the beds close by wafted around them. Sedona focused on those flowers for a moment, seeing some color but mostly shadows within the soft glow of strategically placed landscape lighting.

"Does Del know you're here?"

"No." Tatum shook her head. "I…" The girl's voice faded and Sedona sensed her inner struggle.

"You love Tanner," she said now. The brother might be overprotective. Was possibly abusive. But he'd been the only parent this girl had known.

"Sometimes, I guess."

"And you love Del." Or she thought she did.

"Yes. I do." There was no doubt that Tatum believed the words. And maybe they were true. It wouldn't be the first time a love that was born in high school lasted a lifetime.

She had to look no further than her own parents to see that.

"Does Del know that Tanner hit you?"

"No." No hesitation there.

Time was of the essence. The bottom line was that Tatum had had the courage to reach out for help.

"Do you think Del is the one who reported you missing?"

"No. I messaged him on Facebook this morning to tell him I loved him and that I was leaving but I wouldn't say where I was going. I didn't want him to have to lie when his dad asked him about it.

"I know Tanner turned me in. It's just like him. He did it to Talia, too, the first time she ran away. I can't believe I didn't think of that. I just found out the name of this place and then called a hotline to find out more about it and knew today was the only chance I'd have of getting here." There was absolute conviction in Tatum's reply.

"You mentioned the first time Talia ran away. There were more?"

"The second time she took off, she was eighteen and he couldn't do anything. She'd left a note saying she was moving out so she wasn't, like, in danger or missing or anything. But for years he couldn't find her. When he finally did she was in Vegas and there was nothing he could do to her."

"Did he hit Talia, too?" Sedona kept her tone soft, unthreatening. And tried to stick to the facts, not giving rein to any of the emotions that were creeping up on her.

In a small voice, Tatum said, "Yes, he did. The big kids always hid everything from me like I was too dumb to know what was going on. But one time after Thomas left and Talia and Tanner were in this really huge fight, Talia screamed at him to get away from her and said he'd gotten away with slapping her face once but that if he ever touched her again she'd report him." The girl frowned.

And Sedona could only guess at what Tatum was feeling in that moment.

"Is that why she ran away?"

"I don't know. I was only seven."

"So you really don't know her, either?"

"Talia was like my mother until Tanner drove her away. And she still kept in touch with me. In secret. Until Tanner threatened her or something and made her cut me off."

"How long has it been since you've had contact with her?"

"Almost a year. He caught me talking to her last summer. He'd just found out from an old friend of hers where she was in Vegas and then, just my luck, he comes in from the vineyard and hears me saying her name. Next thing I know, he's off to Vegas and when he comes home he tells me she won't be contacting me again."

"Did she?"

"Nope. She had her number changed, blocked my email and unfriended me, too."

"Even though she communicated with you in secret for all those years?"

"Because Tanner didn't know then. She wasn't really crossing him until he knew and I'm sure he expressly forbade it. You have no idea how convincing my brother can be."

"Is that when you found out she was a stripper?"

"No. Talia told me what she was doing. That's why she couldn't petition for custody and let me come live with her. Because child services would never have approved her for my guardian. She wanted me to know she wasn't ditching me. That she loved me and would take me if she could."

It seemed to Sedona that Tatum had tried to look at other avenues to make a good life for herself. To fix her problem.

Without success.

That was going to change.

Tanner Malone wasn't just dealing with a fifteen-year-old girl anymore. He had Sedona Campbell to contend with now.

For better or worse.

CHAPTER SEVEN

TANNER WAS OUT in the furniture barn, looking under an old claw-foot couch that Tatum had wanted to move into the living room. She couldn't possibly fit under it, but—because he was out of his mind with worry—he had to look everywhere. He hit his head when his cell phone rang. It was Detective Morris.

"The boyfriend repeated that she messaged him this morning. And as he told you, she said she loved him. He also admitted, when we told him we could trace deleted Facebook posts, that she told him she was leaving but wouldn't tell him where she was going so he wouldn't get in trouble."

His heart sped up. And dropped. Tatum had left? Without taking any of her things? Where could she have been going? Harcourt had to have made some provisions for her, given her someplace to hang out....

"We know she got on a bus." Morris's voice was all business. And Tanner's heart rate escalated again. "Heading toward Santa Raquel beach. We've spoken with the driver. He told us where she got off." The detective named an intersection he could place, but wasn't all that familiar with. It was easily twenty miles from the vineyard that was situated halfway between Santa Raquel and Santa Barbara. "Do you have any idea why she'd get off there? Is there someone she knows in the area? Someplace you used to go?"

"No. I... We've never been there. I have no idea...."

He tried to remember, forcing his throbbing head to work overtime. Had Tatum attended a birthday party in Santa Raquel, maybe?

"She loves to go to the beach," he said, for lack of any better ideas.

And there were a handful of them a hell of a lot closer than Santa Raquel. Besides, Tatum knew better than to go to the beach alone.

"We've got officers canvassing the area," Morris told him. "Someone has to have seen her."

He was beginning to think more clearly. He headed to the truck, about to get to know that unfamiliar neighborhood really well. "Was she alone?"

"As far as we can tell. The driver said she was the only person to board the bus about a mile from your place."

He knew the stop. Little more than a bench on a country corner. How in the hell had Tatum gotten there?

Harcourt. He had to have taken her. Had to know where she was.

"He said there was an older woman who got off when she did, but they didn't seem to know each other and went in opposite directions. She didn't fit the description of a druggie or a homeless person and he didn't recognize her from the picture you had of your mother."

Tatum didn't know any other older women that he was aware of. "Harcourt's got to be meeting her later tonight. When he can get away without anyone noticing."

"We've spoken with his parents. He won't be getting out of their sight tonight."

"So if she's waiting for him someplace, she's going to be alone in the dark." He wasn't sure which was worse, Tatum alone with Harcourt all night or out by herself.

Or with Tammy.

He feared that the lesser of two evils was the young man he'd banned her from seeing.

In his truck, driving toward the main road, Tanner said, "Can we call them and have them give him his freedom? Just in case. He could lead us to her."

"I'll give them a call," Morris said, not sounding happy about the prospect. "But if they don't want their son used as bait, I can't blame them."

Tanner could, though. If not for their corrupt son, Tatum and Tanner would still be okay, sitting at home, ignoring each other.

Ringing off, he pushed the pedal to the floor, determined to make twenty miles in fewer minutes than that.

"WE'RE GOING TO have to let the police know where you are." Sedona needed a lot more answers. And had no more time. "They're wasting valuable dollars searching for you."

The eyes that looked over at her were filled with fear. And resignation, as well. It was a look far too mature for a fifteen-year-old girl to be wearing. "They're going to send me home with Tanner," she said, without a hint of a whine. "This will all be for nothing."

"If Tanner's hitting you I can ask for an emergency order to have you kept away from him, at least until the state has time to investigate your allegations."

"I told you, I'm not going to report him to the police."

A response that wasn't all that unusual in domestic situations where the abused also loved their abusers.

"You're a minor, Tatum. And you told me about it. I'm legally obligated to report it."

"I'll just deny having told you. Or I'll say I lied. I thought this was a safe place. Where I could come and just tell someone here and have a place to stay until I can get settled on my own."

"You're fifteen. You not only have to finish high school, but you're under your brother's guardianship. He's legally responsible for you."

"I'm not reporting him." Tatum crossed her arms, her face set.

"Why not? If he's hurting you, he needs help, Tatum."

Her gaze darting around the subtly lit garden, Tatum straightened, flicking her long blond hair over her shoulder. "It'll be my word against his," she said. "I don't have any proof. It's not like I took pictures.

Or even told anyone. They're going to think I'm just a fifteen-year-old kid who's mad at him because he won't let me be with my boyfriend."

Sedona couldn't deny the possibility. She'd already thought of it and had to be straight with her client. Even though, technically, Tatum couldn't be her client without her brother's, or the court's, approval.

"Is that what's happening here?"

"No!" Tatum's eyes widened and she faced Sedona squarely. "I'm pissed at him about Del, yes, but I'm not just a spoiled kid who can't take no for an answer. I'm here to find answers."

"What kind of answers?"

Tatum sat back. "You know, about what someone does when they're a victim of domestic violence."

Tatum could be playing them. She could just be saying the right words. And if she was, she'd be caught out. If she wasn't, and they sent her home…

Sedona couldn't take a chance on sending this young girl back to get beat up on again. Statistics showed that domestic violence issues in the home escalated from incident to incident. The next time Tatum might not just get off with a few bruises.

"I have another suggestion," she said, believing that, under the circumstances, it was the best option for the moment.

"What?"

"I can try to talk your brother, to let him know that you aren't missing and haven't run away so that he can alert the police to drop their search. And then ask him if he'd be willing to let you stay here—even if it's just for a day or two, until we get this settled."

"It'll take a lot more than a day or two for anything to get settled with Tanner. More like a lifetime."

"Either way, we're out of time," Sedona said, aware that Lila would be pacing her office, looking at the clock.

They could only pretend not to see the news bulletins for so long.

"What'll happen to me tonight if I tell the cops that Tanner hit me? Which I'm not going to do. I already told you that. But what would happen to me if I did?"

"I can't say for sure. I can probably arrange to have you spend the night here tonight. But they might come for you in the morning. And then it will be largely up to the court. They'll assign a caseworker to you. And investigate the situation."

They could send her home as early as that night, too. Or the next day. Based on the lack of evidence or witnesses—and if no domestic violence reports had ever been filed for Tanner Malone, and there were no medical records of abuse and no problems reported by Tatum's school, and if Tatum said she lied, they probably would send her home. And just keep an eye on things.

Which, as Sedona knew all too well, so often meant wait until the abuse happened again....

She could contact Talia. See if she could get testimony out of the older sister regarding previous abuse. But again, with no corroborating evidence, and considering Talia's current situation and previous history with her brother, her testimony wouldn't be all that credible. The court could go either way. Unless reports had been filed in the past.

"Even if I talk to Tanner, whether he lets you stay here or insists on taking you home, I'm going to have to report the abuse to the police, whether you want to do so or not."

A caseworker would be assigned. Tatum would most likely still be sent home because, as the teenager said, she could just be a truculent child lashing out for having her boyfriend privileges removed.

There would almost surely have to be another abusive incident before anything more could be done.

"What's your choice?" she asked Tatum, standing up in the dimly lit garden. "The police have to be notified that you're safe, Tatum, one way or the other. Do you want me to call your brother or not?"

It felt cruel, to be putting such a choice to a child who'd turned to them for help. But it was the best she could do. Short of putting the girl in her car and running with her.

Standing, her chin low and shoulders sagging, Tatum gave Sedona Tanner Malone's cell phone number.

"WHERE'S MY SISTER?" Tanner approached the woman with the thick blond hair sitting at the corner table in an upscale sandwich shop not far from the corner where Detective Morris had told him Tatum had exited the bus.

Sedona Campbell, she'd said her name was. And that she'd be wearing navy pants and a jacket with a cream-colored blouse.

"She's fine," the thirtyish woman said. "She's with a couple of friends of mine," she said. "Female friends."

"Who are you?"

Reaching into her pocket the woman pulled out a business card and placed it on the table.

Sedona Campbell, Attorney at Law

He read the name of her firm, but didn't take it in. His heart racing, Tanner stood there, trying to slow his mind, to calm the panic.

He was thirty-three, not twenty. He owned a home, a business.

And he was losing control of his baby sister. Cold sweats swept over him. Through him.

"What does she want?" If their mother thought she was going to ride back into their lives and sweep her baby away, she was wrong.

No matter how vulnerable a girl Tatum's age might be to her mother's false promises of newfound sobriety. Tanner, Talia and Thomas had heard them all too many times. But Tatum…she'd only been five when she'd last heard from Tammy.

"Have a seat, Mr. Malone."

Because he was feeling a bit sick, Tanner did as she asked. He'd be fine. He knew the signs of post-stress-induced anxiety. And knew how to overcome them, as well.

The law was on his side. He had to remember that.

"Tell me how much she wants."

The woman's creamy white brow furrowed. Who had creamy white skin in California? "I'm sorry?"

"You're a family lawyer," he explained slowly. If this lawyer wanted to play games she'd soon find she'd come to the wrong man. He knew all his mother's tricks. Eventually, he'd grown immune to every one of them.

"That's right."

"The only times my family has ever needed a lawyer have been when our mother deigns to make an appearance in our lives." That was true even before she'd left them for good and given him custody. He'd had to quit school to protect the kids from her—and the court system. Not that anyone needed to know... "Tell me, what's Tammy said or done to get to Tatum and how much does she want?"

"I don't know your mother. Or anyone named Tammy."

Leaning back in his chair Tanner feigned a nonchalance he didn't feel. He'd learned early on that if he showed a woman weakness she'd use it to wipe her feet. Spreading his hands and then steepling his fingers, he said, "So whatever she's calling herself this time, how much does she think it's going to cost her to provide the life my sister needs?"

Because Tammy would never admit the money was for herself. To feed her habits. No, she'd blink those big blue eyes and swear that it was for her children.

She'd tried a few times over the past ten years to extort money from them—from him. Playing on his love for his siblings. But it had been a while since he'd heard from her. Three years. He'd looked it up as soon as Morris had left.The longest she'd ever gone.

Sedona Campbell flicked a strand of really long hair behind her shoulder. A move that accentuated her femininity. And worried him. "Let me get this clear," she said. "You think someone has your sister?"

It was like a game of chess. He not only had to plan his moves a minimum of three in advance, he had to assess his opponent, to predict what she was thinking and, more important, to ascertain her next moves before making his own.

"Tatum's a good girl," he said. "A straight-A student who loves to read. She has an appreciation for antiques and nurtures hurt animals anytime she can sneak one in. She also has no problem speaking her mind. She is not the type of person who would just up and leave on her own."

"Especially since you've made her a virtual prisoner out there on that vineyard of yours."

"That's what Tammy told you?"

Ms. Campbell looked at the table. Seeing a chessboard of her own? After a couple of seconds, she glanced back at him. "Let's get one thing clear, sir. I've never met your mother, or anyone else who knows your sister. I am here on Tatum's behalf. Period."

A vise descended upon his chest. And he was sweating again. From the inside out. "You want me to believe that my little sister hired a lawyer?"

"Technically she can't do that without your signature."

Right. Okay. But... "She sought one out, though?"

"She came to us for help."

His feet landed flat with a thud as he sat forward and put his arms on the table. "Who is *us?* Why does Tatum need a lawyer? Where is she?"

He was back to Del Harcourt. This was about that punk kid like he'd originally thought.

But he had the senior Harcourt in his corner. And he'd put his money on the mother standing by whatever Ken Harcourt dictated.

Not that that was necessarily a healthy thing, but it would serve his situation. And theirs was none of his business.

"Your sister is at a women's shelter."

Oh, God, no. "Is she all right? Is she hurt?"

"Physically she's fine. But women, and more particularly teenage girls, don't turn up at shelters just for fun."

"The bastard hit her again?"

"You're saying you didn't do it?"

Breathe, man. In and out. Relax your chest and breathe. "I didn't do what?"

"Hit your sister."

Everything inside Tanner stilled in that moment. His heart. His soul. "Is she saying I did?"

Tatum was pissed at him. But she wouldn't turn

on him. They were tight. More so than the other two. Since the day she was born she'd been his little girl. More daughter than sister. There had to be a misunderstanding. Someone at that shelter, this *lawyer* perhaps, had listened wrong.

"Are you denying that you hit your sister, Mr. Malone?"

"Hell, yes, I'm denying it!"

"But you knew she'd been hit?" The woman didn't believe him. Her disdainful tone was enough to tell him that, but the cool look in her eyes was a dead giveaway, too.

"I didn't know. I suspected. When I asked her about it, she adamantly denied it. She looked me in the eye."

"And that means something?"

"Tatum has lied to me before, but never while looking me in the eye."

People milled around them, talking over coffee drinks and eating freshly baked cookies. Scattered about at various tables. Some had computers. Tablets. It was a gathering place.

And it was like Tanner wasn't even there. He had no sense of reality. No way to wake himself from the nightmare.

"But you saw signs that she'd been hurt? Bruises, perhaps, that she explained away?"

"I grabbed her arm out in the barn when she was trying to run after Harcourt. She flinched. I made her roll up her sleeve. The bruise was faded to yellow, but I was sure I saw the imprint of knuckles. She told me I was crazy. That I see the worst in everything. She said she ran into an antique dresser spindle in the barn."

"Harcourt? Who's that?"

"A rich punk she met at a party a couple of months back."

"I take it you don't like him."

He wasn't all that fond of Tatum's lawyer, either. She looked good enough to eat and had the mind of a barracuda. "I just told you he hit my sister. What do you think?"

"You *allege* that he hit your sister. Other than that, has he given you cause to doubt him?"

"He smokes dope. I overheard him trying to convince my fifteen-year-old sister to try it. I suspect he's trying to get her to sleep with him, too. And he speaks disrespectfully to his perfectly respectable mother." For starters. "Now…I need to see my sister." He'd spoken with her on the phone, briefly, when Sedona Campbell had called twenty minutes before to arrange this meeting. Just enough to be satisfied that she was fine, so that he could alert the police.

"I can arrange a meeting, but I need to speak with you first."

"I believe I'm done talking."

"I'm under legal obligation to call the police and inform them that your sister, a minor, reported abuse at your hands."

He had to see Tatum.

Had to slow down. His nerve endings were tripping over themselves.

Outwardly, not a muscle of Tanner's body moved.

This couldn't be happening. Didn't make sense. He'd made a good home for Tatum. A normal home.

"Or we can handle it another way."

The words were a lifeline. And they told him she was working him. Either she was under a legal obligation or she wasn't. If she had to report him, how could they handle it any other way?

She was the lawyer. She'd know. And she'd figure that he might not.

Eyes narrowing, he watched her. Skipping his next move to wait for hers. Any other time he might have enjoyed the game. But not now, with Tatum's life in the balance.

"Tatum would like to stay at The Lemonade Stand, at least for the night, and for longer if that can be arranged."

"My sister has a home." And, as her legal guardian, he had rights and obligations, too.

"She claims that it's an abusive one."

"Just because she claims it—" which he didn't buy "—doesn't make it so."

While he couldn't believe Tatum would accuse him of something so heinous, so life changing, he couldn't figure out why this lawyer woman would be lying to him. Unless she'd lied about her client, too. Unless his mother really was involved.

And wanted Tatum.

To sell her for drug money? Or have her go to work

so Tammy could stay home with her latest dealer and get high? Stay high?

When people first met Tammy they fell for her vulnerable victim act. Maybe this Sedona Campbell was in the still-believing stage of knowing his mother. Maybe she thought she was fighting for the lives of a helpless woman and her child.

So maybe Tammy had concocted the abuse story and not Tatum. Calming a bit as he thought things through, Tanner figured he'd come upon the more likely scenario. Tatum, and this lawyer, too, were pawns in Tammy's game.

"I'm assuming, since you didn't immediately report me to the police, that you have some doubts about my...sister's...story." Tammy's story, he was pretty convinced now.

The woman—a looker, he couldn't deny that—sized him up. And seemed to be considering him as strongly as he'd been considering her. Because he was right? She had doubts?

Did that mean, if he handled this right, she could become an ally?

"I'm interested in what's best for Tatum."

Not really an answer to his question, but it was enough.

"I'm willing to listen to what you have to say," he told her. He could listen for as long as it took.

And then take his baby sister home.

CHAPTER EIGHT

THE MAN DIDN'T look like an ogre. He didn't seem like the violent type, either. On the contrary, Sedona couldn't stop looking at him. Sure he was tall, his dark hair was a little long, but he moved with slow grace, agile, but not aggressive. Her first instinct was to like him.

He'd taken his seat as though weighing the options. And every move he'd made since had flowed more than jerked. As though he lived his life deliberately as opposed to reacting to it. That was a characteristic she respected.

"First and foremost, I'd like you to allow Tatum to spend the night at The Lemonade Stand." Sedona repeated her initial request. She'd wanted to keep her tone congenial. Nonthreatening. Her words came out as more of a plea than anything else. She'd expected not to like this man. Instead, she wanted to get along with him.

For Tatum's sake. And…just because.

"It's obvious that your sister is struggling. And that she's not happy at home. It's also very obvious to those of us who've spoken with her today that she wants, more than anything at the moment, to spend the night at the shelter."

He watched her. Saying nothing. But his gaze remained direct. Focused.

"We have a bed ready for her. In a bungalow with a woman who lives and works full-time at The Stand. There will be another woman, an employee, who will be awake in the bungalow all night, keeping a watch in case anyone has any problems."

His brow quirked.

"If you allow her to stay, Tatum will be under twenty-four-hour supervision. She understands that if she stays at the shelter, she will not be free to come and go. She's a minor. She can only leave on the say-so of her legal guardian."

"And she wants to stay on those conditions?"

"Yes, sir."

"I prefer not to be called 'sir.' My name's Tanner."

There was no invitation to friendship in the words. More like a simple form of address.

Sedona liked that, too.

Remembering Tatum, a girl without a mother, a girl whose big sister had been out of touch, Sedona tried to keep her guard up against this man. "So, Tanner, will you let her stay?"

"I want to see her."

"I understand. She'd rather not see you tonight, though. She's asked for this one night of peace to figure things out."

"There's nothing to figure out. She's coming home. She has school tomorrow."

Sedona tried to smile. It didn't work. The man barely moved, his facial features relaxed. His voice was so quiet she could only just make it out within the din of the other patrons in the shop. And yet going up against him was like scaling impenetrable rock. Sheetrock. The kind that was strong without bulk.

He was human. When it came to people there was always a way in.

Thinking back over their conversation, she searched for any breach in the facade he presented, any exhibiting of tension. A different tone of voice, or speed of speech. And could only think of one.

"Why would you think your mother hired me? Has she tried to be in touch with Tatum?"

"She's tried to contact us a few times. When she was down and out and needed money or a place to stay. I won't let her anywhere near us. She signed away her rights to her minor children ten years ago, and other than the gift of life, she's never given them anything worth having. I'm not going to have her insidious filth anywhere near them."

There was no venom in his voice. Just calm conviction.

"What makes you think she'd hire me now?"

He looked her straight in the eye. "My mother is ruled by one thing and one thing only—her addiction to drugs. If she's desperate, she'll do whatever it takes. She once promised a guy he could join my sister Talia in the shower if he'd give her a hundred bucks. I'd left to take Tatum next door when Talia got in the shower, not knowing that Tammy had this guy in her room. I traded off with the neighbor, taking the little ones to kindergarten. Tammy got confused and thought it was my day to drive them. I came back and heard what was going on and kicked the guy's ass out of our house."

Sedona believed him. She didn't know why, but she did. "How old was Talia?"

"Sixteen."

Hadn't Tatum said her sister was sixteen the first time she'd run away?

"Did you press charges?"

"I had no proof because nothing actually happened. It was their word against mine. And I didn't want Talia to know what I'd overheard, or what had almost happened to her, which she surely would have found out if we'd gone to court. But I knew, because of our past history with the system, that I stood a much better chance of being believed than Tammy did. So I told her I was going to press charges unless she gave me custody of the kids, then got out of our home and never came back."

He didn't seem to be looking for sympathy. Or even understanding. And he'd given her far more insight than he probably knew or intended. Tonight she saw a man who'd had a lot of responsibility thrown on him from a very young age. And a boy who'd clearly seen and known more than any child should.

She saw a man who'd had a tough life.

And who could have developed an unhealthy view of relationships. And of family.

A man who would resort to hitting his sister if he thought, for one second, she was going to fall into her mother's ways? A man who thought physical discipline was far healthier for his teenage sister than the drugs and sex her boyfriend was using to tempt her away?

The drugs and sex that had ruined their mother's life?

"When was the last time you heard from her?"

"Three years. But it makes sense for her to show up. Tatum's fifteen. Another three years and we'll be home free. She's running out of time if she hopes to milk one last penny out of having given birth."

Wow. How could a person say such words without any hint of bitterness in his voice? The guy was cold as ice—or was healthier than she figured she'd have been if she'd grown up like he had.

"You have a brother, Thomas, correct?"

"Yes."

"How does he feel about your mother?"

"You'd have to ask him."

"I'm asking you."

"Thomas's father was Tammy's dealer. And, I believe, her pimp. When he was five, Thomas disappeared for three days. I never knew what happened to him, but I know he was with his father, and when he came back he didn't talk for more than a month."

"Did you report this to anyone?"

"No. I was ten at the time. My father was dead. I

had no way of providing for my brother and sister and knew that if they took us from our mother, we'd be separated. I just made certain that I didn't leave Thomas or Talia alone with Tammy after that."

"Do any of you have grandparents?"

"Not that we've ever known. From what I gathered, Tammy was a lot like her own mother. Egotistical and immature. Just look at the names she gave us—how cute for her, Tanner, Thomas, Talia and Tatum. Unusual enough to be remembered. Poetic, she used to say. But embarrassing as hell to a kid in junior high."

He paused, like he hadn't meant to reveal so much. And then, when she said nothing, he continued. "According to her, my father's parents were horrified that he'd ever had anything to do with her and denied that I was their grandson."

"And your dad didn't step up and do something?"

"Nope. But he took out a life insurance policy naming me as his beneficiary. In the event of an early death, the money went into a trust that couldn't be touched by anyone but me after I turned twenty-three. He died of a heart attack when I was eight."

So he'd had some money. Sedona was relieved, then pulled herself up short. She couldn't care. Couldn't sympathize with him. She was there to represent his sister and Tatum's charges against him.

"You used the shower incident against your mother because you'd just gotten the means to care for your siblings yourself," she said. Admiring him even while she assessed him for signs of an abuser.

"I had to know that the court would keep us together, yes, before I could take such a strong stand against her."

"Would it have been so awful if you'd been split up?" She had to ask. "Did you ever consider the possibility that your sisters would be placed in good homes where they'd be loved and happy and grow up with nothing more to worry about than brushing their teeth and emptying the dishwasher?"

"My mother wouldn't sign away her rights to anyone but me," he said, seeming kind now, as he explained things to her. "The girls would have been foster kids, not eligible for adoption. Together, at least we had one another. A place of our own where we belonged. We loved one another. And we understood one another's challenges, too, since we'd all come from the same place."

Sedona wondered if the siblings needed one another as much as Tanner had evidently needed them? Had Talia, Thomas and Tatum been his sense of family? Of belonging? And now that Tatum, the last of them, was almost ready to fly the coop, was he having a hard time letting her go? Serious enough to use physical force to keep Tatum with him?

"I am not now nor have I ever been in contact with your mother," she told him, aware of the lateness of the hour. Of Tatum waiting back at The Lemonade Stand, nervous and wondering what was going to happen to her. "Your sister showed up at The Lemonade Stand today, out of the blue. She asked for our help. We're trying to give it to her. That's what we do."

"And she says I hit her."

"That's correct."

His gaze didn't waver. "I didn't."

She believed him. And wasn't sure she trusted her own instincts at the moment. This man was having an effect on her that she didn't understand.

"She's afraid of something, Mr.…Tanner. I've never witnessed nor even heard of a fifteen-year-old begging to stay locked in at a women's shelter before. Not without just cause."

"Harcourt has something to do with this."

"Maybe he told Tatum to seek help."

He didn't flinch. Didn't show any overt reaction at all. Tatum had said her brother was a vintner. That held weight with a wine connoisseur like her. It took real dedication, tenderness, an attention to art, to produce a good wine.

Maybe that was why she felt such a strong desire to like him.

"What happens if I insist on taking her home tonight?" It didn't sound like a rhetorical question. "Other than me royally pissing her off, of course."

"We'd have to call the police. They'd come out."

"Would they take her?"

"They might."

His eyes narrowed, and Sedona was afraid she'd somehow transmitted a compassion she shouldn't be feeling toward this man.

"What are the chances they'd take her?"

She wanted him to trust her. Because Tatum obviously loved him. Not only had she said so, but her refusal to press charges also pointed to an attachment to him. One thing Sedona was already completely sure of—she was already fond of Tatum and wanted to help her and her brother be as happy as they possibly could be.

It sounded to her as though they both deserved a big dose of the secure, happy and loving environment she'd grown up in.

But she could not take even a minute chance of possibly returning an abuse victim to her abuser. Not for any reason.

"Tonight? Not good at all."

That eyebrow rose one more time. And taking a last-ditch chance on a nurturing instinct that had been muted in law school, she said, "Your sister has said that if we call the police, she's going to tell them that she lied to us. She's going to insist you've never hit her. She has no bruises left to show. There have been no prior complaints or reports, no reason for anyone to seriously suspect that this is anything more than a recalcitrant teenager trying to get back at the guardian who thwarted her love life. They might or might not assign a caseworker. If they did you'd have to endure a few visits. And as long as there are no further instances of abuse, you'll carry on as you've always done."

She'd handed the life he wanted back to him on a

silver platter. Tanner Malone continued to watch her, his face as placid as always.

"You knew that all along."

"Yes."

"And you don't know my mother."

His mother. His tell. The crack in his armor. Curious that it had come out just as she'd handed him victory.

"I swear to you, Tanner, I have never met your mother. I'd never heard of any of you until I met Tatum this afternoon."

"I was hoping there'd be mac and cheese on the table when I got home this afternoon."

Random.

"She told us she was Talia when she arrived. Had her older sister's ID."

He didn't say a word, as though waiting to see where she was going.

"We discovered who she was when someone saw the Endangered Missing Advisory on the news."

"She didn't want to be found."

Sedona watched him, wishing she could have even an inkling of what was going on in his mind. She didn't want to send Tatum home with him that night. At all. The girl was struggling, whether for the reasons she'd said or not, Sedona wasn't completely sure. But until she knew the truth behind Tatum's unease, she wanted the girl with the people at The Lemonade Stand. The people she'd turned to for help.

"Someone hit her. I'm one hundred percent convinced of it."

"Believe it or not, so am I."

"But you think you can protect her from it happening again?" Many abusers did. When they weren't in a rage, they were rational. Loving. And truly loved. They wanted more than anything to protect those they loved. She just couldn't see this man as an abuser. Which meant that someone else had hit the girl. Maybe her boyfriend. Or someone else neither of them knew about....

"I'm not sure what I think at the moment." He picked up a piece of straw wrapper from the iced tea she'd ordered but never touched. "I'm afraid that if I push things she'll change her mind and report me to the police. And then we really will have a problem."

Her stomach sank.

"Not because I did anything wrong, but because she really thinks she loves this creep and Tatum wants what she thinks he has. A normal family. A sitcom life. She's impressionable and naive and is willing to sacrifice anything for love," he said, not as though he was surmising, but as though he *knew*.

"Did she tell you that?"

"She didn't have to. I have eyes. And ears. And..." For the first time in a key moment, he glanced away.

"And?"

"I read her diary."

"You breached her trust and impinged on her privacy?"

"Yes." He was looking at her again. "I'm not proud of myself, but yes. And that very same day, I told her

I'd done so. But after she met this Harcourt kid, she started to change, to snipe at me for no reason. I knew something was up and was afraid Tammy had contacted her."

"Why not just ask her?"

"I did. She told me nothing was going on."

"She lied to you?"

"She didn't look me in the eye."

"What did she say after you told her you'd read her diary?"

"We got into a fight about Harcourt."

A fight that had clearly been ongoing ever since.

"She lied to you. Do you think she'd lie to the police?"

"Right now, after today, while she's in his thrall, I think she could do anything to be with him."

"So how does involving the police give her that?"

"They take her from me, she's a fifteen-year-old in the system. Who's going to care what boy she dates? Or even notice whether or not she's seeing anyone on a steady basis, let alone know whether or not he's good to her? As long as she tells her caseworker she's happy and keeps her grades up—and covers her bruises— chances are no one will care."

"But…"

"This kid comes from money," he went on. "A lot of it. And he knows how to play people. He's a real pro."

"Isn't it possible that he really loves her?"

"Sure it's possible. I'm not saying he doesn't. Who wouldn't love Tatum? She's the sweetest, smartest young woman I've ever known. I'm only saying that if my sister stays with him, he's going to ruin her life."

How could he be so sure? Wasn't it possible that his past, his life with his mother, had skewed his perceptions? That he was responding in a knee-jerk way because he was afraid to trust his sister to make her own choices?

But his theory, that Tatum was trying to work the system to be allowed to see her boyfriend, while desperate, wasn't completely crazy.

He tapped the table with his forefinger. Three times. "I would consider allowing her to stay at this…shelter, under a couple of conditions."

"What are they?" The Stand's guidelines were strict. To protect *all* the residents. They couldn't be bent for one.

"I will pick her up every morning and drive her to school. I will pick her up from school every afternoon and return her to the shelter. Other than that, she's not to leave. For any reason. Unless I know about it ahead of time and approve each and every outing."

Turning a child over to her alleged abuser—even for rides to and from school—didn't sound like a good idea. But it was a hell of a lot better than sending her home with him. At least this way they'd get her back every day. Sara, a counselor at The Lemonade Stand, would meet with her each afternoon. And they could put countermeasures in place. If Tatum didn't show up at school, or back at the shelter at exactly the time she should, they would know who to hunt down.

Sedona didn't believe Tanner was an abuser…

"How far is her school from here?"

"Fifteen minutes."

Not enough time to get Tatum on a plane before they'd be on to him. Sedona had the thought—but she didn't really think he'd try to steal her away. There was something about this guy…

"Something" couldn't hold weight in her world. It wouldn't stand up in court.

"If she doesn't arrive at either place, we call the police immediately."

"I'm counting on it."

"What's the second condition?"

"That you represent Tatum, but give me a chance to show you that I am who I say I am. Give me a chance to prove my innocence. Come to our home. Check me out. Spend some time with the two of us together. Spend some time alone with me. Make calls. Ask around. Get to know me. And then help me get whoever made my baby sister feel like she had to run away to a shelter to be safe. I'll pay your regular fee for all your time involved, of course."

His voice didn't break. But there was a definite tremor.

A curious sensation ran through her. *Spend time alone with him. Get to know him…*

"I can't promise I'll help you. The law is the law. Black-and-white. I believe in it and I uphold it. I won't compromise that for you."

"I'm not asking you to."

"Your winery is in the infant stages."

"Yes."

"I know a bit about winemaking and I know that starting up isn't cheap. Where would you get the money to pay my fees?" She had to find out what the man was made of. And if she couldn't read him, she'd find out about him one seemingly innocuous question at a time.

"Tatum's college fund, at the moment. There's enough there to pay four years at any Ivy League school. If I use it up, we'll get loans to pay for her college and I'll spend the rest of my life paying them off if I have to, and it'll be worth every cent. This is my sister's life we're talking about here."

Right. No matter what Sedona was feeling personally, good or bad, the only way Tatum would be able to stay at The Lemonade Stand right away was if Sedona agreed to his crazy plan.

"I'll call Lila McDaniels, the managing director at the shelter. She's the one who'll have to make this decision. She's waiting to meet you."

"Good, I'd like to see this shelter."

"She's not going to agree to that. Not tonight, at any rate. And not while you're suspected of abuse. The Lemonade Stand is sacred. A safe place."

"I want to see my sister."

"Then Lila will have to bring her here."

Sedona didn't want to put the girl through any more that night. But didn't really see a way around it, either. Not when they were so close to keeping her.

And seeing the siblings together, watching them interact, might clear her mind a bit where Tanner Malone was concerned.

In ten years of practicing family law, specializing in victims of domestic abuse, she'd never once, ever, felt sympathy for the abuser.

And that, she told herself, was the reason she had doubts about Tatum Malone's story regarding her abuser.

It wasn't because she found the accused man interesting. No, absolutely not.

"I'll go home and get together a bag for her for school in the morning. She'll want her curling iron and makeup and it wouldn't hurt if she did some studying tonight, either. I can meet you all back here in forty-five minutes if that works."

"I'll make sure it works," Sedona told the man. "And, Tanner? I work for the shelter pro bono. If, at some point, you hire me to press charges against someone else, then we discuss my fees. For now, I'm agreeing to take this on without pay."

Somehow, that made it all seem a little more acceptable.

She stood as he did.

"I pay our way."

"Your sister chose to come to us. And I'm choosing to take this on. But only on the specified conditions. I can't be on your payroll and investigating you at the same time."

With a slow nod, he turned away. Sedona watched him all the way to his truck before dialing Lila's private line.

CHAPTER NINE

OH, GOD, HELP ME. She couldn't see Tanner. She just couldn't. All she had to do was look at him and he'd know what she was thinking. He'd know about Del.

Shaking from the inside out, Tatum sat in the car next to Lila McDaniels and wondered why she couldn't have been lucky enough to have her for a mother. Or maybe a grandmother. She was kinda old. Like maybe sixty or something.

Sedona would make a good mom. But she probably already had kids. And she didn't seem old enough to have a fifteen-year-old, anyway.

"You okay?" Lila's glance made her wish she could just lay her head down on her lap and take a nap.

"Yeah." Putting her finger to her mouth, she almost started in on her nail. And remembered Tanner's words. *If you chew your nails, you tell people you're uncomfortable. Besides, why start a habit that'll be hard to break?*

She'd been a kid at the time. Maybe eight or nine. Before she'd cared about nails.

She'd chewed them behind his back. Probably because, like Talia, she was her mother's daughter. Since she'd met Del, she'd been trying really hard to break the habit.

"You don't have to do this." Lila's voice was soft.

"I do if I want to stay at TLS tonight."

"If we call the police, they might let you stay."

Her stomach cramped at the mention of the cops again. Stupid, stupid her that she hadn't thought about them. About being reported missing or having Lila and Sedona figure out that she wasn't Talia.

Stupid, stupid, stupid not to see that her lie about Tanner, which she'd only told to get into The Lemonade Stand, could get him in trouble. She'd thought just the people at the shelter would know what she'd said, and since they had no idea who he even was, what could it matter?

Del would break up with her if she left TLS and went back home to Tanner. He'd broken up with her on Sunday, after Tanner had kicked him out. Until Tatum had promised to find a way to get around her brother.

Then yesterday, when she'd agreed to go somewhere else—to the shelter—he'd said he missed her so much.

She'd missed him, too. Way more than she'd ever thought she could. She'd felt as if she were going to die with every breath she took. And she'd been scared to death that he'd go off and be with someone else before she had a chance to make things right with him.

Every girl in Santa Raquel was hot for Del Harcourt. Not just because he was rich, but because he was a jock and the hottest guy she'd ever seen.

She still couldn't believe that he'd actually chosen

her. A loser Malone. Not just to hook up with, but to date. He asked her to be his girlfriend. To be exclusive. He said he wanted to marry her. And didn't care that her parents were, like, homeless druggies or whatever.

And it wasn't just to get back at his parents, either. Mr. and Mrs. Harcourt liked her, too. Del's mom had even said Tatum could stay with them anytime she wanted or needed to. If, like, Tanner had to be out of town or anything.

And Tanner was screwing it all up. He'd lied to her about everything and scared Talia off and made Tatum live out on that stupid farm he'd promised they'd fix up so she didn't have to be embarrassed every time someone picked her up or dropped her off. And then he hadn't fixed it. And, besides that, he wasn't who she'd thought he was at all....

Feeling as though she might need a bathroom, Tatum reined in her thoughts as Lila turned another corner. She'd said the coffee shop was only a couple of minutes away. They'd better get there quick.

And when they did, she wasn't talking to Tanner. She wasn't even looking at him. She wasn't going to let him mess her up or make her feel worse than she already did. She just had to show up.

And then she could stay at TLS. And not have to talk to the police.

Even for Del she couldn't go that far. Tanner might be a jerk, but sometimes she still loved him. And even if she didn't, she couldn't be like him. She couldn't lie about who and what he was, or what he'd done.

He might not be the great guy everyone seemed to think he was, but he hadn't hit *her*.

And she wasn't going to get him in trouble. He was still her brother.

But he had to get that he had to let her stay at TLS.

She had to learn to recognize when something was abuse and when it wasn't, and how to live with someone who'd been abused so she could be a good wife to Del.

And maybe someone could help her figure out her brother, too.

TANNER CAME BACK to the table, calm and ready to show Tatum how very much she was loved. Ready to support her in whatever way she needed.

He'd known the time would come when Tatum faced the same struggles Thomas and Talia had faced—the day would come when she'd look in the mirror and see a person born of two drug addicts, neither of whom cared enough for her to hang around, let alone felt any kind of unconditional love for her.

He'd hoped—really hoped—that his own unconditional love would have been enough. She'd only been five when Tammy left.

Tatum remembered her mother. But anytime she spoke about Tammy it was to relate a memory from the good times, the few sober minutes when Tammy would overwhelm her children with love and attention.

Sedona Campbell was the only one sitting in the late-night internet sandwich café when he returned just after nine with Tatum's backpack in hand. He'd packed only enough to see her through this one night.

The attorney looked just as good as he remembered. Beautiful but tired…

"I heard from Lila several minutes ago. She had a hard time getting Tatum to agree to the meeting."

He had a feeling Ms. Campbell had been instrumental in that outcome. He just wasn't sure whether she was playing him, trying to trap him in what she believed was Tatum's truth or if she'd agreed to his proposal with the sincerity in which he'd proposed it.

It didn't much matter to his decision making at the moment. She was his best shot. Until he figured out something better.

And he would—figure out something better. Regardless of how attracted he felt to the woman. He knew not to rely on her.

"I assume that means they've agreed to my conditions."

They hadn't called to tell him otherwise.

"For now."

They were all on the same page, then—settling for something they didn't want to buy time to figure out how to get what they did want. He knew how the game was played.

He'd been playing it his whole life.

Pulling out the chair opposite Sedona at the table for four, Tanner deliberately left the other two seats, opposite each other, open, forcing Tatum, when she arrived, to sit perpendicular to him. As close to him as he could maneuver.

He settled his long legs to the side, and stared at the attorney, liking what he saw. If he had to spend time he couldn't spare convincing someone he was a good guy, then at least he could be thankful that it might prove enjoyable. "Why are you doing this?" The question was slow and deliberate.

"I'm not convinced you hit your sister."

"I didn't."

"I believe someone did."

"I know why you're helping Tatum. And I have a fairly good understanding of why you agreed to my plan. I'm asking why an attorney, who has her own practice, and an A-plus rating, volunteers at a women's shelter." He'd done his homework on her in the half hour he'd been gone. A Google search on his phone took a minute.

"Does it matter?"

"It does if you're predisposed to prejudice against the accused before guilt is proven."

It did because he was curious about her. And he *wanted* to believe the curiosity stemmed only from her connection to Tatum. But he realized that wasn't the case.

"You want to know if I'm capable of giving you a fair shot."

No. Actually, he was just curious. A fair shot hadn't even entered his mind. "Something like that."

"I worked with a battered women's advocacy group

in law school. Extracurricular volunteer activity was a requisite."

"Why battered women?"

Her head bowed and Tanner watched her slender, perfectly manicured fingers smooth the edge of the wood-grain table. He was still waiting for an answer when she glanced up at him.

"My best friend in high school had an abusive stepfather. I'd see the bruises on her and I knew something was wrong, but she claimed she was a klutz. And trying to learn how to Rollerblade. And wearing too-high heels that caused her to slip on the stairs. Trouble was she wasn't a klutz. I never saw a pair of Rollerblades in her room. And the stairs in her house were carpeted...."

The room, which had begun to fill with couples on dates and internet surfers, with kitchen noises and elevator music, faded as Tanner listened to her.

"She used to spend the night at my house once or twice a week, as often as we could get our parents to agree, but never once asked me to stay with her."

He knew that drill. And, until Harcourt, had always strongly encouraged Tatum to bring her friends home. Because she had a home to bring them to.

He'd been able to give her that. And that should count for something.

"I don't know what made me push, maybe hurt feelings because I wasn't welcomed in her inner sanctum. Or maybe it was that I sensed that she needed help but couldn't do anything until I knew what kind of help she needed. Anyway, one weekend when my folks were gone, I asked her mom if I could stay with them in place of the arrangements my folks had made."

"Which were?"

He glanced at the door. Tatum should be there soon. And he wanted a few more minutes alone with Sedona Campbell, too. Sitting with her felt…good.

"I was supposed to go with my brother to his friend's house. Mark's parents were close friends of my parents and our two families spent a lot of time together."

"You have a brother."

"Yes."

Good to know. "Older or younger?"

"Older."

Even better.

"In touch with him much?"

"We're close."

Getting better by the second. She'd know what Tatum had to gain in having him around.

"So you stayed the weekend with your friend…"

"Yes." Sedona stopped, watched him, and he kept his expression bland as always. He didn't know what she was looking for and didn't want her to find something she wasn't wanting to see. "Or rather, no. Her mother invited me. I went. But that first night, her mother and stepfather went out to some party. There'd been some old family friends there. The stepfather was certain the mother had been flirting. He'd also had a lot to drink. My friend and I were in sleeping bags on the living-room floor because we'd been trying to stay up all night watching old movies and we heard them in the kitchen, fighting. At first it was just accusation."

Sedona swallowed. And Tanner wanted to reach out to her. But not like he would reach out to Talia. Or Tatum.

And not like he'd have touched any of the women he'd quietly dated over the years, either.

More like a combination of the two. It didn't sit well, and so he pushed the idea—the whole uncomfortable sensation—away.

"Then what happened?" he asked quietly.

"He said, 'You wanted him to touch you, didn't you, honey? On your breast. Like this.'" She swallowed again. But other than the darkness in her eyes, there was no other indication of the emotion she was obviously struggling with.

"I heard her mother whimper and opened my eyes. Without lifting my head from my pillow I looked at my friend. She was watching me and, barely moving her head, shook it enough to tell me not to do anything."

The door to the coffee shop opened and both of them turned their heads, but the couple who entered was definitely not Tatum and Lila.

"So that was it," Tanner said, with a peculiar inability to let this go. He'd heard stories of abuse before. Could actually recite them. You didn't sit through years of state-funded group counseling without taking in some of the material. "You had to lie there and listen to him beat his wife?"

"Not quite." She glanced at the door one more time,

but if she was looking for Lila and Tatum to rescue her, she was out of luck. "My friend's brother was downstairs and he came up. He offered to take me to my brother's friend's house. I didn't want to leave my friend and when I asked her brother if she could come with me, too, the stepdad came in, grabbed her by her hair and pulled her down to the floor."

"So you had to leave her there."

"I did leave her there. I made a mistake."

"You were a kid. And a girl. Powerless to go up against an abusive grown man."

"I called the police."

"So they saved her."

"No. Her mother denied my allegations. My friend did, too. And on Monday, at school, she pretended like she didn't know who I was. She never spoke to me again."

"Because she couldn't handle what you knew?"

Her gaze steadied, infused with warmth as she leaned toward him.

"How do you know that?" she asked him, and it felt as if it was only the two of them in the large room.

He'd exposed a part of himself he didn't share.

"Do you have any idea what happened to your friend?" he asked, deliberately ignoring her question.

"She got pregnant six months later and quit school to get married. I ran into a mutual acquaintance a couple of years ago and she told me that my friend is now divorced and has three or four kids by two different men. She works at a motel on Highway 1, cleaning rooms. And is a good mom as long as she goes to her meetings."

Headlights showed a car turning into the parking lot. The shelter manager with Tatum, he hoped.

"So you help other women to make up for leaving that night without your friend."

"When I had to volunteer I chose the battered women's advocacy group over the other volunteer choices," Sedona said, a slight edge to her voice.

Which made him ask, "You don't tell that story much, do you?"

"Other than my family, I've never told anyone."

Which begged the question, why had she told him? But he didn't ask. He didn't want to think about why he'd asked such a personal question in the first place.

A fiftyish-looking, gray-haired woman had just walked in the door with his baby sister right behind her.

CHAPTER TEN

"WHAT DO YOU THINK?"

It was late, nearly eleven, and Sedona had to be in court at nine in the morning, had to meet her client at her office at eight to go over her testimony in a cantankerous divorce trial involving child custody issues, but she sat in Lila's office as though she had all the time in the world.

Ellie had probably gone to bed without her.

Lila, who lived in her own house around the corner from The Lemonade Stand, but often spent the night in the little suite off her office, joined Sedona on the couch.

"If the brother didn't do it, and we put her in the system, we likely expose her to whoever she's protecting and greatly increase the probability that it will happen again."

They were talking about Tatum Malone, of course. Discussing the course they were going to take.

"She's said she'll say she was lying about Tanner if we force her to talk to the police," Sedona said. "We've seen no physical evidence of abuse. By law, there's nothing to report."

"We know that a recanted accusation could just mean that she's afraid of retribution if she goes through with pressing charges."

"I don't think so. But I also believe that someone has hit that teenager. More than once."

"I think your plan is the only viable choice at the moment," Lila said after a long pause, her brow creased with a concern she didn't often show.

Lila looked tired out. Something else Sedona didn't see much.

"It just makes you our watchdog," the older woman continued. "And I don't like that at all. If something happens to that child, you'll hold yourself responsible and that's neither right nor fair."

"If we turn her over, we risk them sending her home to him, and then we have no watch at all. What we know is that someone hurt her while she was living under Tanner's roof. And if they take her from him because he might have done it, and he didn't do it, then we risk whoever did do it getting her again. Especially if it's the boyfriend, like Tanner believes. Bottom line here is that if Tatum Malone gets hurt again after coming to us for help, I'd blame myself if I didn't do all that I could."

Lila's nod put a knot in Sedona's stomach. And eased her heart a bit, too. Her world, while volatile, was also pretty predictable. The law was the law. The court generally ruled as she'd expect. And when it didn't, she could find plausible cause, even if she didn't like it or agree with it.

But this…taking on this man who'd already proven himself more than capable of holding his own with her…

A man who spoke to her without saying a word….

What was she doing?

She'd told him about Jolene Raymond. Her high school friend who now cleaned hotel rooms for a living. Jolene had been Tatum's age that night Sedona had witnessed her stepfather's violence. If she'd stayed that night, if she'd been there when the police arrived, would it have made a difference? Would Jolene's stepfather have hit her, and given Tatum evidence to testify against him?

Would Jolene have remained her friend? Let her help?

"Sara's on board with us," Lila said now. "She's arranging to have half an hour with Tatum every afternoon she's here."

"How long do you think we can keep her?"

"As long as it takes."

And Sedona was back to her original question. The one she'd really been asking. "You met him, Lila. What do you think? Am I being a fool to give him the benefit of the doubt? Do you think he's lying about not hitting her?"

"I think Tanner Malone is a man who was raised in a horrid environment. No one comes through that without some kind of consequence. Sometimes good, sometimes bad."

Which told her nothing she didn't already know.

Lila shook her head. "I don't know, Sedona," she said. "Meeting him, I wouldn't think for one second that he'd ever do anything to harm one hair on that girl's head. Clearly he adores her. But I've seen some unbelievable things in this business and I just don't know."

In the four years she'd been working with The Lemonade Stand she'd never heard a word about Lila's life before she'd become managing director of one of the state's most prominent shelters. Didn't even know how Lila got the job.

She'd never wondered more than she did in that moment. Never needed to know more.

But they were business acquaintances. Not confidantes.

There had to be boundaries. Clear ones.

"For what it's worth, not only do I think we're making the only viable choice, I also think it's the right one," Lila said. "The best one for the child. She needs some space and we can give it to her. Hopefully, with you getting a glimpse into her home environment, and Sara having a go at her mind, we'll be able to find the truth. And help her. Sometimes unconventional means are the only way to get our job done."

Sedona stood. "Good," she said, feeling a smile coming on. "Then I'm going home to bed for a few hours. I'll stop by tomorrow after work, and in the meantime, call me if anything changes."

It was all she could do for now. For the rest of the night she was off duty.

Why the hell she took an image of Tanner Malone home to bed with her, she didn't know.

"I'M SORRY…" TANNER uttered the words for the umpteenth time that day as his clipper cut a little deep, as more vine fell than he'd intended—and as he didn't cut deeply enough, leaving too much grape to take up more nutrient than he wanted to expend per fruit. He was in a hurry. Had to be outside Santa Raquel High School five minutes before the last bell, which rang precisely at 3:22 every afternoon.

But pruning had to be done. Everything rested on this summer's crop. He'd managed to attract the attention of a group of highly respected vintners who were counting on him to produce fruit worthy of the high price they were paying him.

He was running his grapes at one hundred percent, which meant one branch to a vine; all other nubs had to go.

It meant less fruit. But better quality. For the best wines.

Because in order to make enough money to put Tatum through graduate school, in enough time to do it, he'd invested a sizable sum on a somewhat rare Italian pinot scion he'd come across through an acquaintance on the internet. He'd grafted the scion with an American root stock—which meant that it had the stamina to withstand American infestation, which the Italian root stocks, raised in Italian soil, could not do.

He couldn't lose this crop.

The only thing more important was his sister. Which was why he'd spent the better part of the day apologizing to his fruit and, at 3:22, was sitting in his truck, watching every kid that exited through the side door. Six words—*Meet me at the side door*—were the only ones she'd spoken that morning.

She hadn't said a word the night before, either. Just shrugged when he'd asked her if she was okay. And adamantly shook her head when he'd asked her to come home with him.

The only time she'd looked him in the eye was when he asked her if she wanted to stay at the shelter. Even then, she'd just nodded.

He'd agreed to a week. But it wasn't in writing.

The crowd of kids blasting from school hallways to freedom in the California afternoon sunshine thinned. Still no Tatum.

Tanner, wearing the stained long-sleeved button-down shirt he'd pulled on with his jeans that morning, and the sandals he'd slipped into when he'd pulled off the waterproof boots he wore in the vineyard, sat up straighter.

Was that Harcourt?

He'd been told the kid went to a private school. He'd never have allowed this if he'd thought the punk would have access to his sister at school.

No way. He'd homeschool her if he had to.

Okay, not that. He'd never meet state requirements, but he could hire someone…

The kid who'd come through the door never turned

around. From behind, it could be anyone. He'd only had a brief glimpse of the face. And…

Tatum pushed through the door, backpack slung over one shoulder, chin to her chest. She was alone.

And unsmiling.

God, had it only been three months since her last post-braces orthodontic checkup when he'd picked her up and she'd come through those same doors in the middle of a group of five or six giggling teenage girls? He'd teased her about their drama. She'd stuck her tongue out at him.

They were a team, him and Tatum. Always had been. Through all of the middle of the night feedings his mother either didn't wake for, or wasn't home to know about, the teething pains and diaper rashes…the first grin. And last bottle.

What had happened to them?

"Hey," he said as she climbed in beside him, acting as though she had the truck all to herself.

His "How was school?" didn't even elicit a grunt.

Pulling out of the lot, Tanner glanced at Tatum as often as he safely could, hoping for a glimpse into what his little sister was thinking.

He knew he hadn't hit her. But something clearly was going on between the two of them. More than just her anger over a boy she'd only met two months before.

He couldn't save her if he didn't find out what to save her from.

"I talked to Talia."

That earned him a brief glance.

"She said you two talked."

He'd had a call from their sister the night before. Late. She'd tried Tatum several times and finally got hold of her around one in the morning.

What adult called a kid at one in the morning on a school night? He'd kept the thought to himself.

And heard that Tatum hadn't had a lot to say to Talia, either.

"I was wrong, Tatum. To think you shouldn't talk to her." In the end, the silence had been Talia's choice. But he'd thought it was probably for the best, and he'd influenced that choice. *Just as Harcourt was influencing Tatum now?*

If he hadn't let Talia sever the family connection, Tatum would've had a woman to confide in. A woman who might've had a chance to steer her right…

Turning her shoulders, giving him as much of her back as her seat belt would allow, Tatum stared out the side window.

As soon as he dropped her off at the shelter he was calling Ken Harcourt. If his kid had transferred to public school, Tanner was pulling Tatum out.

They couldn't stop him. He was her guardian. It would be all nice and legal.

Making the last turn before they'd arrive at The Lemonade Stand and he'd have to watch Tatum walk away, Tanner clutched the steering wheel with both hands. Why had Tatum lied to Sedona Campbell? Why had she said he'd hit her? Did this have to do with their mother?

He knew he'd have to try to find Tammy. He'd never thought the day would come when he'd seek out the woman who'd given birth to him.

But for Tatum, he'd do anything.

Tammy's youngest was lying.

Tanner had to find out why.

Feeling like an unskilled heavyweight on a tightrope, Tanner drove the rest of the way in silence. He might only have seconds left and couldn't seem to find the words to save his family.

Her seat belt was unbuckled before he'd parked in the small public lot in front of The Lemonade Stand. Tatum jerked toward him as he stopped the truck. The unspoken question in her gaze was perfectly clear.

What the hell do you think you're doing?

Tanner glanced around, taking in the nondescript lot, the unremarkable patches of dirt between the lot and the brick half wall separating them from the street, the gray front of a small-looking slab building with a plain glass door entrance.

Tatum wanted to stay *here?*

She preferred this place to the lush green acres and old but statuesque homestead that he'd provided for her?

"I'm supposed to meet with Ms. Campbell," he said in answer to her silent question. He'd left them all at the café the night before. But before he'd gone home alone, he'd driven by the block where The Lemonade Stand was located, behind a series of storefronts. Only a small portion of the acreage was visible from the road. Or visible from the outside at all. Which was the point. But so far, he was underimpressed.

"You can't go in there."

Words. He almost grinned.

"Apparently there's a small public area just inside that door." He pointed to the glass entrance a few feet away. "Ms. Campbell told me I should meet her there."

"Sedona's *my* attorney."

"She's an adult professional. You should call her Ms. Campbell."

"She told me to call her Sedona. And you aren't the boss of me here."

Ultimately, yes, he was. But he didn't figure the point was worth belaboring. Doing so wouldn't win him any points with his baby sister. And Lord knew he needed some. Things were a hell of a lot easier when throw-up meant an upset stomach, whining meant hunger and all-out wails meant anger. Or when, in childish gibberish that only he and Talia could understand, she'd tell them absolutely every thought on her mind.

Out of the truck before him, Tatum headed for the public entrance, though she now had access to a more secure, resident entrance in another location unknown to him.

"Sleep well, squirt. I love you," he said while she was still close enough to hear. He couldn't be sure, but it looked as if Tatum shuddered. Because she was crying?

It took all he had not to run after her. To haul her

into his arms and promise her that he'd make her world perfect again if she'd only give him the chance.

"See you in the morning," he called out instead. And had to give himself a couple of extra minutes before phoning Del Harcourt's father to confirm that his son did indeed still attend a private school for boys, after which he followed his sister into the shelter.

CHAPTER ELEVEN

SEDONA DIDN'T KNOW what to expect as she followed the instructions on her GPS system to the address Tanner Malone had given her the following Saturday. It was her first day outside of court since Tanner's sister Tatum had arrived at The Lemonade Stand.

Tanner was expecting Tatum to be with her. The teenager had refused to come. And before she pushed the issue, Sedona had to find out why.

Or at least try to figure out what the troubled teen was not telling them.

And she knew what she might find—but didn't want to find—was evidence of the truth Tatum was trying to get everyone to believe. After three days of after-school sessions with Sara, Tatum still had not wavered from her story at all. Tanner was the one who'd hit her, but she absolutely was not going to admit that to anyone outside of The Lemonade Stand staff.

Sara, who'd yet to meet Tanner, didn't completely believe that Tatum was telling the truth about the identity of her abuser, but she was one hundred percent certain that the girl had been physically harmed. More than once.

"Are you sure this hasn't been going on for some

time?" the counselor had asked Sedona the evening before when, after a long day at work, Sedona had given up Friday evening with Ellie on her beachfront balcony to meet with Sara at the café by the shelter.

"You think it has?"

"I think Tatum has issues that are deeper than a sock in the arm a week or two ago."

"How much deeper?"

"If I had to guess, I'd say it's been going on pretty much forever—or at least as long as the girl can remember. She's got defenses that have clearly been engrained over a lifetime."

Sedona hadn't wanted to hear the words. And thinking back over them now as she approached Tanner's home, she didn't like the counselor's suppositions any better than she'd liked them the first time around.

Whether Tanner had been the one hitting his sister or not—and she still didn't think so—something was going on here. Something that, according to Sara, had been going on for a long, long time.

She'd seen abused women with their abusers. They flinched. Exhibited some kind of discomfort or fear around them.

The other night at the café, Tatum had clearly wanted nothing to do with her older brother, but she'd exhibited no sign of fear.

Sedona wasn't the least bit afraid either as she drove to Tanner's home. But she *was* nervous. And not just because she wasn't delivering his sister to him. She'd primped like a teenager on her first date as she prepared for this meeting and couldn't quite convince herself that her sweaty palms were due to the malfunctioning heater in her old car.

She was looking forward to seeing Tanner Malone again. The way a woman looked forward to seeing a man... According to the talk she'd had with herself in the shower that morning, she was only excited about seeing him as a means of exorcising his effect on her. Once she saw him again, she'd realize she was overreacting.

Pulling onto the dirt path drive that led to what had obviously at one time been an opulent home, Sedona appreciated the cleanliness of the unlandscaped front. The yard could use some sod. And a flower bed or two.

But the front porch, though old and in need of paint, looked solid. In good repair. As she parked and made her way toward the three cracked cement steps leading up to the front door, she noticed that the porch looked as though it had been sanded at one point, as though someone had been intending to paint but then never completed the task.

"Where's Tatum?" Sedona jumped, her heart squeezing against her lungs for a second as Tanner Malone came around the side of the house, his tone of voice demanding an explanation even while he kept his volume down.

His presence was explosive. At least to her libido, which had apparently not gotten that morning's message in the shower.

"She didn't want to come." And he shouldn't be

surprised by that. As of last night, Tatum Malone still had not spoken to her brother. She climbed into his truck every time she was expected to do so. She rode with him to and from school. But after that first day, she never spoke to him. Or responded when he spoke to her.

It was all in her records, from her meetings with Sara. Tatum Malone wanted nothing to do with her older brother.

"Her appearance here today wasn't up to her. Or negotiable. This is her home. Maybe if she came back, she'd remember that she used to like it here."

They weren't negotiating. They were talking about a young woman's life. And his ground was tenuous. All it would take was Tatum telling the police that he'd hit her and everything would change. At least temporarily.

Sedona had no doubt whatsoever that he knew that. His sister's residency at the shelter was evidence enough.

"I understand my sister is struggling, Ms. Campbell, and no one wants to help her more than I do, but catering to her whims is not going to do it. She's had four days at the shelter, three sessions with a professional counselor. She's still not speaking to me or, it sounds like, to anyone else about what's really going on here. And we have no idea how much time we've got before whoever is influencing her makes another move. We have to know what that move will be, and if you aren't going to find out, I will." He headed toward his truck, which was parked in the circle drive in front of Sedona's old Thunderbird.

A vehicle most guys drooled over and he hadn't even seemed to notice. Not then, understandably, but not the other night, either, when she'd walked him outside after a brief tour of the common areas of The Lemonade Stand.

As Tatum's guardian, he had a right to know where she was staying, since, legally, there was no suspicion, and certainly no charge, against him.

It was a fine line they were walking here. And as she stood there in the dirt with him, Sedona felt as though she was teetering dangerously.

He might not have noticed her car, but he'd noticed her. She'd seen the look in his eye when he'd first come around the corner. She'd seen it the other night, too. Or thought she had. And then convinced herself she hadn't. The slight lowering of his lids, the intensity of his gaze, made her glad she'd taken care with her appearance—for the brief second it had taken her to remember that she couldn't go down that path.

She also sensed his growing frustration as though it were her own. And her heart yearned to help him.

"What are you doing?" He'd opened the cab of his truck.

With one hip lifted up to the seat, he turned to look at her as she came around the front of his truck, her heels digging into the dirt. "Going to get her, that's what," he said. "This clearly isn't working."

"You're disappointed," she blurted out. His feelings

were none of her business. "I understand," she continued without taking time to think. "If you rush out there now, you could certainly bring her home. It's within your rights. But for how long? You going to chain her up here? Hope that she doesn't run from you like Talia did? And what happens if she gets desperate enough to leave that she calls the police on you? Can you trust that she won't lie to them about you?"

He still had one foot on the ground. And was looking toward it.

Sedona was glad. She didn't want him looking too closely at her, afraid of what he might see. She was doing all she could to protect his sister. And would continue to do so.

But she wanted to help him, too. Almost as much. She wanted to know what it felt like to have his affection aimed at her. To have his arms around her.

"She's got defenses that have clearly been built over a lifetime." Sara's words came back to her.

She couldn't let him bring his sister back there. Not until she knew what was driving Tatum away from him.

But he was obviously hurting. And had given his life to raise his siblings...

"Please give her a little more time," she said now. "It's only been four days, Tanner. I know it seems like a long time, but it's not. Why not show me your vineyard? Give me a tour. Show me the house, Tatum's room. Let's have lunch just like we planned. Help me get to know you as you asked me to do."

Her heart shouldn't respond to the prospect. This was business. Period.

"Someone's hitting her and she needs help," she said now, though, of course, she had no solid proof of that. Just instinct. Tatum's word. Tanner's testimony about the bruise on his sister's arm. And Sara's professional opinion, an expert witness who was certain Tatum Malone had issues dating back as far as Tatum could remember.

Enough to build a strong, albeit circumstantial, case.

If she didn't believe so strongly that Tatum needed help, and that she could offer the help, she'd let Tanner bring the girl home. And then see if she and Tanner could be friends—or more.

Worried about where her last thought had come from, Sedona almost walked away.

"I realize she needs help," the man said. The way he stood there easily, one foot flat on the ground while his butt rested against the seat of his truck, accentuated his long legs. Currently encased in the jeans he seemed to wear nonstop, those legs were interesting to her.

And they absolutely should not be.

"It's pretty clear that she's not going to talk to you about it," she said, focusing on the case. Because it really did come first.

"Agreed."

"I know you love your sister, Tanner. Why not give Sara a chance to help her? I swear to you that I'm in touch with them every single day. And will stay in touch with you, as well. You're seeing her every morning and afternoon of every school day. And I'll continue to encourage her to spend time with the two of us together."

With an arm resting on the window jamb, head slightly bowed, Tanner glanced over at her. "I'm not saying how long I'll be patient."

"Understood."

"Fine. For now, you win."

It was a curious turn of phrase. As if they were playing some kind of game. And if that was what this was to him, a game, all three of them were going to lose.

How THEY MADE it to his small winery, Tanner wasn't sure. He was making a name for himself in their tiny portion of the wine-making world, producing top-shelf quality grapes that he sold to larger, established wineries upstate. Producing his own wine was a dream that might or might not materialize into a money-making venture.

"Pinot noir is my favorite wine," Tatum's lawyer told him as she looked over the few dozen cases of bottles he had packaged in one corner of the small barn he used for his own production.

Tatum's lawyer. He had to remind himself. To keep things in perspective. Because if he didn't, his body was going to win the battle he was currently fighting. The one in which he had a beautiful woman admiring his life's work. He wanted to haul her up against him to see how she felt. And to know if she'd like how he felt.

"I'm just experimenting at this point," he told her,

recognizing that kid-in-a-candy-shop glint in her eye. And responding to it, too, in spite of himself. "Those bottles are just for my own education," he clarified. "Until this week, I only had one oak barrel. Now I have four. I'm nowhere near the point where I could actually make enough wine to label and sell it."

"I'd love to taste it."

No one tasted his wine. He wasn't ready.

"I bottled that stuff as an experiment," he repeated.

"So tell me about the process."

It had been clear to him during their tour of his four-acre vineyard that it wasn't her first rodeo. The woman had a wine tour or two under her belt. Or was a damn good study with books and videos. She knew his business.

And he wanted to know her. But couldn't trust her. Because he'd learned a long time ago to trust no one but himself. To rely on no one but himself.

"The barrel can make or break a wine," he explained, anyway. If she was looking to trip him up, testing him to find out if he was legitimate—in wine-making and in his assurances that he'd never, ever hit his sister—he could play along, on both counts, with complete confidence. "Most of a wine's flavor comes from the barrel," he continued. "French oak is widely accepted as one of the best trees for making barrels. Right now, in the U.S., one French oak barrel costs twelve hundred dollars. It will last for three to five seasons. In barrel production, the oak is heated through a special process that caramelizes the inside of the barrel and that's what flavors the wine. As time passes, the wines that pass through the barrel soak up all of those caramelized properties and the barrel becomes virtually useless."

She raised her brows. He'd told her something she hadn't known?

"At that time, you either shell out another twelve hundred dollars a barrel or, like a lot of American wineries, use the services of a cooper, who reburns the barrel, which brings about more caramelizing. That process costs about three hundred and fifty dollars per barrel. That alone means that, until my sister is through college, I can't afford to produce the quality of wine my grapes are grown to produce."

"What about steel barrels? I've seen them in use."

"Vintners put oak chips in them to flavor the wines, but in my opinion, they don't produce the best wine."

"And being the best is important to you?"

She was looking at him then, not his wine. He moved behind an oak barrel to hide his hardness. He promised himself he wasn't going to act like a fool. He also wasn't going to answer her question.

SEDONA SAW CLIENTS all through the day that next week. Still only four years into her practice, she didn't have her own paralegal, but she had a woman that she hired by the case to do a lot of the time-consuming case law research. Everything else—the filings, the phone calls and correspondence, the billing—she handled on her own.

And now, she'd added older-brother-sitting to her list. She wasn't just a lawyer. She had a life. And she wasn't keeping up with it.

Neither could she desert Tatum Malone. The girl and her brother were on her mind any time it wasn't occupied with another client.

Which was why she found herself, the following Wednesday evening, on her way to dinner with her parents, sitting in the passenger seat of Tanner Malone's truck.

She'd issued the invitation under the guise of spending time with him alone—on the way to and from dinner—but she knew that justification was weak. And she'd guessed from his lengthy pause before accepting her invitation that he knew it, too.

She also knew that no matter what might or might not be going on between them, Tatum came first. For both of them. The girl needed help and somehow the two of them had to work together to find the answer.

Despite the sexual awareness between them.

He drove with the same easy grace that he seemed to do everything else. Leaned back, his long legs open to accommodate their size beneath the steering column, one hand hooked over the wheel. He'd picked her up from her two-room office suite, ten minutes from The Lemonade Stand, wearing jeans again, but black instead of blue, so if they bore grape stains, the stains didn't show.

His shirt, another button-down, which was all he

seemed to own, was black-and-white-striped and equally unblemished.

She felt completely overdressed.

"I thought I saw Del Harcourt coming out of Tatum's school again today," he said as soon as she'd buckled herself in.

"But you just called Mr. Harcourt last Wednesday night and he confirmed that his son attends Brophy." An all-boys Catholic school in between Santa Barbara and Santa Raquel.

"That's correct."

"I asked Tatum and she said the same thing."

He drove a mile or two per hour above the speed limit. She was a strict, right-on-the-limit girl. The little Italian eatery they were heading toward, a beach-front place owned by a couple her parents had known in college, was a half hour down the coast toward Los Angeles.

"There's no way she can be seeing him, Tanner," she reminded him, not nearly as convinced as Tanner was that Del Harcourt was the only threat to his sister. Tatum had only known the boy two months. Her issues were years in the making. What if Tanner had been right the first day she'd met him? What if their mother had somehow gotten to Tatum? "She's either at school, with you or at the shelter. She has no time alone right now."

Which was the point. For now, Tatum Malone was safe. It was her goal to keep her that way.

"Do you have any way of contacting your mother?"

she asked now, hating to bring up the woman Tanner so clearly despised, but concerned enough to do so.

"Not really," he said. "Not easily. She changes her last name like most of us change underwear. Legally, and not. But I'm looking for her. Why?"

That surprised her. And yet, deep down, it didn't. Of course he'd be looking for her. He'd be looking for anything or anyone he thought might be a threat to his sister.

"You mentioned, that first night, that you thought Tammy might be behind Tatum's problems. I just think it's best to cover all the bases."

The sharpness with which his head turned told its own story. "Has Tatum said something about her mother? Has Tammy talked to her?"

"Tatum hasn't mentioned her mother at all to my knowledge, except to allude to herself as a loser because of who and what her parents are."

"She said that?" His tone had changed. "She called herself a loser?"

She hadn't meant to hurt him. Didn't want to hurt him. "Yeah."

Tanner drove silently after that. Until, out of the blue, he asked, "What did you tell your parents about us?"

The long glance he gave her had her shuffling in her seat, as if he was asking some intimate, personal question. "Just that you're a friend." He'd called her almost every night for the past week, wanting a report on Tatum's progress with Sara, and a rundown of every breath his sister took while she was at The Stand. He'd even asked what Tatum ate for dinner, as if Sedona would know the answer to that.

Of course, every night after the first time he'd asked, she'd had the answer for him. It was a small enough thing, and if it gave him some measure of comfort…

"So they're used to you bringing men they've never met to dinner?"

He was looking straight ahead now, but his right elbow rested on the console between them, bringing him closer to her side of the car.

They'd talked about other things, too, in those nightly chats. Casual comments that led to another minute or two of conversation. He hadn't seemed any more eager to hang up than she was.

His fresh-air smell filled his cab. Residue from the grapes he spent his days with? Some kind of after-shave?

She couldn't look at his hands on the steering wheel. Every time she did, she wondered how they'd feel on a woman's body. *Her* body.

"No, my parents aren't used to me bringing men to dinner," she had to admit. Because he'd know soon enough as it was. "I haven't brought a man with me to a single family event since I was an undergrad."

His eyes widened. She thought maybe he smiled, but looked away. She didn't want him to get the wrong idea. Her parents were going to be bad enough.

She'd known asking him to come tonight was wrong. A risk. Messy. But she needed to spend time with him, because of their agreement. And she needed their opinion of him.

He'd accepted the invitation so readily... As if he really wanted to meet her parents.

"Between my work, my regular volunteering and my extra time at The Stand with Tatum and Sara, I haven't seen my folks in over a week. If I canceled on them again, they were going to be hurt."

She wanted to know what her folks thought of him. Because she'd invested far too much of herself in the Malones and didn't know why. She didn't trust her judgment. And couldn't walk away.

All firsts for her.

"Why haven't you brought anyone home since college? Something happen?"

"Yeah, my folks embarrassed the heck out of me, hinting about marriage. And the guy made fun of them. He was history and so was introducing my male friends to my family."

"They want you married, and if you give them an inch they'll take a mile."

Sedona glanced at him. Was he guessing? Reading her mind?

"Something like that."

Taking his eye off the crowded highway for a second, he looked at her and back to the road. "You're, what, twenty-eight, twenty-nine?"

It was none of his business. "Twenty-nine."

"You have no significant other, at least not that your folks know about, and haven't had since college?"

She had no reason to feel defensive. He wasn't married, either. "That's right."

"How come?"

"Excuse me?"

"You're gorgeous." The words sounded both complimentary and commonplace at once. As if they were discussing accepted fact. "And smart and successful. Surely you've had offers."

Not as many as he'd think. None, actually. She'd never been close enough to a guy to get that far. Her nipples were tingling. Not appropriate under the circumstances.

"I'm..." She started to fill in the blank with her standard "picky" or "choosy" or "not ready" comments, and said, instead, "Not willing to settle."

"I'd guess it would be hard for someone like you to find a guy who met your standards."

He didn't sound judgmental. Or critical.

She almost let it go at that. Watched him drive with that bland, satisfied-with-life look on his face when she knew his life had been hard, horrible in some ways, and was currently challenging him, as well.

But where she usually felt compelled to stay quiet, she suddenly wanted to talk.

"My folks were high school sweethearts," she said. They had another twenty minutes to fill before they got to the restaurant. Where Millie and Chuck Campbell would already be stationed at the best table in the house, overlooking the Pacific Ocean, with cloth napkins on their laps and an opened bottle of pinot grigio between them.

They'd be quietly sipping, talking about the stock market, discussing odds. Disagreeing about some. And that night, even though they were both retired, they'd go home to their separate computers and make some changes to the few portfolios they still managed.

"My dad is the only man my mother ever kissed. They both went to UC, majored in business and opened a stock brokerage together, which they ran successfully for thirty years. They had my brother and me, took adventurous family vacations and basically taught us that we could be whoever we wanted to be, do whatever we wanted to do, as long as we were honest, worked hard and listened as much to our hearts as to our heads."

She paused, but he didn't respond. She wasn't even sure he was listening anymore.

"They've been in love for more than forty years, and while they disagree on a regular basis, it's obvious to anyone who knows them that they never lost the spark that first drew them together."

Still nothing. Tanner drove as though he was alone in the car. Because he couldn't relate at all to what she was saying? Because he didn't really care?

She was giving him a real part of herself and he'd probably just been making conversation. How did this man constantly make her feel so stupid? And yet... so alive.

"You're not going to settle for less than that." His

words, as softly spoken as always, fell like a cannon-ball into the truck.

She stared some more. Who was this guy? And what was he doing in her life?

He glanced over at her. "Am I right?"

"Yes."

With a slight nod, he drove on.

Not sure what had just happened, why Tanner Malone, a man with a traumatized sister and no answers, seemed in tune with her psyche in a way that felt like an invasion of privacy, Sedona watched the side of the road, the trees, the greenery, the occasional glimpses of high cliff and ocean below. And then asked, "What about you? You ever bring women home?"

"Never."

"You're thirty-three," Sedona said, kind of hoping to get into his skin just as he'd done hers. Even while knowing that she couldn't be there. Shouldn't even want to be there. "You haven't ever had a date?"

"I didn't say I don't date. Just that I don't bring women home."

"Why not?"

But she thought she knew. And had her supposition confirmed as he said, "Because Tatum's home life already had enough inconsistencies. I wasn't going to bring her any more emotional confusion."

"You're giving up your own family-making years to raise her."

"A choice I made willingly."

"And these women you date, they're okay with that?" She should just let it go. Couldn't. And was uncomfortable about that, too.

"I don't date anyone enough for her to get attached. Tatum's always been emotionally vulnerable. Needy. Like this little puppy that only wants to please and is so afraid of displeasing she always has to check out a room before she enters it."

Sedona sat up straight. *This* was why she was spending time with him. Because he'd asked her to get to know him and Tatum. So she could help them.

His being with her had nothing to do with *her*.

The man was diabolically smart. Was he also as pure-hearted as he seemed to be? As black-and-white as she was?

She'd never been so precariously balanced on the line between right and wrong. Never been so confused.

"I've always feared that if I brought a woman home, even casually, just for dinner, Tatum would get attached to her and be broken-hearted if things didn't work out. And in my experience—" he sent her a pointed look "—in the end, it never works out."

Maybe purposefully, maybe not, he'd just handed her pieces to the Malone puzzle she had to solve. Not sure where to place them, Sedona filed them in her memory and said, "That's because you haven't met my parents yet, but you're going to—" they were pulling into the restaurant "—in about two and a half minutes." Unless she missed her guess.

She'd told her mom that Tanner drove a dark blue

Ford truck. They'd be sipping wine and watching… surreptitiously, of course. Both watching, neither mentioning the watching to the other, but both knowing that they were doing it.

And…*yes*…just as she stepped down from the truck, even before Tanner had come around the hood to join her, she saw her mother and father walking together, hand in hand, out to the parking lot to greet them.

For a second, noticing the unconcerned expression on Tanner's face, she felt sorry for him.

He had no idea what he was getting into.

And no idea how much love and happiness he'd been denied, growing up as he had.

CHAPTER TWELVE

"I'VE CROSS-HARVESTED a couple of varietals that have proven to do well with our central coast weather and am experimenting with various soil sections on my land. On most of my acreage, I've got French pinot plants on American stems and am currently running them at one hundred percent. I've had eight good harvests. I handpick, leaving behind any clusters that aren't ripe or have bunch rot, and I destem before crushing to lower the developments of tannins and vegetal flavors. Last year I produced small batches of both pinot grigio and pinot noir. I'm most pleased with the grigio but consider that an easier, more novice wine to perfect as I don't have to factor the skins into the process...."

Chewing slowly, barely conscious of the seafood fettuccine she'd ordered, a personal favorite and only ordered on special occasions, Sedona listened while Tanner held court at a dinner that was giving her insight into the man—and giving her an opportunity to know him, which was so much more than their original deal had specified. She was supposed to be checking him out for Tatum's sake. Not her own.

"So your white juice never touches the skins?" Sedona's mother, Millie, was asking.

"I crushed them with skin contact for six hours. I wanted to extract tannin from the skins to encourage protein precipitation and also to increase the pH of the juice. I harvested on the modest pH side and was concerned that the juice might be a bit too acidic."

He'd ordered the spaghetti with meat sauce and had nearly finished his meal. The glass of pinot he'd had from her parents' bottle was half-gone. Sedona was ready to finish off the bottle and order another.

In twenty-nine years of living she'd never felt so off-kilter. Or unsure.

TANNER WAS EARLY the next morning, sitting outside the public day care owned and run by The Lemonade Stand, waiting for Tatum.

"My parents really liked you," Tatum's attorney had told him the night before during their drive home.

For a second, he'd wanted her to really like him, too. And had stopped the old yearning immediately. He'd learned early not to want things from others.

"You fit right in."

He'd learned to adapt.

To be happy where he was.

And still, all the way back to her car, he'd been aware of Sedona Campbell, his sister's beautiful, well-read, wine connoisseur, compassionate attorney, sitting in his truck, so far away and far too close. In the dark of the cab, with her scent filling his lungs and the obvious approval of her parents ringing in his ears—as they'd told him he was welcome at their home anytime, hinting that perhaps the upcoming Sunday dinner wouldn't be too soon—he'd wanted their date to have been just that. A date.

She couldn't tell them that he was supposed to be no more than a job to her. Naturally they'd assumed he and Sedona were friends.

He hadn't expected to care what they thought.

He'd wanted to take her home, to his bed, and make love to her. Absurd. He'd had sex many times. In many beds. He'd never once had a woman in his own bed.

He spent every night at home. Alone.

Because that was where Tatum needed him.

When she was home and when she wasn't. She needed to know he was there. Always. For as long as she needed him.

The door to the day care opened, and he saw Tatum step out.

She was a beauty, that little girl in a young woman's body. Too pretty for her own good. Every day she looked more and more like their mother, and Tanner's fear escalated. With her naturally tanned skin, a gift from the biracial father who'd been supplying their mother's drugs in exchange for sex, that long blond hair and perfect figure, she was a walking temptation for men. Men who might hurt her.

He'd be damned if he'd let that happen. He waited for her to look at him. To give him any kind of recognition. God help him, he needed her this morning. Needed to know that he had someone.

"Hey," he said when she climbed in without so much as a glance in his direction.

What had he done to her? Why did she suddenly hate him so much? The questions raged in his mind during the far too short trip to school, as he ran through past conversations with her, wishing he could find the key to bring her back to him.

"I had dinner with your attorney and her parents last night."

It was Thursday. She'd been at the shelter for a week and two days. A week and two days without saying a word to him. They'd never gone twenty-four hours without speaking before. Even the summer he'd made her go away to camp, she'd called him every night. He'd made special arrangements with the camp director to allow her to do so because it was the only way she'd agree to go.

"You'd like them. Their friends own this Italian restaurant down the coast, the bread sticks were just as you like them, butter but no garlic, and the whole time I was eating I was thinking about how much you'd love the fettuccine."

He was dying to ask about her homework. To know if she'd done any studying for the October exam. She was taking it for the first time in the fall of her junior year as recommended—so she could re-take it several times to better her score. Her future rested on those scores.

"I just want you to know that I take full responsibility for whatever has gone wrong between us, Tay. I raised you to be as you are, and whatever I've done, I'm sorry. I'll do whatever it takes to make it right. Go to counseling. Whatever."

He wasn't great at begging. Detested the thought of it. But for Tatum…

He pulled into school and she was going to leave him to another long day alone at the vineyard worrying about what was going on with her. Trying to figure out a way to make things right again.

Something that didn't involve Harcourt. He loved Tatum too much to let that screwed-up boyfriend ruin her life just so Tanner could have her back in his.

Every day that he'd dropped her off, the last thing he told Tatum was that he loved her. People needed that. To know that they were loved. To be told. Often.

Today the words clogged in his throat. She didn't want his love. Maybe she'd outgrown him. Didn't need him anymore. He'd known the day would come.

But not at fifteen. They had three more years to get her all grown up.

She opened the door, hitching her backpack on her shoulder in one movement.

"Bye," he said, and waited for her to leave him.

She jumped down. Turned to slam the door. Just like always. "Bye."

At first he thought he'd imagined the word.

But it rang in his ears.

A glorious chorus.

Tatum was speaking to him again.

"YOU TASTE SO GOOD...." Del's lips covered Tatum's again and she leaned into him in the backseat of his car, wishing they could just be together forever. In their own home. Where no one could ever again tell them they weren't allowed to see each other.

He stuck his tongue into her mouth—something that had excited her beyond belief the first time he'd done it.

She liked it now, too. A lot. But she needed to talk to him and they didn't have much time.

Breaking away from him, but not so far that his hand fell away from her breast underneath her short-sleeved cotton shirt, she said, "I think I'm going to be at the place where I am for a while."

Del still didn't know where she was. She'd told him it was for his own good. But really it was for her own. Sara told her that she had to learn to look to herself for her happiness before she looked to someone else. And the only thing that made her feel happy at the moment was living at The Lemonade Stand.

"What about us?" Del asked, frowning, teasing her nipple at the same time. He knew it drove her crazy. But she didn't want him to stop.

Because it drove him crazy, too. Which kept him hooked on her.

"It's just for a little while longer," she said. "Until I can figure out what to do, how to make Tanner give me my freedom." She wasn't really clear on the "until" part of it. Not until she figured out all the abusive behavior stuff and how to stand her ground and not be afraid.

"You just need to come live with us," Del said, his eyes big and lonely-puppy-looking until she just wanted to melt right into him. "Mom said you could."

"You asked her?"

"Yeah. She wanted to know why you weren't coming around and I told her that you were staying at a friend's house for a while."

"Did you tell her why?" Her stomach cramped up again, which was happening all the time. She didn't want Del's mom to think badly of Tanner. No matter what he'd done or was, he was still her brother. And he'd done a lot for her.

Still did.

And, okay, she loved him. Most of the time.

"I just told her that you and Tanner had a fight."

"What did she say?" It was important.

"That it had to be hard for him, being so young and raising his siblings. That's when she said you could stay with us."

Wow. That was cool. Something to think about.

But...

"For right now, I think I should stay where I am," she said. "Tanner's being cool about it and..." She needed Sara and Sedona. And Lila and Maggie and Lynn, too. Growing up alone with Tanner she hadn't realized how much she'd missed having another female in the house.

"He's not doing it to you again, is he? Pulling you back in with all that talk about loving you when he doesn't even take the time to find out who you are and what you want? You know how Tanner is, telling you whatever he has to tell you to get you to do what he wants. What is it, school again? Because he thinks you'd be happier at some school back east than you will being my wife?"

She shook her head.

He licked her lips. "Just think, baby, if you were at my house we could have all the time we wanted for this." This time when he kissed her, he slid a finger across the crotch of her pants.

And she pulled away. She needed to think. To know she was doing what was right for her. Just like Sara said. Not be pressured into doing things to please others.

Like Tanner. Who'd lied to her.

And Del. Who loved her and who she loved to distraction, but…

"If you were at my house, Tatum, I could take care of you all the time. You wouldn't have to worry anymore about anything or anyone, ever. You could have all the clothes and jewelry you want, too."

"From your dad, you mean." She didn't like Mr. Harcourt any more than Del did. And didn't need to take one single counseling session to know that he was abusive. Or to know that Del was a victim. "We don't want to owe him anything," she reminded him.

"I have an inheritance from my mom's side, too. And I know other ways to make money."

She was kind of worried about that. But now wasn't the time to get Del to see that getting his friends whatever they wanted, for a price, wasn't as cool as he thought it was. One thing at a time, just like Sara had said.

"I just… This place where I am…it's a place where Tanner can't come get me and take me home." She kissed him then, just to prove to him that she was really serious about him. About them. "I don't want him to keep us apart," she said, giving him "the look."

He put her hand on his crotch and she recognized the hard feel of him.

"Then at least think about taking part of me home with you," he said, rubbing her hand against him. "If you'll have sex with me, I'll know you're mine and then I can relax."

He made her hot. And she was curious about sex with him. She thought about it every night. Especially since Maddie had talked to her so openly about her and Darin having sex. Maddie really liked it and said that it made her feel completely in love with Darin and kept him completely in love with her.

Which was what Tatum wanted with Del. To know that she had a family of her own forever and ever. That she didn't have to worry about being a single woman out in the world like Talia. Or their mother.

Tanner thought school would keep her safe. But he was a guy. What did he know?

"If I do it…will you be okay with me staying where I am for a while longer?"

"Yes." He sounded so sure.

"You promise?"

"Of course, I promise. I told you. I love you and want to marry you. As soon as we're old enough. So will you do it? Soon?" He pushed his thing up against her.

"Maybe," she said. She needed to think. "Probably," she added.

According to Sara, every man who hit someone wasn't an abuser. When Tatum had asked, she'd said there were some situations where a man was driven by circumstances to use force, but that didn't necessarily make him an abusive or violent man.

But sometimes the victim of abuse made excuses for a man, thinking he wasn't abusive because she loved him and understood what made him act as he did.

And that was where it all got so confusing. How did she know if she was making excuses or just loving a person and everything about him? She made mistakes and apologized and anyone who loved her accepted her apology and let the mistake fade away. Shouldn't she do the same?

Sometimes she even made the mistake again. But Tanner had always forgiven her. Because he'd known she didn't *mean* to make that mistake. Or because he loved her, anyway.

Just like she'd always loved him.

Until she'd found out that he wasn't who she thought he was.

The horrible sick feeling she'd had that afternoon a couple of months ago, in his office when she'd found out he'd been lying to her all her life, came back again.

He hadn't just been lying about their mother wanting her, like she'd thought, but about himself.

And if she didn't know him, then maybe things she knew, things she'd tried her whole life to forget, weren't what she thought they were, either.

Or maybe they were.

Sara told her that the hardest part was knowing when someone was telling you something to manipulate you, or to get you to do what they wanted, and when they were really trying to help you or to tell you something valid that you didn't already know.

Like her mother. Sara had asked if Tammy had been in touch with her. Of course she hadn't been. Tanner would never allow it and Tatum was glad about that. But they'd talked about people telling lies to make you feel good so you'd do what they want.

Tammy would do that.

But what about Tanner? Would he?

Sara told her to listen to her own heart. Separate and apart from what anyone else told her. She told her not to let anyone convince her to do anything that didn't seem right to her. Not ever. And to ask for help if she ever felt pressured, or unsure.

Del picked up her hand, slid his fingers up and down

her ring finger. She thought of the day he'd taken her shopping for diamonds. She'd picked out her engagement ring. It had been the most romantic, best day of her life. "You know no one's going to love you as much as I do."

She loved it when he said that. And Del Harcourt not only wanted to give her respectability, he loved her enough to beg for her. "Yes," she said now, feeling as if she might start to cry.

Why did life have to be so complicated? Why couldn't Tanner just see that she'd met her Prince Charming and let her go have her own life? So what if she was only fifteen? He'd been younger than that when he'd started taking care of Talia and Thomas. And then she'd come along and he'd been a dad to her, too.

"So tell me, what's Tanner been saying to you in the truck all week? You seem upset. Has he been getting to you?"

She shrugged. "We don't talk."

"At all?"

"I haven't spoken to him at all. And I won't, Del. I told you that. I'm not going to give him the chance to try to manipulate me, and if I start listening to him, it could happen without my even knowing it, just like you said. I had no idea how much I believed everything he said until you pointed it out to me."

"It wasn't really me." Del's voice had grown still. "It was only after you found out he'd lied to you about his—"

"I know." She cut him off. If she hadn't been so shocked the day she'd found the paperwork in Tanner's desk, she never would have told Del about it. Sometimes, she wished she hadn't. Every time he mentioned it, her heart broke a little bit more. Not because of what she'd found out. But because Tanner had been living a lie, even with her, when she'd thought they were the only ones who really knew everything about each other.

He'd told her that was what made the difference with family love—you knew your family members at their worst so you didn't have to hide. And all the while, Tanner had been hiding. Preaching one thing and living another.

"Just promise me one thing." Del interrupted the confusing muck of thought that kept giving her a headache, pulling her onto his lap and laying her head against his shoulder. It made her feel better. Which was why she knew she was meant to be with him. That they were meant for each other, just like he'd told her. "Just promise that you won't go back home to your brother, and I promise you that I will wait for you. No matter what."

The horrible knot left her stomach and Tatum almost felt like laughing. Something she hadn't done in a long time. Del really loved her as much as she loved him.

"I promise," she said, knowing it was a promise she could keep. Even if she had to tell little lies about Tanner, or threaten to tell them, to get him to let her stay.

After all, he'd told her lies about him, too.

SEDONA MET WITH a new client on Friday. A seventy-five-year-old woman who'd been married almost sixty years and wanted a divorce. She and her husband lived in an active adult community and she'd caught him in bed with another woman. A sixty-year-old widow who'd moved in down the street from them. She'd been hesitant to take on the case. Had suggested arbitration to the mother of four—and grandmother of ten—but in the end had agreed to represent her.

She'd written a summary judgment on a frivolous lawsuit against another client of hers. The woman's ex-husband was suing her for having the locks changed on the family residence, causing him to have to sleep in his car because she'd also emptied the joint bank account, when, under an emergency order, the court had granted her both sole occupancy of the residence and the six hundred dollars that had been left in the account after the louse went to Vegas for the weekend and managed to use up the four thousand dollars she'd just deposited.

She'd represented a mother in a custody hearing and had planned arguments for the case she was taking to court on Monday. A couple of friends from law school invited her out for salad and wine, but she was tired and ready for some Ellie time, so she asked them for a rain check. Locking up her office, she headed for home, and then decided to make a stop at The Lemonade Stand.

Parking in the back lot, she used her key card to enter the private inner sanctum of the many-acre facility, breathing in the fragrances of flowers and freshly mowed grass, compliments of the new landscape design artist who was engaged to marry Lynn Duncan, the center's full-time on-site nurse practitioner.

The Lemonade Stand—where, when life handed you lemons, you made lemonade—had a resortlike feel, with meandering walkways, manicured grass and flower beds everywhere she looked. The idea was to give its female residents a sense of self-worth, of being treated well, to raise their expectations of what they deserved, and how they could expect to be treated so that they wouldn't settle for anything less than decency.

They were required to treat themselves, and others, with respect. Encouraged, through action as well as word, to expect respect.

As she strolled the grounds, Sedona let the peaceful atmosphere wash over her. Bathing her with a reminder of the world she'd grown up in. A loving world. Reminding her that she deserved a home, a life, as full and complete as the one her parents had built together.

She took a minute for herself, and then made her way slowly up the walk toward Maddie Estes's bungalow. She'd spoken with Tatum Malone a couple of times that week, spoken with Sara every night, just to check in, but she hadn't seen Tatum in several days.

The dinner hour had passed and she'd expected Maddie and Tatum to be settled in for the night, but found the two with backpacks on their shoulders, heading out the door of their bungalow.

"We are going to the younger girls' house, Sedona,"

Maddie said in her slow, slightly garbled drawl. The woman, in her midthirties, was educably slow from birth and unable to problem solve a lot of the time, but she was a superb caregiver.

Tatum wasn't a child. And Sedona had promised Tanner that the young woman would be in her bungalow by seven each evening.

"Gwen's husband is off tonight," Tatum said before Sedona could speak up. "Maddie and I aren't allowed to stay alone, so we're going to share the spare room over there." Tatum pointed to a bungalow across the quad. "We did it last weekend, too."

She hadn't been told. But there'd been no reason for her to be. She was Tatum's lawyer, not her babysitter.

"We have to share a queen-size bed, but I do not kick at night," Maddie told her.

"I guess Darin will be glad about that." Sedona smiled at the woman who'd been badly beaten and locked in a shed by her ex-husband. And who, after a couple of years of healing and working at The Stand, was now engaged to marry another mentally challenged individual.

"Yes, Sedona, he will like it that I do not kick him when he is trying to sleep. I think I will be sleeping with him soon. How long is it until June?"

"It's six weeks until the wedding," Sedona told Maddie. "Think of last Friday when Tatum first spent the night with you and the girls. It's been one week since then. You do that six times and it will be your wedding day." She turned to Tatum. "Can we talk for a couple of minutes?" she asked the girl when she'd really just intended to make a quick stop to see for herself that Tatum was doing all right.

"Of course." Telling Maddie she'd meet up with her at the bungalow, Tatum walked with Sedona farther along the cement pathway that wound past bungalows and through the grounds.

"Maddie's pregnant."

"I know."

"I think it's kind of cool that she and Darin can have a kid, and all."

"They'll be living with Darin's brother, Grant, and his soon-to-be-wife, Lynn, who will be helping raise the child."

"But Maddie takes care of Lynn's little girl, Kara, all the time."

"She follows the lists that Lynn leaves her and knows to call for help immediately if something doesn't go exactly as planned."

They'd reached the playground area and Sedona sat in one of the leather swings, while Tatum took the one next to her, lightly kicking off.

"I want to be a mother." Tatum's voice took on a longing note. "I think that's the coolest thing about being a woman, being able to grow a human being and love it and keep it safe."

When Sedona's thoughts immediately flew to the boyfriend Tatum had told her about, the boy Tanner had forbidden her to see, she was afraid she was thinking for him. Worrying about how he'd feel if he could hear his sister's thoughts. Instead of assessing for herself.

"I'm sure you'll make a wonderful mom someday," she said. Most girls had dreams of motherhood. She had.

"Not if my brother has his way." The girl's tone of voice changed completely.

"Why do you say that?"

"All Tanner cares about is me going to some Ivy League college and having this great career. He says that way I'll be safe and secure for my whole life, but that's a lie. Tanner tells me I always have to tell him the truth, but he lies to me."

Did he lie to Sedona, too?

"When does he lie to you?"

"All the time."

"Give me an example."

"He said that I would love high school and I don't."

"That's kind of an opinion, not really a lie," she said, even though she could see how Tatum felt lied to. "Give me another example."

"He told me that my mother wanted me but was just too sick to take care of me. But I remember things and Talia told me the truth. Our mother is a druggie prostitute loser."

"Okay, when else?"

She listened as Tatum listed other innocuous instances of Tanner telling her things to protect her from truths he didn't think she should have known.

She tried to hear the duplicity in his intent, to accept

what Tatum was trying to tell her. And didn't believe that Tanner Malone was a liar.

"I'm not sure how much longer your brother is going to allow this arrangement to continue," she said as Tatum continued to push off the ground softly, swinging herself lightly back and forth.

The girl's head jerked toward her, her pretty gray-blue eyes sharpened by fear. "He can't make me go back there, can he?"

"I'm not sure why you don't want to go." She hadn't meant to have this conversation tonight. "I've been to the farm, sweetie. I've seen your room. It looks like your brother has done all he can to show you how special you are, how much he loves you."

"I can't go back there, Sedona. Please don't make me."

Tatum's face tightened with panic.

"It might not be up to me," she told the girl. "But I promise you that I will continue to do everything I can to help you. I'd be able to do a better job, though, if you'd try to cooperate a little. I can't tell how Tanner treats you until I see the two of you interacting. Until I see you together."

Tatum skidded to an abrupt stop and stood up. "You're trying to trap me, aren't you? Just like he does? You're trying to get me to agree to something that I just told you I don't want to do."

Someone had done a number on this girl.

"No, I'm not." Sedona stood, as well. "I represent you first and foremost," she said, with a strong reminder to herself, as well. "My parents invited your father over for dinner on Sunday. I'd like you to come with us. You'll like my folks. And you won't have to be alone with Tanner, or go home, but I can still see how he treats you."

Tatum studied her for a long moment. "So this is to trap him."

"Not to trap him." *Trap* was such a strong word. And not anything she wanted to do to Tanner. What she wanted was to help him. "Just to understand how to help you." How to help them both.

God help her, she was in too deep. Was losing what little bit of perspective she'd been pretending to have.

And if she admitted that? If she recused herself from the situation, what would happen to Tatum? Would Tanner be willing to let his little sister remain at The Lemonade Stand if Sedona reneged on her part of the deal?

She couldn't take that chance.

But she could bring the problem to two people she trusted with her life. Maybe not the specifics, but the people. She could see if her parents still liked Tanner as much when he was around his little sister.

"I need to see you and your brother interact, Tatum. Please come with me on Sunday. I promise I won't leave you alone with him."

Those unusual blue eyes gazed over at her. "You promise?"

"I do."

"Okay, I'll come. But I'm not going to talk to him." The girl's pain was clear to see.

Sedona's heart lurched.

But it wasn't until she was on her way home that she admitted to herself that her heart wasn't just hurting for Tatum. But for Tanner, too.

CHAPTER THIRTEEN

HE'D BEEN TAKING Tatum an outfit each day when he picked her up from school, for her to wear the next day. She wasn't returning them and he could only surmise that she was laundering them herself. He waited to do his own laundry, thinking that she'd be handing him a bag of dirty clothes and he'd throw all the jeans in together, like always. And Sunday morning, when he finally had to break down and wash his clothes or have nothing to wear to Millie and Chuck's that afternoon, Tanner made himself a promise.

He was going to pick Sedona up, and then Tatum, for the drive to dinner. And on the way home, he'd drop them off in the same order. Sedona first. Leaving him alone in the truck with Tatum. At which time he'd drop her off, too.

In her own room.

He was going to dinner. And then, everyone else be damned, he was bringing his little sister home.

He'd given them their chance to help her. Time was passing and nothing was changing. He'd done just fine helping Tatum since the day she was born. He'd find a way to get her through this, too.

With that thought in mind he canceled his participation in the private wine testing he'd been scheduled to attend that afternoon, put his clean jeans in the dryer and, with an old pair on, went out to spend a few hours with his vines.

"THIS WAS SEDONA'S room when she was growing up." Standing in the upstairs hallway of her childhood home, Sedona watched as Tatum stuck her head in the door of the yellow-walled room. "It's nice," she said, polite as always.

It had been a mistake bringing her here. She'd driven to the shelter after church, wanting to spend some time with a couple of the other residents before Tanner came to pick them up for the drive to her folks' house. She'd also wanted to be there with Tatum to make sure the young woman didn't back out of her promise to spend the afternoon with them.

Tatum had been joking with Maddie when she arrived. Teasing her about the *X*s in her dough while they stood at the kitchen counter making peanut butter cookies together. She'd been patient with Maddie's valiant attempts to place her fork exactly in the middle of the ball of dough—and as happy as Sedona had ever seen her.

And she'd clammed up the second she'd climbed into the backseat of Tanner's truck.

The girl was reticent at dinner, too.

Sedona's mother, who knew only that Tanner was Tatum's guardian and that brother and sister were at odds—and that Sedona was friendly with both—had seated Tatum between herself and Sedona, placing Tanner on Sedona's other side.

"I'd like to see your vineyard," Chuck was saying to Tanner as though the two had been buddies for years. They'd chatted outside while Chuck grilled their steaks. Tatum had glanced out at them several times, as though keeping Tanner in sight, and Sedona was anxious to ask her father what Tanner had had to say.

For Tatum's sake, of course.

"You're welcome anytime," Tanner said over a bite of steak. "But it's not that impressive." Listening to Tanner conversing with her father felt…good.

"Yes, it is." Tatum's voice slid into the conversation naturally. Sedona could feel the sudden tension emanating from her brother at the tone. "It's small by winery standards," the girl continued, looking at Chuck, and nowhere else. "But the vines are trellised and healthy, his grape size and color is as good as any you'll see anywhere else and there isn't a single weed in four acres. He spends enough time out there."

The last sentence might have held a touch of resentment, but there'd been no doubting the pride in the rest of her soliloquy.

It was also clear to Sedona that Tatum didn't just live at the farm—she was a part of it.

They moved to the deck after dinner, the adults having one glass of wine apiece, sipping slowly from a bottle her father had brought back from France with him. Tatum sat first, settling on a bench on the far corner of the deck, looking out at the ocean beyond.

"You ever think about getting on a boat and sailing away?" the teenager asked Sedona as she sat down next to Tatum.

"I used to come out here when I was a kid and dream about all of the worlds that were out there for me to see," she said.

"So what happened?"

"What do you mean?"

"Why are you still here?"

"Because I grew up," Sedona told her. "And I realized that while I wanted to visit different worlds, my life was where my heart is. And that's with my family."

Tatum glanced over to where her brother sat in a patio chair perpendicular to her father. "I think he would have liked to travel," she said. "But instead, he just made stuff up and then must've started to believe it was true."

"What stuff did he make up?" Sedona held her glass of untouched wine, needing to help this young woman more than any client she'd ever had. Tatum shrugged, her long blond hair falling around her face like a shroud. "Just stuff," she said. "You know, like who we are and stuff."

"Who you are?" She wanted to know, to understand. To fix this one.

"Like us as people. Like having people think we aren't who we really are."

More chilled than the glass in her hand, Sedona said, "I don't understand."

"He lets people think that we're these decent people,

winegrowers, a family that is, like, you know, normal. And we aren't. You know, stuff like that."

No, she didn't know. But she wanted to.

"You don't think you're normal?"

"We're white trash, Sedona." The girl's voice was pained, as though she was imparting a horrible secret. "We come from trash and we're nothing but trash."

"There's nothing trashy about you."

"My mother's a hooker. My dad was a pimp. Tanner's the only one of us who had a decent dad. We aren't like you, with smart parents who have money and a real house...."

Yeah, maybe it hadn't been a good idea to bring the girl here.

"Wait a minute, young lady," Millie said from behind Sedona while the two men remained deep in conversation—about wine varietals probably. Sedona had no idea how long her mother had been listening in. Tatum, apparently, hadn't realized they'd been overheard, either, as stared at Sedona's mother, a look of shame on her face.

"You had no choice about who you were born to," Millie said, sitting down on the bench on the other side of Tatum. "Your brothers and sister didn't, either. And that doesn't define you. You are a product of the choices *you* make. Tanner is a product of the choices *he* makes. He chose to be a vintner, and by the sounds of things, he's a pretty darn good one."

Silent, Tatum looked at her brother. Seeing him differently? Or seeing something they couldn't see? "You see Chuck over there?" Millie asked, pointing to her husband. And Sedona knew what was coming. Should have thought of it herself.

"His daddy was a rapist. Raped his momma and she had him. She couldn't stand to look at him, though, because he reminded her of what had happened to her, so she gave him up for adoption."

"How does he know about her, then? If he was adopted."

"Because when he was about your age, he decided that he had to know who he was, and figured the only way to do that was to find out where he'd come from. He talked to his adoptive parents, and they agreed to help him find his birth mother."

"And they found her?"

"Yes, they did, but she didn't want to see him. She told his adoptive parents why, and they talked about it and decided the best thing was to tell him the truth."

Tatum's mouth hung open. "What did he do?"

"He went a little crazy for a while. Drank too much. He got in a car accident, but luckily no one was hurt. And his parents told him that he was at a crossroads. They would pay for him to go to college and make a life for himself. Or he could choose to move out of their home and find his own way."

"And he chose college?"

"And never looked back," Millie said.

Looking at Tanner again, Tatum didn't seem any happier. Her expression didn't lighten. She didn't smile.

But when Sedona came back from the restroom a few minutes later, she noticed that the teenager had moved on the deck and was sitting several feet closer to her brother.

And throughout the rest of the afternoon, though there was no visible softening in the young woman toward her brother, Tatum didn't let Tanner out of her sight.

DRIVING HOME FROM the shelter Sunday evening, Tanner wasn't in the best of moods when his phone rang. Seeing his caller's name didn't improve his emotional state all that much.

But he answered. Because when it came to his siblings, he always would.

"So how'd it go? Is she home?" Talia got right to the point. They'd been in touch, pretty much every day, but only to speak about Tatum. Talia was never going to forgive him for the lover she'd lost. The baby she'd given up for adoption.

"No." They'd outwitted him this time—Tatum and her lawyer, a woman who inspired his trust even while he knew that she'd take his sister away from him in a second if she thought it was the right thing to do. "Sedona was waiting for me at the shelter this afternoon. She left her car there."

"You think they knew you intended to take her home?"

"No." Probably not. But maybe.

"You need me to come home? Maybe if I'm there…"

"Is she answering your calls yet?"

"Not since that first time." Last year he'd have been happy to hear that, seeing it as a sign that Tatum was choosing wisely. Now her refusal to speak with the older sister she'd once idolized scared the shit out of him.

"Then I'm guessing it wouldn't help any to have you here."

"Your way with words amazes me, big brother." Talia's drawl almost made him smile. "I thought maybe you'd like the company. I don't see you as too happy rambling about in that big old house by yourself."

"I'm pruning."

"Ah, the vines. Maybe if I came home you'd actually let me try a bottle of Malone Maison wine."

"I don't have the label yet."

"But you will have, Tanner. We both know that."

Because he didn't give up. Because he was tenacious. Because he'd had to be and had wanted his siblings to know that they didn't ever have to settle for less than the best. Less than what they wanted.

"So there's no change, then?" Talia didn't seem as eager to hang up as he was.

"No."

"She didn't talk to you at all today? Didn't this lawyer's folks think that was a little odd?"

"No, she didn't speak to me and I don't know what they thought about it," he said. "Chuck Campbell talked about wine. Millie makes a great broccoli salad.

Sedona seems to get along well with her folks, and Tatum was her sweet self with all of them."

There. Had he given her what she needed? Could he hang up now?

"This lawyer, she's close with her parents?"

"How the hell would I know?"

"You're good at reading people, Tanner."

There'd been no sarcasm in the tone. Nothing negative.

"What happened today isn't important. What matters here is what happened months ago."

"What was that?"

"A teenage asshole went after our little sister, trying to get her to do drugs and have sex with him."

"You could have trusted her."

Read: *you should have trusted me*. But he had trusted Talia. And she'd ended up pregnant at sixteen by a man older than Tanner was.

He wondered, not for the first time, if Talia ever had thoughts of looking up the son she'd given away. Just to see how he'd fared. But he didn't ask.

"She's vulnerable," he said instead, sparing his sister the trip down memory lane. "You know how sensitive she is."

"And impressionable."

"She's not hardened like the rest of us." And dammit, he'd sworn that he'd see that she grew up that way. That one of them had a chance to see beauty first in the world.

"I can't believe this is all over a guy."

If Talia had been around, if he hadn't made her see that she'd become too much like their mother to be a role model for Tatum, would she have seen signs he'd missed?

"Doesn't make sense to me, either," he said now. "But one thing's for sure, I've either royally pissed her off, or someone's got some kind of hold on her."

"You still think it's Tammy?"

They'd agreed—him and Thomas and Talia—that the woman who'd birthed them didn't deserve to be called "Mom." Those days of the three of them banding together against the world seemed so long ago.

Like a different lifetime.

"I think it's possible."

"I've done what I can to find her and I've come up with nothing."

"I haven't been successful, either," he said now, surprised at how difficult finding Tammy was proving to be. Granted, he'd never tried before, but he'd always assumed that if he had, it wouldn't have been that hard to locate her.

Tammy had always told them that if they wanted her, she'd be there. He'd actually believed her.

"I've got someone looking for her," he told Talia now. He'd hired a guy.

"You hear from Thomas yet?"

"No."

"Did you say anything in your messages about Tatum?"

"No."

"It's been almost two weeks. Maybe you should call him again."

"Okay." Or… "You could call him."

"Nah. You do it."

He would. But… "Maybe it's time you did, too."

"I don't think so. It's not like Thomas has any power to get Tatum to come home. Hell, she hardly remembers him. I just thought, maybe he'd want to know. But it's not that big of a deal."

From the day he'd left, Thomas hadn't instigated a relationship with any of them.

"We're family, Talia. It's time we remembered that."

Their family connection went soul-deep. But the truth was, sometimes, in a day-to-day world, it was easier to try to forget.

"It's pretty clear that Thomas has no interest in remembering that." Her words held no rancor.

And because he agreed with her—maybe even understood, somewhat—he didn't push the issue.

"And let's face it, Tanner, he sure as hell wouldn't want to hear from me. Like you made clear last year, I'm Tammy's daughter."

He shouldn't have said that. He'd just been so shocked. And afraid when he'd found her being pimped out by her own husband…

"You're one of us, Tal."

"But you don't want me to come home."

"You're welcome here anytime." The words felt good. Damn good.

Talia's silence shamed him. He'd been protecting

Tatum when he'd come down hard on Talia for the choices she'd made. But she was his sister, too. And he'd let her down.

"I, uh, have some vacation time coming," she said. "I thought…maybe…I'd head your way."

"When?" Anticipation swept through him for the second it took him to quell the useless emotion.

"I'm not sure. I'll let you know."

Translation: *not now and maybe never.*

"Sure, you do that," he said. And rang off. He was home, anyway, pulling into the driveway. He had to be up early in the morning. One of his back quarter irrigation lines had sprung a leak and he had no idea how long it was going to take him to fix it.

Plumbing was a bitch.

CHAPTER FOURTEEN

THE WEEK FOLLOWING Sunday dinner with her folks, Sedona spoke with Tanner Malone almost every day. Something was making her keep in touch with him. A need to keep him content because every day that she pacified him was another day she bought for Tatum to heal.

Or something deeper, more personal. Not giving herself any slack, she tried to be completely honest. To be fully aware of her motives so that she could make changes where appropriate, if necessary.

"How was Tatum today?" she asked the second he picked up her phone call Thursday night—their daily calls had been growing steadily longer.

"I got a 'hey,' and a 'see ya' today. 'Hey' this morning, 'see ya' this afternoon."

Her heart catching, she sat on her balcony, watching Ellie stare out toward the unlit shore where they could hear waves they couldn't see.

"She loves you."

"But you still aren't sure I didn't hurt her, are you?"

Tomorrow was Friday. The last school day of the week. The last day of the week he'd see Tatum.

"What are you doing this weekend?" *No, Sedona, you're crossing a line.*

"Working. I've still got an acre to prune, weeding to be done and some trellises need maintenance."

She couldn't be concerned about him there, all alone—a good man whose only goal was to serve his family.

A man like her father?

"Why?" he asked into the silence that had fallen. "You want some more time to observe me? There's a private wine tasting in Santa Barbara, at the home of a vintner I'm sure you'll recognize. You could see me interact with my peers. Find out if any of them exhibit any fear toward me. Or drink enough wine to loosen their tongues and tell you how I treat my sister." His tone was light.

But the undertone caught at her. Was he aware of her fear that they were moving into territory that would make them more than just lawyer and client's brother?

Were they doing that?

Did he want to? When she realized she was afraid to ask him, afraid he'd say no, she said, "I'm going to be spending my weekend with briefs, and writing the first draft of a summary judgment," she said. She couldn't allow her boundaries to shift any further.

Couldn't care, other than from afar, objectively.

And if her body tingled every time she heard his voice…if she woke up sweating in the middle of the night with thoughts of him naked beside her…that was information she was keeping to herself.

But on Friday morning, as she drove to work, and then again, in the afternoon, as she stopped in at home to let Ellie out, she was thinking about his wine-tasting invitation, envisioning what it would be like to go. To be with him among his peers, listen to his voice take on that note of passion it got when he talked about varietals and stems and growing techniques, to see him smile.

Lost in her daydream, it took a couple of seconds to realize that something was wrong with Ellie. She'd been quick to dart out her doggy door due to the length of time she'd been alone, but now she stopped cold. The dog's little scrunched-up furry face turned to look at Sedona—and that was when she noticed the water spraying straight up in the air like a geyser, soaking everything in its path, including her balcony. Water was puddled at Ellie's feet, soaking her paws.

Taking stock of the situation—a landscape irrigation system blowout underneath Ellie's patch of grass—she grabbed up the dog, and hurried with her out the garage door, through the garage, to the garden area at the right of her driveway.

"Sorry, girl, this will have to do," she said, while Ellie, for once not the least bit timid, went forth to do her business. Sedona turned the shutoff valve for the outside irrigation.

And an hour later as she sat in on the tail end of Tatum's session with Sara, Sedona thought of Ellie and the ease with which she'd adapted to a change Sedona would have bet she wouldn't tolerate and said to Tatum, "Sometimes we think we have to coddle those around us, we think they can't do things for themselves, and instead, what we're doing is holding them back. Sometimes we just need to let them try."

Tanner's little sister quirked her head, her brows drawn together as she sat on the couch in Sara's office, next to Sedona and across from the counselor. "You're saying you think Tanner's trying to coddle me because he thinks I need it, but really he just needs to let me try things?"

Well…yes, but, really, it wasn't her job to speak for him.

Most particularly until they knew why Tatum was so adamantly against going home.

"I think it's important to understand why people do what they do," Sara jumped in when Sedona couldn't come up with a right answer. "It explains things. It helps us understand. And those things are vital to living happy, healthy lives. But it's also important to keep in mind that some things people do are just wrong, even if we understand the reason."

"Like someone hitting someone else."

"Yes."

"Even if they caused it?"

Sedona's back muscles stiffened. Sitting straight up, she tried not to show any kind of reaction, not to move the air in the room at all. She couldn't have an effect this. Her job was to listen—and then to act on the provable facts.

"How would someone cause themselves to be hit?" Sara's quiet voice brought a measure of calm to the room.

"I don't know. Like maybe just keep pushing for what they want, what they need, what matters most to them, and not listening to what other people need. Like not putting as much importance on others' needs."

"Do you know someone in that position?"

"No."

"Do you think that's why you were hit?"

"No. I don't know." Her face lined with deep emotion, a mixture of fear and worry and something else Sedona couldn't define, Tatum looked from one to the other of them.

"Who told you that you don't put equal importance on the needs of those around you?" Sara leaned forward, her elbows on her knees.

"I don't know." Tatum looked down as she spoke and Sedona's breath caught. She glanced at Sara, who met her gaze and nodded.

"I think you do know," Sara said.

At which Tatum glanced up wide-eyed and said, "It's not anything any one person told me," she assured them both. "It's just…something I've pretty well, I mean, I just figured it out. Del and I talked about it, too. About how we have to make sure we think of each other in our relationship, not just of ourselves."

"Did Del Harcourt hit you, Tatum?" The question blurted out of Sedona's mouth before she could stop it.

"No! Of course not!" The girl didn't hesitate for

a second. "Don't even say that," she continued more calmly. "Del would get in so much trouble if someone even suggested that he did. You have no idea."

"Who did hit you?" Sara's quiet question fell into the taut silence.

"I already told you."

"You said Tanner did."

The girl nodded, her blond hair falling over hunched shoulders to hide her face again.

"So your brother hit you."

"I told you, you don't know him."

"But you do."

Tatum nodded again.

"You think you know him better than anyone else?"

"I know I do." There was no mistaking the derogatory note in the teenager's voice. And Sedona's heart sank again. But she couldn't help grabbing on to the fact that Tatum hadn't been able to out-and-out say Tanner had hit her, the way she had when she'd first come to them.

Because he hadn't and they were making progress with her?

Or because she was starting to miss him and was thinking about going home no matter what he'd done.

Sedona believed it was the first.

And had not one piece of provable evidence to back up her hunch.

"Who's Ellie?"

Looking a little desperate, Tatum was focusing on

Sedona. "You said that you'd planted grass for Ellie and the irrigation hose blew."

Right. She'd turned off the water to the outdoor watering system. But the problem awaited her.

Sedona almost welcomed it. "Ellie's my housemate," she said. Finding a picture of the little poochin on her phone, Sedona showed it to her.

Tatum glanced at the picture, her expression flattening. "We had a dog once," she said. "It ran out in the road and got hit by a car. Tanner wouldn't let us have another one. I got to keep a kitten with a hurt paw until we found another home for it. And there was a bunny who'd been abandoned—I fed him until he ran away, but that's it."

Wow. Sedona looked at Sara again, who seemed to have picked up on the same thing. Tatum's resentment against her brother was not dissipating.

"Anyway, call Tanner," the girl continued. "He installed four acres of irrigation for his grapes. I'm sure he can fix it for you."

Such mixed messages the girl was sending. She resented her brother, and yet needed him in the picture, too. She seemed petrified at the thought of going home with him, and yet trusted his abilities.

For Tatum's sake, Sedona needed answers. She also needed her irrigation system tended to as soon as possible. The days were getting warmer and if she didn't get the water back on, she was not only going to lose Ellie's grass, but the hundreds of dollars of landscaping and flowers that she'd planted around her house.

And so she did as her client suggested. During her nightly call to Tanner Malone on Friday, she set up an appointment for him to come out to her place on Saturday and take a look at her irrigation system.

It was business. Not a wine tasting.

HE WORE JEANS. Blue and faded. With a black polo shirt that Talia had bought him the last Christmas she was home. It was name brand. And generally hung in his closet.

Pulling into the driveway of the address Sedona had given him, Tanner looked around. Her home was much smaller than he'd expected when she'd named the Santa Raquel neighborhood where she lived. It was the most modest place on the secluded street that backed up to a private beach.

And way out of his price range.

He was there to do work. Not to compete. Or socialize.

But as he got out of the truck and walked back to get his plumbing toolbox out of the bed, he enjoyed the view of the ocean that beckoned beyond Sedona's bungalow. And of the woman herself, too, as she came down the steps.

"Nice dress." He said it because it was true. He probably shouldn't have. Now they both knew that the spaghetti-strapped ankle-length piece of cotton that hugged her figure had his attention.

"Thank you. Do you want me to turn the water on so you can see the leak?"

A reasonable person would assume that he'd also noticed the perfectly shaped feminine body housed by the dress, as well.

Sedona was a reasonable person.

"Just show me where you saw the geyser and we can go from there," he said. He hadn't slept with a woman in a while. And had been taking this one to bed with him, via cell phone, every night for more than a week. The longest relationship he'd ever had with a woman who wasn't related to him.

Her sandaled feet moved easily along the walkway beside her house. He followed, not quite as easily. He'd noticed that nicely rounded rear before. Of course. Pretty much every time he'd seen her.

He just hadn't ever seen it at home. Or in such a thin piece of cotton. He was pretty sure she was wearing a thong.

She'd known he was going to be there.

So maybe she'd wanted him to see her this way. Maybe she'd been aware that he was attracted to her.

"See that slight indentation?" She was pointing to a crevice in the dirt in the middle of a small grassy patch. Bending down, Tanner spread the blades of grass with the fingers of one hand, resting his other arm against a bent knee.

"I see the problem. It's—"

His explanation was broken off by the high-pitched yelp of the four-legged munchkin-looking thing that bounded down the steps of the back deck and headed straight for him.

"Ellie," Sedona said, half sternly, but with a bit of a chuckle thrown in.

The creature, a cross between a puppy and a gremlin, stopped about three feet away from him, still yelping.

Sedona bent to pick it up, giving Tanner a very clear glance down the front of her dress.

He knew more about her underwear now. Not the bottom half, but the top. It was absent. She was braless. And had rosy brown nipples that were ripe and hard.

"You're staring," she said, straightening immediately, holding the critter she'd called Ellie to her chest.

"What guy wouldn't?" He looked her in the eye, not sure whether or not she knew what he'd seen.

She didn't back up, or look away, either. "One who's lived his whole life in Santa Raquel and should be used to beach attire."

"I don't get to the beach much."

"Apparently not," Sedona said, chuckling, and Tanner hoped she didn't pay as much attention to his private parts as he had to hers. He was hard as a rock—a fact his tight jeans weren't doing much to disguise.

And, of course, an observant lawyer such as herself wouldn't have missed that fact.

"You've got a bubbler," he said, pointing to the ground. "A hole in your irrigation line."

He could tell by the way the soil gravitated in one spot.

"Can you fix it?"

"Of course." Wasn't that why she'd called him? Because she knew he was experienced with irrigation systems?

"I meant do you have what you need to fix it?" She held the little dog with one arm now, and gestured toward her problem piece of grass with the other.

"Yes." He didn't elaborate, but the couplers and spare line he'd need for splicing, the tools and plumber's glue, were all in the back of the truck. "It should only take a few minutes."

Her smile fell a bit. Like she was disappointed.

"But since you're dressed so nice and all—" he didn't smile "—I could still take you along to the wine tasting."

She buried her face in Ellie's fur, watching Tanner.

"You know you want to," he said.

"Yeah, okay, I want to."

"So come with me." Was he really so close to begging this woman? This lawyer who could, at any moment, decide to help keep his little sister permanently away from him?

Being emotionally vulnerable, other than with his siblings, was unacceptable. So Tanner told himself he had to keep Sedona close, to get as far inside her as he could, physically or otherwise, if he was going to thwart any attempt she might make to take Tatum away.

He told himself it was all about Tatum.

But he knew it was a lie.

And when she accepted his invitation and his day instantly brightened, Tanner wasn't happy at all.

CHAPTER FIFTEEN

SHE TASTED A little too much wine. But as much wine as she'd tasted in her life, she'd never been to a private vintner party—never had so many varieties of exquisite wine in one setting.

"He's never brought a woman to one of these before." The man who spoke had just walked up behind her, coming to stand with Sedona at the windowed wall of her host's living room, overlooking the ocean.

She tried for a chuckle that came out sounding more like a full-bodied laugh reminiscent of the petit Syrah she'd just sampled. "Don't make too much of it," she said, listening for Tanner's voice at the bar off to her right. All afternoon she'd been aware of his presence, had known, even as she mingled with the twenty or so people in the elegant room, where he was every second. She could feel him there—close.

And told herself that was because he was the only person in the room she knew.

"We're just friends," she thought to add. If she remembered right, Tanner had said he'd known the man most of his life.

"He used to work for me, did he tell you that?" Ron something-or-other asked.

"No."

Ron, an aging hippie with a long silver ponytail and an even longer beard, shrugged, the half-filled glass of wine in his hand a lighter hue than the liquid Sedona had most recently consumed. "Kids come cheaper than grown men and he was willing to work during the day."

"Other kids weren't?"

"I won't say they weren't willing, but the rest of them were in school."

"Why wasn't Tanner in school?"

"Don't know," Ron said, his brows loosely drawn together as he glanced sideways between her and Tanner, who was still deep in conversation with a couple at the bar. "I never asked. I just put him to work whenever he came around."

Tanner had cut school? To make money to supplement the government assistance his mother wasted away on her booze and drugs?

"How old was he?"

"Never asked that, either."

Wanting to tell the man that perhaps he should have, Sedona swallowed the urge and instead asked, "Did you ever know him to have a temper?"

"Tanner? You're kidding, right?"

She focused, wishing now that she hadn't allowed herself to consume both the white and the red tasting flights that afternoon. "I just…I've never seen him lose his cool," she improvised, "and…you know…everyone gets mad now and then."

"Tanner's the most mild-mannered individual I've ever met," Ron said, his gaze serious. "I watched that boy step in front of a fist aimed at his little brother once. I'd just dropped him off home and glanced back to see him into the house. That's when I saw this man haul off to hit the younger one, and like a panther, Tanner slid in to take it. Then, as though nothing had happened, he put his arm around the little guy and calmly walked into the house. The moment's as clear as if it just happened."

"Who was the guy?" she asked. And then, "No, wait, you didn't ask, right?" That was the wine talking. And maybe a piece of her heart, too. The piece that was crying for the young man Tanner had been.

"I didn't ask, no," Ron said. "But I also never saw him around again."

"How often were you around to see?"

"I made it my business to stop by the boy's house every day for a while after that, just to make certain that there was no more of that nonsense going on."

"So you knew Tanner's mother, then?"

"Tammy? There aren't many people in their neighborhood who didn't know her. Nice lady, when she was sober. Just didn't happen all that often."

"But you didn't turn her in."

"Actually, I did. Twice. Both times the kids were questioned. She was questioned. They all went into counseling. I know because Tanner didn't come around to help as often when he had to go to sessions, and things would be better for a bit. But it didn't last."

And Ron hadn't been able to, or maybe hadn't wanted to, do anything about that?

"I offered him a room at my place, but he wouldn't leave those kids. And he swore that he'd take them and run if I turned them in again. Said he was doing just fine, and if they got reported again, the state would split them up. I didn't have the heart to do that to him. So I just made sure there was always lots of work for him."

The man's gaze toward Tanner was filled with regret.

"You wish now you'd done it? Turned them in again?"

"Hell, no," Ron said, glancing back at her. "I wish he'd met you ten years ago. All Tanner needs is a good woman and I'm guessing, no matter what you say, if he brought you here, you're that woman. I know Tanner."

Liquid fire shot through her. Because of the wine.

She could *not* be turned on by the idea of being Tanner Malone's woman.

"I TALKED TO my folks about you."

Glancing over at the woman in the passenger's seat of his truck as they sat in her driveway Saturday evening, Tanner liked the relaxed way Sedona's head lay back against the seat.

"You did?" he asked. She'd had quite a bit more to drink than he had. Not so much that she was drunk, but enough to have loosened her tongue.

And he was willing to take advantage of the windfall.

"Yeah."

"Why did you do that?"

"Because I never have trouble maintaining professional boundaries."

So one could infer from her statement that... "But with me you do?"

"I like you."

It wasn't enough for him to go on. "Let's walk," he suggested, afraid she'd get sleepy and go inside, leaving him to replay the afternoon as he tried to figure out Sedona's place in his life.

He was afraid that the evening might end before he had a chance to kiss her.

Because if she liked him, she'd help him get Tatum home. He really, really needed his desire for this woman to be for that reason only.

She took him down to the beach and was fine walking in the sand as soon as she took off her sandals, but didn't seem the least bit inclined to continue the conversation they'd been having in the truck.

"So what did your parents have to say about me?"

Obviously, they hadn't said anything too awful. She'd invited him to her home. Was now alone with him outside in the dark.

"Mom thinks that Tatum adores you, but that there's been a serious breach of trust between you two."

His heart thudded deeply in his chest. Was she about to tell him that she'd decided to help Tatum leave him? The sand gave way beneath his feet, making walking more difficult.

"And your father?"

She was only a foot or so away, but he had to raise his voice to be heard over the surf.

"He thinks you're getting a bum rap all the way around."

He let the sound of the waves cover his silence. Let them be the conversation. He should get whatever information he could from her and go. Figure out what he was going to do if she decided that Tatum was right, that living with him on the farm wasn't best for her anymore.

But a war was raging inside of him. Between guardian and man. His entire adult life had belonged to the guardian. Tonight, the man was fighting for life. He wanted these few minutes with Sedona. Wanted to relax and enjoy the peace that she seemed to bring into every room she was in. Into every space she occupied—even outdoors.

He matched his long-legged pace to her more sedate one, listening to the waves. They'd rush angrily forward, and then, spent, retreat more quietly out to sea.

Much like the emotions that assaulted him, still, after so many years of schooling them. He'd feel the surge, and then, with a deep breath, wait for the wave to quietly retreat back from whence it had come.

They reached a fence, marking the end of the private beach, and Sedona headed up along the fence line, a little farther from the water.

Her hand brushed his and his fingers burned to take hold of hers, to grasp them and hang on.

"So why are you telling me this?" he asked, because it was all he could do.

"Honestly?" She kicked at the sand, sending it shooting in front of them. "I'm not sure."

"Guess."

Head bent, she continued to slowly traverse the beach and he shortened his pace once more.

"I like you." She repeated what she'd said earlier, but with a deeper note to her voice.

"And that's a problem?"

"It is if it gets in the way of my professional judgment."

And yet, that was just what he was hoping for. Or was he just hoping she liked him? Separate and apart from his little sister.

"So don't let it."

"I'm trying not to. But…"

Another surge of emotion hit him at that "but" and he waited for it to dissipate before saying, "What are you afraid of?"

She shrugged again. Her shoulders, accentuated by the thin cotton straps of her dress, seemed so feminine to him. So…in need of protection.

"I guess that you'll like me, too."

"And that would be so terrible?"

"That depends."

"On what?" A dog barked in the distance—the deep bark of a big dog—and the beach was pitch-black. Glancing the few acres between them and a half wall that separated the beach from the yards beyond, he noticed a few lights on, but knew that the people in those homes couldn't see him.

He liked it that way. To be able to observe without being seen.

To know without being known.

And he was tired of it, too. So tired…

Where in the hell had that thought come from?

"On whether or not your sister is better off someplace besides your home."

"She isn't."

"So you say."

"So I know."

She stopped, moving closer to him until he could see into her eyes. And, he was afraid, until she could see into his.

"I believe you, Tanner." Her whisper was so soft it was almost lost in the sound of the surf.

And he bent his head. The move wasn't premeditated in that moment, though it would have been if he'd thought about it. Problem was, he wasn't thinking. He touched his lips to Sedona's and just…felt.

Her lips. Her kiss. Searing desire. And more, too. He wanted the kiss to go on forever. To transport him out of the life he'd been born to into a world where he was just a guy, free to love this smart, beautiful, successful woman.

And then she pulled her lips from his. "But…" she said, her voice thick. "If I find out that your sister's fear stems from you, as she says it does, then I'll have no choice but to turn you in."

She wasn't going to be wooed. No matter how much she wanted him. He could see the truth in the stiffness of her shoulders. A contradiction to the tautness of those unfettered nipples touching the front of her dress.

He could taste her desire for him in her kiss, see it in her eyes, and could hear the conviction of her purpose in the tone of her voice.

"Fair enough."

"It's not fair at all. To any of us."

He needed to argue. To keep her on Tatum's case because he'd already won half the battle. She believed him. For now.

And because he knew more than anyone that life wasn't fair.

"So recuse yourself," his traitorous self, that emotional being who'd been forcing himself into Tanner's life of late, suggested.

"Believe me, I've thought about it." Sedona started to walk again. He took her hand. She held on.

And it felt good.

Better than he'd imagined.

"So do it."

"And risk having Tatum go to the police about you? Risk another attorney making her feel as though she has no other choice?"

God, no. He dropped her hand. What in the hell was he thinking?

He hadn't been. And that was the problem.

"What did your parents say about us?" She'd told them that Tatum and Tanner were at odds.

"That I should trust myself and listen to my heart. And Lila believes, as I do, that there's too much risk to Tatum if I abandon her. Something is obviously going on with her. Until we find a way to get her to tell us what it is, we can't know what's best for her. She's engaging in her sessions with Sara. Paying attention. Asking questions. She's just not talking yet, beyond what she's already told us."

"So trust your heart."

As long as it was telling her to trust him.

"I'm trying."

Which was more than he could say for himself. Walking her up to her door, Tanner said good-night to Sedona without touching her again.

Because he knew, even if she didn't, that he'd given up trusting anyone too long ago to remember.

CHAPTER SIXTEEN

SHE'D IMAGINED WHAT having sex would be like since she'd fallen in love with Del. Especially since Maddie talked about it so much. Her friends said the first time hurt. But that it didn't have to if you did things right.

As long as she was really turned on. And Del was patient and tender. Romance was supposed to help, too.

But it was a little hard to have romance or expect patience when you were in the backseat of a car skipping out of an English class that you'd really wanted to attend.

"I have to be back in twenty-five minutes, max," she said, sliding into Del's car Monday afternoon—a week and a day since she'd had dinner at Sedona's parents' house. A week and a day since she'd been anywhere except The Lemonade Stand and school.

Del had hung out at two different parties over the weekend, Friday night and Saturday night. He'd come pretty close to hooking up with someone, according to what she'd seen on Facebook.

She'd texted him, all night both nights, asking him about the girl. He'd promised he still loved her, but he was tired of being all alone. She had her new friends, people who cared about her and were helping her. She got to live with a roommate and choose her own meals every night and go to bed when she decided to. He was still forced to live like a prisoner in his father's house.

And his old man had been in a particularly bad mood on Sunday. He'd broken his golf club and taken it out on Del.

Tatum's heart bled for him and she had to see him. The only time he could get away from Brophy and sneak over to her school had been during English. And so here she was, dressed in a skirt, just like he'd instructed by text that morning, and climbing into his car parked by some bushes on the street just behind the high school.

"Come here, baby," he said, already in the backseat.

Her foot got caught in the seat belt up front as she attempted to climb over. And she hit her head on the overhead light.

Del didn't seem to notice her clumsiness. His eyes glowed with happiness and pleasure as she settled down next to him.

"That's too far away," he said, his voice all low and hoarse sounding, as he pulled her onto his lap. She could feel his penis pushing into her underwear.

And suddenly she just wanted to get it over with. There'd be time for romance. And patience. When she and Del were married and had a home of their own.

This day was about him. About putting him before her. He was being so good to her, sticking by her while she did nothing but tend to herself at The Lemonade

Stand. She was so busy figuring out her messed-up life, she hadn't been much of a girlfriend to him at all.

And still he'd stayed faithful to her. Only wanting what was best for her. And like he'd said from the beginning, if you wanted a relationship to work, you had to think about the other person, too, not just push for yourself.

She'd been pushing him to stop smoking dope at the time. And had grabbed that joint from him and thrown it in the ocean. That had been why he'd hit her that first time. He'd just been throwing his arm out to save the joint. And she'd been too close.

"Come on, baby, move with me here," he said now as he pushed his penis harder against her crotch, while she just sat there with that heavy feeling she got every time she remembered worrying about someone seeing the bruise.

If she'd told how she got it—because, after all, it was just a mistake—she'd have had to tell on him for doing drugs. And he'd promised her he was going to stop.

Del's lips closed over hers. His tongue touched hers, and she forgot everything. Her crotch started to tingle and get all warm and wildly weird-feeling and she knew she was doing the right thing.

She was thinking about him. Because he was so good to her.

His hands slid up her thighs, smoothly, like he knew exactly what he was doing. That was Del. Always so in control and sure of himself. Capable. He could do anything he wanted to do. And always kept his promises to her. He'd be a good man. A good father.

His hands were in her panties. He'd asked her to wear a thong, but she didn't have any. Her big brother saw her laundry, or he had until she'd started staying at The Lemonade Stand.

Thoughts of Tanner, of sweet Maddie and Sedona and the rest of them, wiped out all of the delicious warm feeling, leaving her nervous about the time.

And wishing Del wouldn't touch her.

Almost as if he could read her mind, he kissed her again. God, she loved his kisses. From the very first night she'd met him, she'd lost it when he kissed her. He'd gotten hard that first night, too. It had been her first personal experience with the way a man's penis grew.

He pulled her panties down and left them dangling on her left ankle. His pants were already undone and she realized they had been before she got in the car. He wasn't wearing any underwear. He already had on the condom.

And before she could have second thoughts, or really even a first one, he'd shoved himself up inside of her vagina and she thought she was going to die. It burned. Like ripped skin. All the way up inside her. She hurt so bad she figured she had to be gushing blood.

Thankfully, Del didn't move. She'd heard that guys went in and out, but Del didn't. He must have figured out that he'd done something wrong. That she was hurt.

And how the heck was she going to explain it? Was she hemorrhaging?

"God, baby, that was fantastic...."

It was?

Afraid to pull herself off from him, afraid of how badly it was going to hurt, and of the blood that would rush down when she did, Tatum tried not to cry.

"We need to set a date to do this every Monday," he said, and jerked, pulling himself out of her as he pushed her over to the seat next to him and did up his pants.

She stared at his penis. The condom was completely full. There was no blood there.

"I don't mean to rush you," Del said, leaning over to give her a quick kiss. "But you better get your underwear back on and get back to class."

Wow. That was it?

Stunned, Tatum did as she was told, managing to figure out that while she was bleeding, it was a little enough amount that her panties could handle it.

He said something more to her. She could hear his voice. She just wasn't paying all that much attention. Opening the door, she slid out.

"Hey, baby, what about my kiss?" Del's eyes glowed. His smile was huge and made her belly flip-flop. Leaning back in, she kissed him. Really kissed him. To see if the feeling came back.

To her surprise, and huge relief, it did. So maybe it was like they said, the first time wasn't so great, but the next time would be.

Not that she was in any hurry for a next time.

"I love you," Del said, tweaking her nipple outside her bra and shirt. She tingled there, too. In a good way.

"I love you."

"You gave me the greatest gift a girl could ever give a guy today," he said, his gaze completely serious. "You gave me your virginity. Thank you, babe."

And just like that, she was ecstatically happy again. Del wasn't just out to get some. He valued what she'd done for him. He valued her. "You're welcome."

"And remember," he added just before she shut the door, "it's all mine. You don't lift that skirt for anyone but me."

Hardly. She didn't even want to lift it for him again, and she was in love with him.

But she promised she wouldn't and when, as she hurried back toward the high school, she looked back to find him still watching her, when she saw him smile and wave, she knew that she'd done the right thing.

THE NEXT WEEK passed in a bit of a blur for Sedona. May was approaching and in another few weeks Tatum would be out of school.

As would many other kids whose lives would be drastically changing that summer, whether they knew it yet or not. Why people waited until vacation time to split up, she didn't know, but typically, she had twice as many new clients in the summer months as she did during the winter.

She spoke with Tanner every night, because she'd

made a verbal agreement to try to get to know him in exchange for Tatum's residency at The Lemonade Stand. And because she wanted to. She couldn't pretend anything different.

She could sense his growing frustration and wasn't sure how much longer he was going to be patient with Tatum's stonewalling them all so she could continue to live at the shelter.

Sedona wasn't sure how much longer she could continue her balancing act, hoping that Tanner had done nothing to warrant his sister's aversion to coming home.

Why would a fifteen-year-old girl prefer being locked in at a women's shelter every night to living a normal life?

She talked to Tanner, lay in bed at night and tingled as his voice came over the line. One night, late, in a low, sexy voice, he asked if she had regrets about her lack of a love life and she told him about the lonely law school years, when it seemed that life didn't exist outside case studies and torts. He asked about her toughest case—just an overview, not personal details. She told him about the few times she'd had to excuse herself to the restroom after court to allow herself to shed the tears that sometimes welled up inside her.

And one night he confessed that he didn't know what he was going to do when Tatum left for college. "Other than the vineyard, my whole life has consisted of looking after my siblings, and even the vineyard was for them. To have a way to support them," he'd said, his voice softer than usual. "I'm not sure I'll know what to do when I'm no longer a guardian. Based on these past weeks, I'm going to suck at living alone."

Staring out her window at the blackness of the beach in the distance, she'd listened to the waves through her open window. She'd been living alone for almost ten years. Since she'd started law school.

"Maybe it's time you started thinking about a life for yourself." Her parents had encouraged her to make her own way. To find out what she wanted and focus on obtaining it. She couldn't imagine not having had that chance.

"Sounds lonely."

Sometimes. A lot of times. But it was wonderful, too. Straightening her legs, she'd moved them along the cooled softness of her sheets, and thought about evenings like the one she'd just spent—when she could come home, bathe and crawl into bed without having to answer to anyone.

"It's nice now and then to have some hours without any expectations on your shoulders." Then she'd told him about long days and being able to come home and not have to do anything, to answer to anyone or have anyone expect her to do something for them.

"Yeah, but what if you'd come home to find a plate of your favorite food warming in the oven, a glass of wine waiting and, while you undressed, your bubble bath being drawn for you?" She'd thought maybe his tone had changed. And she might have imagined the difference.

Moving her legs again, pulling them tightly together, she'd allowed her mind to play out his imagined scenario.

"What's the wine?"

"My pinot grigio."

Her toes had tingled. Along with every other part of her.

"Would I be drinking it alone?"

"Depends." His tone had changed. Most definitely.

"On what?" So had hers.

"On whether or not you'd like me to join you in that tub."

"Hmm." She'd never actually shared a tub with anyone.

"Is yours a double-wide garden tub?" He'd dropped his voice to just one step above a whisper.

"Yes."

"Plenty big enough for two."

"Mmm-hmm."

"Was I out of line when I kissed you the other night?"

"Yes." She'd agreed to get to know him. Not to get physically involved.

"Did you like it?"

Black was black and white was white. She'd never settled for shades of gray. "Yes."

She'd heard some rustling. And then he'd said, "Yeah, me, too."

It had been a long day. And maybe that was the reason coming home to hot food, a glass of wine and a shared bubble bath had sounded so very much better than lying in bed alone with no one there to know or care that she'd come home late and exhausted.

"You kiss…for someone who's never been involved in a committed relationship…you do it…well." The darkness had taken away most of the embarrassment she'd felt for having made the admission out loud.

"So do you."

Did that mean her kiss had had the same effect on him as his had had on her? Maybe she should have poured herself a glass of wine before she'd climbed beneath the sheets. Or maybe she should have called him first.

"I…I've never actually quite felt like… Your kiss had… It was…good. Different."

She was normally quite eloquent.

"Would you like it to happen again?"

She'd closed her eyes. Listened to the ocean. Thought of hot baths. And warm nights out on the sand. "Yes."

"Yeah. Me, too."

Liquid had pooled inside her. Opening her eyes, Sedona had sat up in bed, upsetting Ellie, who'd tucked herself into a ball on the pillow next to Sedona's. "It's not a good idea, though."

"Why not?"

Because a fifteen-year-old girl was depending on her to make the right choice if it came down to choosing between her and Tanner.

Truth was, each day, as she got her Tatum report

from Sara, coupled with the few times she'd stopped in at The Lemonade Stand to see the girl, or spoken to Lila about Tatum's future, she knew she couldn't trust herself to be alone with Tatum's brother.

According to Sara, Tatum was exhibiting signs of trust issues that reached beyond the scope of being recently hit. So even if Del Harcourt had been the one to leave the physical bruises, there had to be something else driving Tatum's behavior.

Something the girl didn't seem to be able to talk about. Due to the very real confusion the teenager exhibited, Sara suspected Tatum might not remember everything that was driving her fear. That perhaps the recent events in her life, having been hit, had triggered something else inside of her.

And so on Thursday night, when she was overtired and wanting to make love to a man she wasn't sure she could trust, when, during their longest conversation yet, he was at the most open and vulnerable point she'd ever known him to be, she said, "We'd like to put Tatum under hypnosis."

He was a practical man. And too controlled for her to know who really lived inside the facade he gave to the world.

"What? That's crazy! Why?"

She'd both expected, and dreaded, the response. Someone with something to hide would find any form of mind release therapy threatening.

But she explained Sara's theories, anyway, adding

that Sara would need to speak with him herself before proceeding.

"Hypnosis is for circus acts," he said, all evidence of emotion wiped from his voice. But she was on to him now. The calmer Tanner got, the more something raged inside of him. Not raged with anger. Just raged. As though he fought silent battles that he didn't dare let the world see.

And so she patiently relayed the research she'd done before making her call that evening. Citing scientific evidence of the successes renowned psychotherapists had experienced with the therapy.

"It won't work unless we have Tatum's full cooperation," she added. "If your sister doesn't believe in the treatment, then she'll be resistant to the level of relaxation that must be reached in order for hypnosis to produce any true results."

"Has anyone talked to Tatum about it?"

"Not yet. Not without your approval."

Which probably was not on its way. She could hear his "no" loud and clear.

He asked a couple more questions. She answered them.

"Who would do the hypnosis? And who would be in the room?"

"A psychiatrist that Sara works with. And Sara, the doctor and Tatum."

"Let me talk to her about it tomorrow," he said after an inordinately long pause, a note of defeat in his voice. "If she wants to try this experiment, if it will somehow give her the excuse she needs to open up and tell us what's going on, I won't stand in her way. I want my sister well, Sedona. Well and back home where she belongs."

There was no doubting the truth in *those* words.

TANNER DIDN'T GET to talk to Tatum the next day. Instead, he spoke with Lila McDaniels, the shelter's managing director, who called to tell him that his sister wasn't feeling well and would be staying home from school that day.

Tatum had a sore throat and Lynn, the nurse practitioner, had already seen her and was running a culture. They'd call him as soon as they knew anything.

He called the high school to let them know that Tatum wouldn't be at school that day.

The attendance counselor wasn't in, but the school secretary assured him that she'd pass on his message.

She also asked how he was doing. How his wine was coming along. And whether or not he'd been to the new steak house up the coast.

He'd made the mistake of sleeping with the woman once—after Talia had left and before Tatum started high school. She never missed a chance to let him know she wouldn't say no to a repeat performance.

But Tatum didn't like the woman. And so he wasn't bringing her home.

Period.

Pretending he was getting another call, he rang off before she pinned him down to a definitive answer on the steak house front. He wasn't going to sleep with her again—which meant no dinner, either—but he didn't want to hurt her feelings.

Let her think he was too busy to date. He'd found the excuse usually let him off the hook without any ill will.

One thing was for sure. With Tatum in a shelter for abused women, threatening to have him arrested for something he hadn't done, he didn't need an enemy from Tatum's school.

SEDONA WASN'T GOING to call Tanner Friday night. After spending the entire night before dreaming about having sex with him, she needed a break.

Tatum's throat culture had come back negative and after a day lying on the couch in Maddie's bungalow with Maddie fussing over her and bringing her tea, the teenager was feeling much better. Just to be sure, Sedona stopped by the shelter. And was told that, since Tatum hadn't been at school, she hadn't spoken with Tanner.

"Did he call you?" she asked as she perched on the edge of an armchair in Maddie's living room while Maddie had dinner with Darin and his brother, Grant, at Lynn's larger bungalow on the edge of the property. The June double wedding was looming closer and it seemed as though everyone at The Lemonade Stand was catching the fever of excitement that Maddie didn't have the ability to contain.

"Yeah, but I didn't answer."

Understanding that the girl needed this space, supporting her right to have the time to work through whatever was traumatizing her, Sedona also felt a strong pang for the man who was now going to have three days without a word from his little sister instead of just the two she knew he'd already been dreading.

It also meant another three days before they could make arrangements for the hypnosis. Another three days of a stand-off that was getting harder and harder to bear.

"I think he had something in particular to talk to you about." The line she was treading was stretching too thin. If it broke she would have no one to blame but herself.

"What?" Tatum asked.

She was the girl's lawyer. Owed Tatum her loyalty.

"I'd rather he spoke with you about it." She chose her words carefully. "I don't want to influence your conversation."

Nodding, Tatum turned her face toward the television that she'd muted when Sedona had walked in. Some reality show was on.

Sedona, who faced far too much reality in the course of a day's work, didn't watch them. She didn't watch much television at all, preferring the sound of the ocean for company over laugh tracks and rehearsed speeches.

She stood. "So you'll take his call?"

"Yeah." Tatum seemed unhappy. Not so much afraid as concerned. "I need to talk to him about my cell phone, anyway," she said. "My month of grounding from my smartphone is almost up."

TANNER HAD JUST come in from the vineyard on Friday, satisfied that his crop was healthy and going to produce as planned, and was on his way in to shower when his cell phone rang.

Thinking of Sedona, and then of Tatum, his heart leaped as he grabbed the phone from the holster on the waistband of his jeans.

"Mr. Malone?"

He didn't recognize the voice and steeled himself. "Yes?"

"This is Nancy Pawloski calling from Oceanside High School."

Tatum's school? "Yes?"

"I'm the attendance counselor, sir."

Returning his call from the morning. "Oh, hello. She's fine," he said now. Lila McDaniels had phoned him that afternoon to tell him so. "It's not strep so she'll be back at school on Monday."

Hand in his pocket, he stood in the living room he and Tatum had arranged together, staring out at the dried-up yard and dusty roundabout. He'd meant to lay sod. And plant flowers...

"I'm glad to hear that, sir."

Heading toward the shower, he said, "Thanks for calling. I should have let you know and I'm sorry." He'd been pruning when Lila had called.

He stood in the bathroom, pretending not to notice his sister's empty spaces, and heard, "It's not a problem, Mr. Malone. I'm glad, with as much as she's been feeling unwell lately, that you've had her checked out. Glad to know that she's fine."

His reflection in the mirror shocked him. Not only because of the lines that had formed around his frown, but because he looked so...old. And worn. "She's been feeling unwell a lot?" he asked, schooling his voice to a calmness he didn't feel.

"She's missed nine classes over the past month."

What? Heart thudding heavily, Tanner waited for the intensity to pass. "There must be some mistake in your record keeping," he stated calmly when he'd regained control of his emotions. "I drive Tatum to school every day. And watch her until she's inside the door," he added, just so there'd be no further misunderstanding. "And I pick her up every afternoon."

"There's no mistake in the record keeping, sir. Several of Tatum's teachers have reported her leaving class due to illness. She always returns, and it's not always the same class so it's not a big deal. Girls go through things and it's not uncommon for them to need to leave class at this age. Teachers report every incident, as a matter of rote, and it's up to me to chart them and watch for trends. I've just been starting to get concerned enough about Tatum to call you, but then you called this morning."

Watching his expression in the mirror until the tension had eased he asked, "Did she say what was wrong?"

Gather the parameter of the problems, then find the solution. Every problem had one.

"Just that she wasn't feeling well. We usually assume that means cramps."

"Nine times in a month?" He wasn't accusing. He just needed to know.

"It does seem a bit excessive, but it happens. I take it she didn't tell you about the situation? Probably didn't want to worry you."

The situation? The man in the mirror didn't look like him. The panic was unacceptable. And Tanner looked away.

The counselor continued. "Thomas, he's made good for himself, largely because of your support. And Talia, you kept her at home and in school as well as any parent could have done. And now Tatum, she's such a good girl, Mr. Malone. Straight As. Polite and thoughtful and—"

"Excuse me." He didn't need a history lesson. "I'm sorry, but have we met before?"

"Not directly, no. But I've been with Oceanside schools for twenty years, starting out as a teacher's aide. I had both Thomas and Talia in my class."

And obviously the gossip mill worked as well in the adult sector of the public education system as it did among its students.

Tanner pulled himself upright. The thought was unfair. And unlike him. The personnel at Oceanside public schools had been a godsend to him. Many times. Supporting his right to have custody of his siblings, helping him pick up the slack a time or two in the early days…he owed them.

"I'll talk to Tatum," he said now. "If there's more going on with her health, I can assure you, she'll be seeing the doctor immediately."

"I told Tatum you'd want to know."

"You've already talked to my sister about this?"

"Yes, sir. Her chart flagged me and I called her in yesterday afternoon. I told her that I'd be calling you."

He didn't know how to respond without giving himself away.

"She said that you wouldn't care, but I knew you would. Girls have a way of underestimating the opposite sex, you know? A lack of outward affection translates as a lack of caring," the woman said, the compassion in her voice mostly lost on him.

Had he just been counseled to show his sister more outward affection? When, at the moment, he was afraid to touch her at all for fear of being accused of bruising her?

"I'll have a talk with her," Tanner said, making up his mind once and for all. Tatum had to come home.

And tell him what was going on. She had to let him help her.

Especially now that school was involved. A lifetime of keeping himself one step ahead of the system that would split up his family was too much a part of him, too fully engrained, for him to ignore.

That thought done, he completed his phone call and immediately dialed another number. Sedona Campbell's time was up. He'd have liked to tell her in person, but when he got her voice mail, he figured that worked just as well. His message was curt and to the point. He'd give Tatum the night to rest, and in the morning she was coming home.

He and Tatum would get this done. Whatever it was.

And things would be okay.

Somehow. Some way.

They always were.

CHAPTER SEVENTEEN

SEDONA HAD NO business stopping by the Malone vine-yard Friday evening. She knew it. Tanner would know it. But as soon as she hung up after a very disturbing phone call from her brother, Grady, who'd called to tell her his wife had been unfaithful, and then heard Tanner's deadpan message on her voice mail, she climbed back into her car and headed out to the country.

Ellie had done her business and had her dinner. But she wasn't happy about being left again so soon.

Sedona wasn't all that happy with herself. But she didn't turn around.

If she was using Tanner's attraction to her to further a business goal—the need to keep Tatum and Tanner Malone from exploding into a crisis mode that would necessitate legal intervention—then so be it.

Bottom line was, her client, Tatum Malone, was not ready to come home.

And if her heart was reaching out to Tanner because she was falling for him…if she was on her way to his place because he was hurting and she couldn't stay away?

Shaking her head, Sedona pushed harder on the gas pedal.

She figured if Tanner was in from the vineyard, he'd hear her old Thunderbird coming up the long laneway. He'd have plenty of opportunity to avoid seeing her.

He was waiting on the front porch when she pulled up to the house in a cloud of dust. He didn't come down to greet her, though.

So, taking a deep breath, she made the short climb up to him, hoping that, in her black pants and black-and-white tailored jacket, she looked more professional than she felt.

The first whiff of fresh masculine scent, and her confidence in her ability to walk the thin professional line weakened. The hair hanging down the back of his neck was still wet. He'd just come from a shower.

He didn't say anything. Just watched her step up next to him. And she had a vision of him minus the jeans and polo shirt he'd obviously just donned.

"Please don't do this, Tanner." She stood there, nose to nose with him, staring him in the eye—and pleaded.

When he turned his gaze to the horizon, her heart sank.

Sedona felt as if she was in the middle of a tornado—the calm eye of the storm part. Knowing that destruction was coming and unable to prevent it. To protect those she cared about.

"Why?"

The countryside was quiet. An occasional car drove by on the road but it was far enough away that she could barely hear it. There were no animals milling

around. No waves bringing unending conversation—
an unrelenting promise of life. Just quiet.

Was this what Tatum was running from? The quiet?

Or had Tanner provided his sister an oasis of peace
out here? A place where delicate grapes grew strong
and healthy?

Turning, she stood side by side with him, staring
out at his horizon. "I stopped by The Stand on my way
home tonight." She spoke softly, withholding judgment. She had to persuade him.

For his sister's sake. But for his, too. Not that she expected this distant, self-possessed man to believe that.

He didn't seem to have heard. And yet she knew he
was listening.

"Tatum agreed to answer her phone if you call her
again. She agreed to speak with you."

She glanced over as she spoke. His chin stiffened,
but there was no other reaction.

"I didn't tell her why you were calling," she added,
just to be clear.

Tanner had trust issues. She'd known that going
in. Growing up the way he had, a guy would be hard-
pressed not to have an issue or two.

Looking to the horizon again, she said, "Last night
you agreed to give hypnosis a chance. Today you're
saying time's up. What happened?"

He didn't trust. But he also didn't go back on his
word.

Or make hasty decisions.

Two things she'd learned about him in this time of "getting to know him."

"If you force this issue, she could still go to the police." A cheap shot, maybe, but also true. Sedona was certain Tatum would be lying if she told the police that her brother was the one who'd hit her. But that didn't mean the teen wouldn't do it. If she felt forced to do so in order to stay at The Lemonade Stand.

He stood, hands in his pockets, staring out as though he was on the old porch all alone.

Man against the world.

Man holding the world on his shoulders.

An overwhelming need to hold him swept over her.

"She's just agreed to speak with you, Tanner." If he forced Tatum to come home, what little bit of opening she was giving him would certainly slam shut again.

His face implacable, Tanner stood a few seconds more and then turned. His gaze swept over her, before meeting hers, and lingering.

And then he left. Without a word. Not a goodbye. Or any indication that he'd be back.

She watched his retreating back through the glass of the screen door until it disappeared into the house, fighting tears.

Was that it, then? He was just dismissing her?

His look hadn't been dismissive.

But she was equally certain there'd been no invitation issued, either.

If ever a man could be an island, it would be Tanner. But the more he looked only to himself for strength, relied only on himself to carry the world's burdens, the more he compelled Sedona to show him a different way.

Which was ridiculous. He wasn't her problem. Or even her client.

Her mind made up to leave him to create his own future, she took a step down to the driveway. Noticed how the dust covered the top of her expensive and stylish blue leather pump.

There was something wrong with the picture. A successful woman, dressed smartly, listening to her head and not her heart. It wasn't the life she'd promised herself she'd live.

It was the career she'd chosen.

As long as she'd been waffling, he'd had a chance to return. Glancing behind her she saw the empty doorway he'd passed through. He hadn't come back.

He also hadn't shut the front door.

Nor had he locked the screen door.

Without really making up her mind, Sedona turned, climbed back up to the porch in her dusty blue pumps, opened that storm door and entered Tanner's home uninvited.

HE'D OPENED ONE of his own bottles of wine. Because he'd provided it for himself. A reminder that he could and would always take care of his own. On his own.

He'd poured a glass. Closed his eyes while he'd taken the first sip—allowing his focus to rest fully in that moment of taste. He had high expectations for the pinot grigio.

And wasn't disappointed.

Opening his eyes, Tanner pulled a pan from the cupboard beside the stove, filled it with water and, lighting the gas burner of the claw-footed iron stove the old-fashioned way, he put the water on to boil.

The cupboard to the right of the stove, quality white barn-siding like all the rest, held the boxes of macaroni and cheese. They bought them by the case. He was down to three boxes.

Taking one down, he left two behind.

And heard the screen door open, followed by the clack of heels on the hardwood floors coming through the living room to the dining room. Heading straight in his direction.

Picking up the bottle of wine, he filled the second glass he'd pulled down to the counter. Lifted it and handed it to his guest as she came into the room.

SHE DIDN'T HAVE to see the unlabeled bottle on the counter to know that Tanner had just offered her a glass of his own wine.

Warmth pooled within her again.

Respecting his need for silence she accepted the gift, took a sip and savored the ever so slightly acidic liquid rolling on her tongue.

Not a hint of sweetness, like a Riesling or a Moscato, yet not too dry, either. She tasted a hint of orange, not lemon, some apple and maybe a little pear.

Swallowing was smooth, no stinging in her throat. Overall…exquisite.

Lifting her glass to him, she smiled. He nodded. And turned to pour macaroni from a box to a pan of boiling water on an antique stove her mother would die to own.

"She's missed nine classes in the past month."

Holding her glass with both hands, Sedona stared at his back. And then watched his hands as he grabbed a wooden spoon and stirred the macaroni. That backside, those pecs—and a wooden spoon in a pot of elbow noodles. The combination was sexy as hell.

And sad, too.

"I don't understand," she said, sipping from her wine. She had to be careful. The stuff was so good she could easily get herself into a state where she wouldn't be safe to drive. "You take her to school every morning and pick her up every afternoon. She told me you watch her go into the building and are there watching when she comes out again."

Tatum had been complaining—or rather, explaining. Giving an example of how Tanner treats her like child. How her brother refused to see that she's a young woman, able to make decisions for herself. To take control of her own life.

At least to some extent. The teenager wasn't crying out for an apartment of her own. Or even a car.

She just wanted some say in her life.

A completely healthy and necessary step in the growing-up process.

And an issue between her and her brother. But certainly not the real problem between them.

"She's been leaving class on the grounds of feeling unwell."

Other than that morning's sore throat, no one had said a word to her about Tatum being sick....

"And because she's not here, I have no idea if she's under the weather or not. It's pretty easy to fake wellness for fifteen minutes at a time, which is all I ever see her."

She didn't miss the complaint in his tone. Or the derision.

And, God help her, she understood. What they were doing to Tanner...ripping his family apart for seemingly no known reason...it wasn't fair.

And was completely necessary, too.

What in the hell did she say to him?

"I'll talk to Sara and Lila and we'll bring the matter up with Tatum."

"I'd appreciate it."

He stirred. An unnecessary act at that stage of the boxed macaroni and cheese process.

Sedona was afraid to move, to break the thread of trust she was pretty sure he'd just handed her.

"You're going to let her continue to stay at The Stand?"

"For now."

He wasn't giving her a mile. Or even an inch. But there was a centimeter there. Or a day or two.

"YOU HAVE DINNER YET?" Tanner ripped open the packet of cheese sauce powder and poured it over the drained macaroni and butter mix in his pan, stirring until the pasta was coated with orangey cream sauce.

"No."

"Are you staying?" Did he get down one plate or two?

"Yes."

Two plates.

And a little more wine.

TATUM'S CHAIR WAS still empty. But Tanner enjoyed dinner a hell of a lot more than he had anytime recently. As he glanced up and saw Sedona delicately putting a forkful of macaroni into her mouth, her perfectly straight white teeth showing for a second before those sexy lips closed over the utensil, it occurred to him that she was the first adult woman to ever sit at that table with him.

It was the first time a grown woman had graced his dinner table since his mother left.

He reached for his wine. An obvious solution to salve the thickness in his throat. And followed it with a bite of macaroni.

If he'd known she was coming, he might have thawed some pork steaks. Tatum loved his vinegar and Worcestershire marinated grilled pork.

Sedona didn't regale him with useless chatter. But their silence wasn't awkward, either. Or filled with the tension that had permeated any time he'd spent at the table with Tatum in recent months.

Sedona had cleaned her plate. And almost emptied her second glass of wine. He opened a second bottle. The night was early. And he was going to spend it with his own success.

Holding the bottle up over her glass he glanced at her. She covered the top of her glass with her hand and shook her head. He filled his own, rinsed the dishes and put them in the dishwasher Tatum had insisted he buy for her for Christmas one year.

When he returned to the dining room, Sedona was still there, babying the tiny bit of wine that was left in her glass.

Didn't much matter to him if he enjoyed his wine there, in the living room, or out in the barn. At the moment, not much mattered.

Not even the fact that he'd promised himself, and all three of his siblings, that he would always be sober.

For thirty-three years he'd kept that promise. And what had it gotten him? A big old rambling house for company. A sister who preferred a women's shelter to the home he'd provided for her.

Tonight he was going to feel what it felt like to be drunk. Must be something to it. The power of the drunk had been far more compelling to his mother than any of her four kids had been.

Even Tatum, as perfect and beautiful and sweet as she'd been, hadn't been enough for their mother....

"My brother called tonight."

Sedona's voice flowed right into the moroseness of his self-pity as though it belonged there. She'd finished her wine. Was looking at his newly opened bottle. He'd yet to sip from his third glass of wine. Three was all he'd ever allowed himself.

But tonight he was going to drink as much as it took.

"How's he doing?" he asked, staring at his glass of wine. Lifting it to his lips. Sipping. Enjoying the flavor. The trickle against the back of his throat.

Wine was meant for appreciating. Not for obliterating.

"His wife was unfaithful to him."

Tanner's attention was no longer on his wineglass. "He called to tell you that?"

"Yeah."

"Wow."

It wasn't as though he was a big believer in fidelity. Still…

He held the stem of his glass, gliding his fingers up down the smoothness of polished crystal. The glasses had been a gift from Thomas—his little brother had used his entire paycheck to buy them secondhand before he'd left for New York—in celebration of Tanner's purchasing the farm to build a Malone family home and start a winery. Prior to that, they'd lived in subsidized housing and, for a while, a small rental.

"Who's the guy?"

"So stereotypical—her personal trainer."

"Does she work?"

"No. Grady's a pediatrician, I think I told you that.

He and Brooke had agreed, before they married, that she'd be a stay-at-home wife and mom."

She might have told him. He didn't remember either way.

"She'd had some problems with postpartum depression after Cameron was born. She'd been feeling fat and ugly and Grady hired the trainer for her so she'd feel good about herself."

"I guess she felt a little too good."

He was watching her, and it hit him that if she were his woman, he'd rather die than find out that she'd been unfaithful to him.

Going completely still, he waited for the sensation to pass. And then took a sip of wine. A small sip. He knew how to make the third glass last.

Sedona helped herself to another glass of wine.

"Are they divorcing?" he asked, maybe just to keep her there. Keep her talking to him.

As soon as she left, he'd have no excuse to put off getting drunk.

"No."

She didn't sound at all happy about the fact.

"Brooke's pregnant."

She might have mentioned that before, too. Marriage and babies weren't things he generally committed to memory. They were outside his frame of reference.

"So they're going to try to work it out." He felt as if he was drowning, and the sensation had nothing to do with his wine consumption. "Makes sense," he added. "For their baby's sake." And the other kid, too.

Tanner was all for dads being decent and standing by their kids.

He just didn't have a lot of experience with ones who did.

"He's not sure the baby's his."

"Oh." Ohhh. Now he got it. She was talking to him because of his mother. This Brooke, she was the baby-daddy type, too.

"Yeah."

Leaving his glass of wine on the table, Tanner pushed it away. "I admire him," he said, sitting back in the old wooden chair, hardly noticing the slats digging into his back. "He's standing by the kids."

"He can still be there for his children, even if they aren't married."

"You think he should leave her." Interesting. She was a divorce lawyer, after all.

But she believed in once and forever.

"I think Grady so badly wanted what Mom and Dad have that he jumped too soon, trying to capture something that has to settle upon you. And now, with this..."

"Maybe his wife won't stay with him and it will be a moot point."

"She's staying." Her derision was clear.

"Because of the money?"

"That's what I think. Grady says that she's horribly sorry, has asked for his forgiveness and desperately wants a second chance. He says that he's been neglecting her, spending all of his time with his sick patients instead of being at home with her and Cameron. I guess he's been working about eighty hours a week."

"So maybe she does love him." But it was probably the money.

"She claims the baby is his. Like she thinks Grady won't test to find out as soon as the baby comes."

"You think he'll leave her if it isn't?"

"No."

"But you think he should."

"She was unfaithful to him. She could be carrying another man's child. That's broken marriage vows in my book."

His, too. "But what if they really do love each other? What if it really was like Brooke said? Maybe you'd make the same choice," he told her, slouching back in his chair.

"I'm not going to settle, if that's what you mean."

"And you think Grady's settling."

"I think…" She sipped. He waited. They stared at each other. Tanner wasn't sure what was happening, but he knew something was. Knew that he could put an end to it—and wasn't going to.

Not that night.

"I don't know what I think." Her words, when they finally came, sounded strangled.

And the unusual depression that had been threatening to bury him earlier that evening faded back into obscurity as he leaned over to kiss her.

CHAPTER EIGHTEEN

SEDONA DIDN'T WAIT for Sara or Lila to speak with Tatum. Saturday morning, she was up before dawn, watched the sunrise on the beach with Ellie and pulled into the back entrance, and her private parking spot of The Lemonade Stand, just as the teenager was exiting the cafeteria with Maddie.

"Let's go," she said, walking up to take the girl's elbow.

Tatum didn't resist. Or hold back at all. "Where are we going?"

Tatum wasn't allowed to leave The Stand without Tanner's permission.

"Just for a drive." She'd hung around with Tanner for another hour and a half after dinner. Wine-free. He'd poured a third glass, but hadn't finished it. She hadn't finished hers, either, though they'd stayed at the table. Talking. With an occasional stolen kiss that neither of them mentioned.

And before she'd left, while standing at the door pretending as if they hadn't just spent the evening flirting with sex, she'd made a promise.

Tatum stopped. "We're leaving The Stand?"

"Yes." Sedona's focus was on the girl's best interests. This morning, alone and sober, she still believed keeping this promise to Tanner was in Tatum's best interest.

"Does Tanner know?"

"Yes."

Tatum nodded then and resumed her step, but with silence and a little less enthusiasm in her gait.

Sedona stepped carefully, as well, knowing that she was close to falling off her tightrope.

"Where are we going?" Tatum finally asked as she buckled herself into the front passenger seat of Sedona's old Thunderbird.

Sedona had debated this part. What did she say? How best to perform the experiment? If she said too much, Tatum's reaction would be skewed. If she didn't tell her that they were driving by the home she shared with her brother, the girl might feel as though Sedona was teaming up with Tanner to make her go home.

"What's up?" Tatum was frowning now. She turned in her seat and the belt grabbed at her top, raising the bottom hem above Tatum's low-rise waistband, exposing her belly button.

It was pierced. With a gold ball loop.

"When did that happen?" Sedona hadn't meant her tone to be so sharp. But Tanner was starting to trust her. And she'd given him her word that Tatum would be completely monitored at all times while she resided at The Stand.

"A couple of months ago," she said. Before she'd come to the shelter. Starting the car, Sedona headed out of the parking lot, still not sure if she was going to tell Tatum where they were going, or let the girl figure it out on her own.

"Del likes belly button rings," Tatum offered, her voice softening as she tucked a strand of naturally blond hair behind her ear. "He thinks they're sexy."

But Tatum wasn't sure she wanted to have sex....

"Does Tanner know you pierced your belly button?"

"No."

"You didn't need his signature?"

She shrugged. "Del did it. He talked to some people and we watched some videos on YouTube and it hardly hurt at all." Tatum's words tumbled over themselves. "My friend's mom let her have it done and she went to a shop and it got all infected and gross. Mine has never had a problem."

"So why not tell your brother about it?"

She was trying to keep an open mind. Had to keep an open mind. Tatum's friend's mother let her have a belly button ring. And Tanner approved of all of Tatum's friends...

"Duh, Tanner?" Tatum sounded about twelve. "You really think he'd go for that? And besides, if I'd asked, and he said no, he'd have been checking to make certain I didn't do it, anyway. This way he has no idea. And doesn't have to worry about it."

"Did you talk to him about belly button piercings?"

"Not specifically. I wanted a triple piercing in my ear and he said that I had enough body piercings with the two in my ears. He thinks nose and eye and belly-button piercings make a girl look wild and loose and I have my mother's genes, you know." Tatum stared out the window as they drove, seemingly unaware of the turns Sedona had made, taking them out of the small town toward her brother's winery. Of course, there were other locations in the same direction.

Like Santa Barbara.

A mall.

"Did Tanner say that? That you have your mother's genes?"

"He didn't have to. But Del says that Tanner thinks that if he doesn't control every single thought in my brain I'm suddenly going to become a whore and a druggie. I never saw it that way, but once I thought about it, I knew he was right."

Sedona's instincts screamed so loudly she squirmed in her seat. *Harcourt* again. Just like Tanner kept insisting. But Tatum had only known the kid a couple of months and Sara said they were dealing with issues dating back a lifetime.

"Sometimes he makes me feel like maybe I do have a whore gene or something."

"Who does? Tanner or Del?"

The girl's gaze shot toward her. "Tanner, of course." But Tatum didn't sound as sure.

"The choice to live like your mother did is just that. A choice. Spurred on by environment, maybe, but not heredity."

"Talia's a stripper. And I'm not stupid. I know she probably does guys for money, too."

"She grew up in your mother's environment. You didn't." Tanner had made sure of that. And Sedona could see why.

"Your school called," she said next, being purposefully vague. No reason to deliberately antagonize Tatum's negative feelings against her brother by setting him up as a tattletale.

Tatum's head turned sharply toward her, a look of fear there and gone. "What for?" she asked more calmly than she looked.

"They're concerned because you've been feeling ill so much lately. I guess you've had to leave classes nine different times in the past month."

"Just sick to my stomach," Tatum said quickly. Too quickly? "I get bad stomach cramps when I get upset. Ask Tanner, he'll tell you. I threw up the first three days of junior high."

She'd ask.

"This past month has been a lot more stressful than junior high," Tatum continued.

"You're sure that's all it is?"

"Positive. As soon as I feel better I get right back to class." Tatum didn't hesitate in her response and Sedona wanted to believe her.

She took another turn. A more certain one. Leading to the road Tanner and Tatum lived on.

"Where are we going?" Tatum's voice was filled with mistrust.

She might have played this one wrong. The last

shreds of the rope she was walking could be unraveling and she had no other plan. No safety net.

For any of them.

"We're driving by the farm," she told Tatum straight out. The girl had obviously guessed, anyway. "Tanner is out in the vineyard this morning."

"You're taking me home?" The horrified look Tatum was giving her caught at Sedona. Taking her breath.

The experiment was to assess Tatum's reaction.

"Just so that you can get some things," she said quickly. "Your brother agreed that you had the right to choose your own outfits and pick up anything else from your room that you wanted."

If, in return, Sedona watched Tatum while she was home, to see that Tatum loved things about her home, that she missed being home.

"And you swear he's not there?"

"He promised he'd vacate."

"And he's just going to let me take whatever I want?"

"He agreed that you had the right to do that." After Sedona had explained that Tatum was a young adult who, without making accusations of abuse, could go to court and petition to have his guardianship removed. That the court would give her request credence simply because of her age. Not that they'd grant it, but that they'd at least entertain the motion.

Curiously, Tatum didn't say another word after that. Sedona wished she'd just gone right on talking. She needed to know what thoughts were racing through

Tatum's brain. Needed to find the missing pieces in Tatum's story before it was too late.

SEDONA CAMPBELL WAS a witch. There was no other explanation for the way the woman could sway him from his course. From what he knew to be smart and safe. After a lifetime of having to watch every move, every second, he knew better than to blindly turn his home over to an attorney who had admitted she would represent his sister in Tatum's attempt to get away from him.

Sure, Tatum would be there, as well. But his sister couldn't be expected to know how sly people could be. She didn't know that people were, basically, untrustworthy.

She didn't know because Tanner had made it his life's quest to raise Tatum in a home where love and safety were the defining factors. He'd given his life so that she could grow up with a heart filled with all the good things he and Thomas and Talia had been denied—faith, hope.

And trust.

Unfortunately, he hadn't counted on the Harcourts of the world preying on Tatum's innocent, naive, loving nature.

Sitting on the cement floor of the antique barn, where he'd gone when he'd heard Sedona's car pull in, knowing that his baby sister and her attorney were in the house, Tanner leaned against the wall, closed his eyes and breathed.

Sedona was going to see that Tatum loved her home.

She was going to notice a bit of longing in Tatum's eyes. Some hint of missing all that had been dear to her.

Maybe, if he willed it hard enough, Tatum would break down and agree to come back home.

A trickle slipped down his face in spite of the eyes he'd closed.

SEDONA WATCHED THE girl closely. Was there any particular place where Tatum's features froze up? Where they softened? In the living room, did she exhibit any sense of fear? Or in her bedroom?

Tanner expected her to see some longing in Tatum's reaction to her unexpected homecoming.

She was looking for signs of a return to a crime scene.

She didn't really see either. Tatum entered the house calmly. Looked around casually, but didn't show any overt reactions of any kind. Until she stopped in the middle of the living room, looked up and waved at the smoke alarm before heading for the stairs and her room. The girl could have been in the house the day before for all the reaction she showed.

Because she'd promised Tanner, Sedona followed Tatum up the stairs, to continue to watch for reaction.

"What was that about down there?" she asked as Tatum went straight to her drawers and started pulling out pajamas and underwear—leaving more in the drawers than she was taking. As if she wasn't going to be gone too long.

Interesting. If Sedona had been running away from an abuser, and had a chance to get her things, she figured she'd take everything she could get her hands on—as quickly as she could get her hands on them.

"What?" Tatum asked, reaching into the closet and coming out with a medium-size roller suitcase that she calmly opened and started to fill. Neatly. Methodically.

"Greeting the smoke alarm."

"It's part of our security system." She shrugged, looking embarrassed. "I... It's a stupid kid thing. It scared me when Tanner had the system installed because I thought it meant people could see me, but he didn't want me in the house alone without it and told me it was my friend. I guess greeting it is just habit."

"He has cameras in the house? He watches you all the time?"

"No, mostly it's just motion sensors, but there are like these nanny camera things that he turns on whenever we leave," Tatum said, putting in a tablet, a couple of ink pens and passing over everything else on her desk to move to the hanging clothes in the closet. "He's always been really paranoid and was afraid Tammy was going to come back. They were up in our old house, too. The one we lived in with Tammy. So if she did illegal stuff we could prove it. And not be blamed for it."

"That smoke alarm is a camera."

"Uh-huh." Tatum pulled out a few shirts, finishing with a couple of pairs of shoes that she zipped into an outer compartment on the case. "There's a motion sensor in it, too."

"Does he watch the security tapes every time he comes home?"

"Usually I did. Tanner gets a lot more upset about Tammy than I do. He lived with her a lot longer than I did and knew her a lot better, too."

"Have you ever thought about finding her?"

A blouse in hand, the girl turned and looked at her. "What for?" Her frown looked completely perplexed.

"I'll take that as a no."

"After what she did to my brothers and sister... there's no way I'd have anything to do with her. It would hurt Tanner too much."

She felt like an interloper standing there in the middle of an intimate family moment. And couldn't help noticing, again, how homey the room was. From the paint on the walls, the professionally framed artwork, the bulletin board filled with personal mementos and photos, to the thick down coverlet and matching shams and throw pillows. It was nice. Felt similar to the room she'd grown up in. "Did you ever notice anything on the tapes?"

"No, but Tanner did once."

"Tammy was here?"

"No, he saw Talia taking cash out of his desk." Tatum left her bag, pulled some things out of a drawer in the bathroom across the hall, put them into a side pocket, grabbed one of the three stuffed butterflies from her bed, tossed it on top of her clothes and zipped up the suitcase.

She turned to Sedona. "That last time Talia ran away, when she was eighteen, she took Tanner's emergency cash with her. But she knew the camera was on. There's a little light by the television that tells us. She knew Tanner would know she took the cash."

"Do you know how much it was?"

"Five hundred dollars. It's always been that. Until Talia took it, it was the original bills he earned from his first summer job baling hay. When she took those, he put five one-hundred-dollar bills right where he'd left the other five."

"And it's still there?"

Tatum shrugged. "I haven't looked, but I'm sure it is. He told all of us that if we ever needed money in a hurry for any kind of emergency, that's where it would be."

"He thinks of everything." She murmured the words, mostly to herself. And wasn't sure if she was impressed. Or worried. Was he really as selfless and thoughtful as he seemed? Or was he obsessive and manipulative and she just didn't want to see that?

What she did know was that the more she learned about Tanner Malone, the more danger she was in of falling, like Alice, into the rabbit's hole.

If she wasn't careful, he was going to take up permanent residence in her heart.

CHAPTER NINETEEN

TATUM DIDN'T SEEM to be the least bit uncomfortable in her home. She didn't seem to fear, at all, that her brother might show up at any minute and confront them.

She also didn't seem inclined to linger.

She gathered her things and, without any long or last looks around, headed out the door and down the stairs.

Until she passed by a large antique wood desk set by itself in a corner of the living room. Tatum turned her head away from the desk. Sedona was on her other side, watching her, or she'd have missed the way the girl's eyes closed and lips tightened for a brief second before she squared her shoulders and moved on by.

Sedona followed her out.

Tanner had given them an hour. They'd taken less than fifteen minutes.

SEDONA DIDN'T DRIVE straight back to The Stand. She pulled into a big-box store first, finding a parking spot farther out in the lot—one with no cars on either side. Her car had enough dings in it already. "Tanner gave me some money for you to get any incidentals you might need," she said.

Expecting her client to hop out of the Thunderbird, excited about spending the free money, Sedona was surprised when Tatum didn't even unbuckle her seat belt. "I don't need anything from him."

Her pretty face was stony.

Sedona turned in her seat. "What's going on?"

"Nothing."

"Tatum." She waited until the girl turned those striking blue-gray eyes on her. "You were fine a few minutes ago and now you're not. What happened?"

Was the desk where Tanner had turned on Tatum? Maybe they'd had an altercation while he'd been sitting there and he'd grabbed her arm to keep her from running off.

Maybe she'd been emotional, as hormonal teenage girls often got, and had been flailing out at him and in trying to restrain her he'd knocked her into the desk.

Sedona had spent the past seven or eight minutes trying to rein in her suppositions.

Her fears.

Tanner would not intentionally harm his sister. She just could not believe differently.

"Nothing happened."

"That's it, then."

Starting the engine, Sedona threw the car in reverse. "What's it?"

"I can't represent you if you aren't going to be honest with me."

"I…"

Sedona glanced over, her look warning Tatum not to lie to her.

"Okay." The girl's whole demeanor changed. Sedona pulled the car back into its spot and cut the engine.

"I'm listening."

"I…just… It doesn't have anything to do with… anything."

"Fine." She'd be the judge of that.

"It's not like… Tanner doesn't even know I know and…"

"Know what?"

Tatum's eyes held a pool of emotion when she glanced over. Emotion Sedona couldn't translate. It wasn't fear.

But Tatum's struggle was obvious. The girl was having a hard time talking about whatever was bothering her.

"This thing that Tanner doesn't know you know… does it have something to do with the reason you say he hit you?"

She almost choked on the words. Tanner's claims that he had never, ever physically hurt his baby sister rang so true to her.

But this was Tatum and she had to reach the girl from her own frame of reference if she hoped to discover the whole truth.

"No. I told you, it's nothing to do with anything."

"Except that it upset you."

"Yeah."

Tatum's gaze pleaded with her to let it go. Which made it even more paramount that she not do so.

"Does Del know about it?" The girl fancied herself in love. Could very well be in love. And it appeared that, until she'd been banned from having contact with him, she'd told Del everything.

"Partly."

She remembered the hardcover book she'd seen Tatum pack. The book Tanner had admitted to her he'd read. "What about your diary? Did you write about it in there? Maybe if you show me the page I could read about it."

"No, it's not in there. It's not, like, a big deal."

Using her most serious lawyer voice Sedona said, "I need to know, Tatum."

When Tatum looked up at her, her expression was skewed, twisted, a cross between pissed and belligerent. "He doesn't have a high school education, okay? He's a dropout."

Phew. Something they could handle. "Del, you mean," she said. "He's dropped out of school and no one knows you know and you don't want Tanner to find out."

Because Del's quitting school would prove Tanner right, the boy wasn't a good catch for his sister. And Tanner's desk must be synonymous in Tatum's mind with the man himself....

"No." Tatum's voice came quietly. "*Tanner* doesn't have a high school diploma. I'm talking about my brother. And it's not like I care about the school part.

I'm sure he quit to take care of me. But he *lied* to me. Do you have any idea how it feels, knowing that?"

The air left her lungs. She was staring. Knew it. And couldn't seem to make herself move.

It didn't matter. Dropping out of high school wasn't a crime. And Tanner had clearly made a life for himself and his sister, but...

He was a man who valued formal education above all else, yet had none of his own. Which had to hurt him like hell.

"He acts like I'll be a total loser if I don't ace my college entrance exams next fall, even though I have my whole junior year to take them and I can repeat them in my senior year, too, if I want. He thinks I have to go to some Ivy League school like Thomas did. He always says that it takes higher education to make it in this world. That's why Talia turned to dancing, because she didn't think she could make it doing anything else without college."

"Did she tell you that?" Of course, there were other ways to make money. Loads of them. Thousands of people made good livings every day without college educations. Better than good in a lot of cases. But...

"No. I just figured it out for myself." Tatum shrugged. "Why else would she be dancing...like that...you know?"

"Well..."

"Don't you get it, Sedona? He's like... I've been trying my whole life to live up to his example, to be as good as he thinks I can be because he gave up so much. And now I find out that he's been lying to me from the very beginning. Like he didn't think I was even good enough to know the truth. Or like he was ashamed and thought I wouldn't love him enough. Or maybe he thought I was too stupid to make my own choices and would quit school like he did. I don't know. I just… It's like our whole lives…how do I know what else he's said that's a lie? I just… There are things… and now I don't know what to believe and…he let me down, you know?" Her eyes were filled with tears. "And I didn't even see it coming. Up until then I believed every single word that ever came out of his mouth. I believed in him. I thought he was like…kind of this god, you know? I feel so stupid and…"

Sedona completely got it. It wasn't so much that Tanner hadn't finished school, as that he wasn't who she'd thought he was.

And he'd been all she'd had.

"Is this why you don't want to go back home? Because you're not sure you can trust him?" People came and went from the store. Baskets rolled by in the parking lot. And Sedona took a shot in the dark.

"No!" The immediacy and intensity of Tatum's response was convincing. "I told you this has nothing to do with anything. You just asked me what went on back there and that's it."

"Being home reminded you?"

"Walking by his desk reminded me."

And Sedona remembered something else. "You said Tanner doesn't know you know."

"That's right."

"So how did you find out?" Had their mother been in touch, after all? Or was there someone else from their past bothering Tatum? Like her father, maybe?

"I saw an application for a GED tucked away in his desk."

Which was somewhat circumstantial, but could have been there for any number of reasons, none of which came immediately to mind.

"It might not have been his," she pointed out.

"It was filled out. It listed the online credential that showed that he'd completed necessary course and testing work and he just had to send it in."

"So what were you doing in his desk?"

"Looking for Talia's new phone number. I knew once he found her again, and she crossed over to his side and cut me off, that he'd have a way to contact her."

"Did you find it?"

"No."

"Did you ask him for it?"

"No. What was the point? He'd already laid down the law where she was concerned."

Tatum sounded more resigned and downtrodden than combative at that point.

"And you didn't tell him you saw the GED application, either."

"No."

"How long ago was this?"

"Six weeks ago. It was after I met Del and Tanner

was already making noises about not liking him and I knew he'd ruined Talia's love life when she was about my age and figured she'd help me know what to do."

Six weeks. A couple of weeks before Tatum ran away to The Stand. But after the first time she'd been hit, according to what she'd told them on the day she'd come to them. She'd been hit twice—a month before she'd arrived, and then again the week prior to her arrival. Those facts were ingrained in Sedona's mind.

Tatum had insisted that today's upset had nothing to do with her reasons for being at The Stand. And now Sedona believed her.

"How about if we go in and see if there's anything you need?" she asked, smiling at the girl. "Shopping always makes a girl feel better."

Tatum sat still for a moment and then, with a nod and a smile that seemed warm and genuine, opened her car door.

"He sent it in," she said, just before they entered the busy store.

Sedona, whose mind was racing with implications and ramifications, and a bit of her own stupor, as well, said, "What?"

"Tanner, he sent the application in."

"How do you know?"

"Because I checked. He had a handful of envelopes to mail right after that and the next day, when I came home from school, I looked in his desk and the application was gone."

TANNER HATED HIMSELF for his weakness, but five minutes after he'd heard Sedona's car arrive, he'd stood at the window in the barn that would allow him to see the front driveway, and waited to see them leave again.

Just so that he could see Tatum at home.

And see Sedona with her.

He'd hoped to see Tatum smile. To show some sign that she missed home.

He hadn't seen her face as she walked out the door.

Still, he had seen her.

The way she'd strutted down the porch stairs, with confidence, but no hurry…he knew that walk. She still felt like this place was home to her.

He knew all her walks. Her mad stomp. Her hurried skip. Even her fearful rush—the time or two they'd had weather warnings and she'd come running to hide her head in his shoulder.

So…the place he'd provided was still home to her.

It wasn't much. But he'd take it.

And the next time she came home, she'd have a fresh new welcome—a home that reached out to her from the second she turned into the driveway.

They'd picked out the paint color together a few years before. A pale yellow with white for accents. He'd tried to talk her into semitransparent stain. She'd wanted neon yellow solid color. They'd settled on her color and his penchant for a more sedate shade.

He'd rented a sander some time back and the wood, while old, was under roof and in good repair. A trip to the home improvement store and he had the couple of gallons of yellow and the gallon of white exterior latex paint that he needed. Rollers, extension handle, brushes, tray, liners and stir sticks were all out in the barn already—waiting. Left over from the interior work he'd done, mostly to Tatum's specifications.

And two hours after his sister had left their home with her attorney, he was dressed in old khakis and a white T-shirt, with yellow paint on the toe of his tennis shoes, rolling new yellow paint on top of old sanded wood.

He had more pruning to do. Cleaning that needed to be done in the winery and in the house. The pH levels to test. Today, the painting came first.

And when he heard the car in his driveway, he wanted to pretend to himself that he hadn't been waiting. For her to call. Or visit.

He and Sedona were…something. Only a fool would deny the way he felt compelled to follow her every movement when she was around. Or the fact that he slept better the nights they talked.

Strange thing was, she seemed as captivated by him as he was by her.

And so he denied himself the right to watch her get out of her car and make her way up to him. He could hear every movement she made, the opening of the car door, its closing, the soft movements of dust with each step she took….

"You got an extra brush?"

Unless she'd changed in the two hours she'd been gone, and there'd hardly been time if she'd taken Tatum shopping as he'd asked her to do, she wasn't dressed for painting. She'd been in jeans that morning but they'd been newer looking. And her short-sleeved top had laced up the front, like a shoe.

He couldn't let her paint.

Turning, Tanner met her gaze in spite of himself. And knew she'd come with a purpose. He didn't ask what it was.

"Is it true that she threw up three times in the first week of junior high?"

"Yes."

Sedona's shoulders relaxed and Tanner felt as if he'd passed some kind of test. But then, that's what life was, he reminded himself...a series of tests. One after another.

"So she's prone to stress-related nausea."

He frowned. "She used to be. There haven't been any incidents in a while."

"Not that you've known about."

True.

But he should have known.

"She says the stress of the past month has been getting to her and she leaves class when she feels nauseous but returns as soon as she's better."

This wasn't just a temper tantrum. Not that he'd really thought it was. But...his baby sister was stressed to the point of nine bouts of a condition he'd thought they'd licked.

"She knows to take deep breaths and think of being

cuddled up in her soft down comforter with someone who loves her watching over her...."

They'd found the solution together. It had worked.

"So you believe she's telling the truth about the absences from class?"

He studied her. The thick, long blond, wavy hair and blue eyes. And couldn't deny that she didn't have to speak for him to hear her.

"Do you?"

"I want to."

"Me, too."

She nodded. So did he. And knew there was more. His paint was going to dry on the roller.

"You don't talk about yourself much."

So this was personal? Not what he'd been expecting.

"I do."

Shaking her head, Sedona picked up a roller and headed to the end of the porch he'd started with. Dipping it in paint, she was down on her knees at the left edge and started to paint with slow even rolls. Just enough pressure. Just enough paint. Taking her cue—and the opportunity to work without further conversation—Tanner moved beside her, back to the right side of the same end of the porch, painting while standing up with the extension rod hooked to his roller.

"You shouldn't be doing that in such nice clothes." No matter how much money she had to replace them.

"It's latex paint. A little hair spray or isopropyl alcohol rubbed in before throwing them in the wash, and they'll be clean as new."

Hmm. Good to know.

He concentrated on the soft brush of paint on wood.

"You talk about your grapes, your wine, your siblings, but you don't talk about yourself."

They were back to that.

"You just summed me up. I grow grapes, dabble in winemaking and take care of my sister. There is nothing else."

"There's so much else."

Like the searing flood that swept through him at the depth of emotion in her tone. His rhythm faltered, leaving him with an unacceptable bubble of paint.

He fixed the glitch and moved on. Coating several more floorboards on his half of the porch. Keeping time with her. Deciding that Tatum's choice, to paint the porch yellow, while unique, was not bad.

"She knows that you didn't graduate from high school."

Tanner froze. Everything inside and out just stopped. And then his heart pounded. Forcing him to breathe.

The pole beneath his hands dug into his skin and he couldn't let it go. Couldn't do anything but listen to the roaring of his circulation in his ears.

There were some things that were a man's business alone.

Eventually he started to paint again. Because he had to do something. Had to get out of the moment. Leave it behind.

And not think. He had a right to some privacy.

"She doesn't care about your lack of formal education…." The words made him cringe.

He gripped the pole tighter in his hands.

"She feels betrayed, Tanner. Lied to. In the most elemental way. She feels like she doesn't know you. And isn't sure she can trust you."

His heart lurched. He'd never betray Tatum. Never. She was his little angel. The thing that pulled him out of bed every morning.

He painted. Emptied the tray, poured more paint. And continued. Sedona spoke a time or two. Mentioned that the color was good. And that it looked like one coat was going to do it. He heard her.

"There was never enough money. I found a guy, Ron—you met him at the wine-tasting—who'd give me work during the day when the kids were in school. That way I could make certain there was food on the table for them and the rent and utilities were paid, and they could have the money they needed for school and other things. Most days I was home by the time they got home from school in case Tammy was drunk or had company. I got in trouble with the truant officer and the courts were going to get involved, which meant they'd split us up. My only option was to take away their truancy card so I quit school."

"Why didn't you tell your brother and sisters?"

"I didn't want any of them to know, to feel responsible. Or blame themselves. And later, when I managed to make a success of this place, I didn't want them to use me as an example of how you could succeed without an education. If Tammy had had some schooling, I really believe she'd have made different choices…back in the beginning. She was smart, a good student, going places in spite of her mother and the home she'd grown up in, and then she met my dad. She thought he loved her. Turned out he was just using her. Judging her by her mother. He thought she was a cheap lay. But she got pregnant and had to quit school to have me and…"

He was saying too much.

They passed the middle of the porch where the stairs were. His plan, before he'd started, was to paint all the way across and climb over the railing down to the ground from there, giving the porch a chance to dry before tackling the spindles and railing that ran the perimeter of the porch and down the three cracked cement steps.

And silently, they reached the other side. As though they'd choreographed their motion, Tanner held his roller, and set the paint tray on the rail just as she placed her roller on the tray. She climbed over the rail first, and he followed, after which she grabbed her roller off the tray he now held and finished the last foot of board left between the spindles.

It was plain and simple and boring—and perfect, too, the way they worked together without words. But the worst part was then they were done. Wiping her hands against each other, as though she had dust there to brush off, Sedona pulled her car keys from her pocket.

"If you have any hope of helping her, Tanner, you're going to have to deal with this. She doesn't trust you now."

Without trust there was no truth.

Without truth, there was nothing to be gained.

Things he'd learned in a different kind of school—the school of "life with Tammy." Things he'd taught his brother and sisters.

Tatum.

Without another word, or even a look, Sedona headed toward her car. She'd drive off—back to her secure, beautiful world. Her beach house and puppy dog. Her career. Her parents who adored each other. And her.

What did a successful lawyer do on a gorgeous spring Saturday afternoon? When she wasn't accompanying a self-made vintner to wine tastings?

She rounded the hood of the old Thunderbird.

"Wait."

Keys in hand, Sedona stopped, but took a minute to look back at him.

"Have you ever soaked macaroni in cold water until it softened enough to chew and eaten it for breakfast, lunch and dinner?"

Her expression shadowed as she shook her head.

Macaroni and cheese was a symbol to the Malone children. A sign of having enough. Even now that they could afford filet mignon.

For him it would always be about having the milk

and the butter and the heat to make the boxed food just as it was intended.

Sedona came a little closer and he backed up. She needed something from him. He wasn't sure he could give it to her.

"Tammy thought she was a great mother. And she was. On her good days. On the bad ones, which were more common, she seemed to hate the kids, blaming them for all of the things they'd taken from her."

Tanner took a second to breathe, and hoped he'd be able to give her enough.

"I didn't tell anyone I quit school. Tammy never asked. I was six months from graduation and Thomas and Talia thought I graduated early." Because he'd told them he could. He'd wanted them to believe that he had. "If I'd told them I quit, they'd have felt responsible, or followed suit, and seeing what had happened to my mother, I just couldn't take that chance."

He felt naked. Exposed. And was getting no feedback.

"When graduation time came, Talia was pissed that I wasn't going to get the chance to wear a robe and graduate with circumstance, so she baked this cake to surprise me and we had our own private celebration."

The cake was supposed to have been a double layer, but, at eleven, she wasn't all that proficient of a baker yet. She'd frosted the thing the second it came out of the oven and the top half had slid halfway off the bottom and broken.

She'd started to cry and, sitting her on his knee,

he'd sat there and eaten every bite, to prove to her how good it was.

And any residual sting from his inability to graduate had slipped away.

He'd had a bigger purpose. His siblings relied upon him.

It suddenly occurred to him to wonder how Tatum had found out he'd never finished high school.

But he didn't ask.

In the end, it didn't matter. What mattered was that she no longer trusted him. "Thanks for your help with the painting," he said when panic started to rear itself and he knew that he'd pushed himself as far as he was going to go. "Let me know what I owe you."

With the last inane parting remark, he turned his back on the most beautiful woman he'd ever known and left her standing in his dust.

CHAPTER TWENTY

SATURDAY WAS WARM for the last week in April. Sunny. A perfect day to be on the beach. Not in a swimsuit, perhaps, but certainly in jeans and a short-sleeved shirt.

Sedona put off a couple of college friends, both unmarried professionals, who'd invited her to join them in L.A. for the night. They all had season tickets to an off-Broadway production house, but Sedona donated her ticket more often than not. She'd thought maybe this week she'd go. Lord knew she needed some time away.

But she also knew that a play, even talking with her friends, wouldn't be enough to take her mind off of the Malones' problems.

After leaving Tanner's place, she stopped by her office, worked for a couple of hours, had a good conversation with a lawyer who she occasionally hired to do research. The semiretired family lawyer had found case law to support a property settlement battle Sedona was facing with one of her more wealthy clients. The case had to do with a woman inheriting family money separate and apart from the marriage and being allowed to keep it outside of marital assets.

It was good news. And it barely inspired a smile.

She couldn't keep pretending that she was only Tatum Malone's attorney—that the brother and sister and their lives and fates meant nothing personal to her.

So she went home and ran on the beach instead. Ellie wasn't happy when she headed out without her, but sometimes a woman had to take responsibility for the things that ailed her and work off steam before she combusted.

It was while she was spraying sand behind her that she knew what she had to do. Out of breath and sweaty, she stopped right there. Dropped down to the sand, facing the water, reached into the pocket of the sleeveless running shirt she'd pulled on with her Lycra shorts and tennis shoes and pulled out the cell phone that she always carried with her.

When it had just been about Tatum, about the girl's claim that her brother had just recently started hitting her, when she'd bargained Tanner's permission for Tatum to stay at The Stand in exchange for getting to know the real Tanner, there'd been no reason to contact Talia Malone.

It wasn't just about Tatum's allegations against her brother anymore. It really wasn't about that at all. It was about a big brother who'd fallen off his pedestal and a young girl in trouble, a girl with no one to trust and nowhere to turn.

As she tried to sort out, in her own mind, what role she played in the brother's and sister's lives, she wasn't coming up with any acceptable answers. Nothing that was black-and-white. Nothing that made logical sense to her.

So she listened to her heart. And, on her phone, she accessed the cloud that stored all of her client information in separate files. Tanner had given her Talia's number in the very beginning. Told her she could call his sister at any time to check up on him or his version of the truth.

He'd issued the permission as a challenge. Almost daring her to call, because not to do so would be paramount to trusting him.

At the time, she'd opted to give him the benefit of the doubt.

She was about half a mile from her place, but still on private property. She didn't personally know the people who were out on the beach behind her. There was a group of guys playing volleyball, and a little farther down, a couple with two children had spread out a blanket with a cooler and while the man grilled, the woman was building bucket castles in the sand. Turning back around to face the waves that were predictable only in their constant presence, she chose the number she wanted and pushed Call.

The voice that answered was so like Tatum's she almost hung up. She couldn't risk liking a third Malone.

Talia had her own problems with her brother. Sedona couldn't take on any more....

"Talia? This is Sedona Campbell calling. I'm—"

"Sedona. I'm so glad you called," the woman interrupted, and Sedona knew instantly that the person she was speaking with was much more mature than Tatum. "I've promised myself not to stick my nose in things for fear of messing them up further, but I'm worried sick about Tatum, and Tanner, too, if you want to know the truth."

The truth. That was exactly what she needed.

And so she asked Tanner's second youngest sibling about the time Tanner had hit her.

"He didn't hit me," Talia said. "Not like you make it sound. I'm surprised he told you about it, though. He doesn't usually talk about the things that bother him most."

Feeling as though she was at the foot of the grail, possibly about to unearth the lost secrets, she asked, "So what happened?"

"I was telling him about something I'd overheard a teacher say to another teacher about Thomas. I told Tanner that I thought the guy should go eff himself. He slapped my face. Not hard enough to knock me off balance, but it stung. Mostly it shocked the words right out of me."

"Did you cry?"

"No, I'd passed the crying stage of life by the time I was five," the woman said laconically, and Sedona guessed that she wasn't exaggerating. "I just stood there, staring at him. I couldn't believe he'd actually struck out at me. For a second I thought he was going to cry. He told me that I wasn't ever to speak like Tammy again. That if I talked like her people would assume I was like her in other ways. And then he started apologizing all over himself for his reaction to my words. He said there was no excuse. That his actions were in no way a reflection of me, but of himself. He rocked me like a baby, begging for my forgiveness. And then made all of my favorite foods for every meal the following week. I think it scared the heck out of him," Talia said.

"Your words or his reaction to them?"

"Both. In any case, his reacting so out of character was exactly what I needed—though I could have done without the sting to my face. I've been through some pretty hellish situations but I've never once forgotten to keep my mouth clean. Funny thing is…Tanner was right. No matter who you are or what you're doing, people respect you more if your speech is clean and kind. They give you more credence, anyway."

That still didn't make hitting his sister okay.

"Did he ever strike out at you or Thomas again?"

"I don't think he's so much as killed an ant since that day," Talia said, her voice sounding sad. "Tanner was so good to all of us, but who was ever good to him, you know? Who watched out for him?"

Sedona had been asking that same question for weeks. And needed there to have been someone.

Because she feared that otherwise it was going to be her now. And it couldn't be.

Still… "You held a grudge, though," she said, staring out at a boat on the water. A smaller vessel, but large enough to take on the Pacific Ocean.

"No, I didn't." Talia's reply left no room for doubt.

"I am far more like Tammy than Tanner wants to believe," Talia said. "What I did was hold on to the memory of Tanner's vulnerability that day. And when it served to my advantage, I'd pull out the reminder and throw it in his face."

Sitting there in the sand, Sedona could almost feel the sharply tipped words piercing her chest. Tanner made one mistake, albeit a huge one, and rather than knowing forgiveness, he'd known retribution.

Was it any wonder the man had faith in no one but himself?

The true wonder was that he still loved as fiercely as he did. Tatum. Thomas. And Talia, too.

"As kind as he was to us all, as self-sacrificing and loyal and loving, he didn't deserve that from me," Talia said now. "I paid for it, though, when I turned sixteen and he had my boyfriend thrown in jail."

"For statutory rape."

"He told you about it."

"Some. In two sentences or less. Tatum told me more."

"Tatum was only five at the time. She can't remember all that much. And I only told her a little bit about it myself, later, when we were in touch."

"She told me that the guy wanted to marry you and Tanner wouldn't allow it."

"I was pregnant. At sixteen. Just like Tammy had been with him. He saw history repeating itself. I saw myself making a new history. One that started somewhat the same but had a happy ending. Tanner's dad wouldn't marry Tammy. As a matter of fact, he never even acknowledged her when she told him she was pregnant. She told me that she'd later heard that he and his friends had sought her out because they figured she'd be an easy mark. And so, she became one."

Tammy Malone hadn't had it easy, either. But she could have made different choices. For her children, if nothing else.

Sedona hoped she never met the woman. She might be tempted to lower herself to Tammy's standards just long enough to voice what she thought about a person who'd learned only one thing from her mistakes—how to repeat them. And then made four innocent children pay her dues.

"I gave my baby up for adoption," Talia said. "That's different from Tammy, too. I'm thinking about looking him up. Once I get my life settled. You, know, just to make sure he's okay. But I don't regret giving him up. I gave him a chance for a normal, loving life."

"What did Tanner have to say about it?" It was something she'd wondered.

"He told me that he'd support whatever choice I made. He said he'd help me out financially and welcome the baby into our home if that's what I wanted. The only condition was that I agree to finish school. He also said that if I wanted to give the baby up for adoption, it wouldn't be a wrong thing, that I shouldn't feel guilty for doing so. I already knew that, of course. Growing up in our house, the hope of being adopted was like thinking about what you'd do with the money if you won the lottery."

Sedona could try to imagine...but that was all. As soon as she hung up from Talia she was going to call her mother. Thank her and her dad for the gift of a loving childhood. She'd taken them and her life growing up for granted. As if happiness was normal.

"If it wasn't for Tanner I don't know what any of us would have done...."

Sedona held her tongue. Told herself this wasn't her business. Other than representing Tatum in case of a legal battle, she had no rights. And then she said, "He needs you," anyway.

"What?"

"I'm not trying to interfere in your life, or your livelihood, but if there's any way you could move home, even temporarily, I think it would help your brother a lot."

Talia's sharp intake of breath was clearly audible over the phone. "He told you that?"

She could hear the children laughing on the beach in the distance. And then screaming with glee, as though someone was chasing them.

Would she ever have a little one of her own? Would Talia have another chance?

"No, he didn't," Sedona had to say. "I'm sticking my neck out way beyond my means here," she continued, with the sudden feeling that she was fighting the case of her life.

And she was off the clock.

"I don't think he hit Tatum, Talia." She spoke slowly, as though in court facing a jury, choosing every word with precision. "But someone did."

Pausing to let her words sink in, she continued. "I found out today that something else happened recently, completely unrelated to Tatum's claims of abuse. I'm not at liberty to disclose the particulars, but Tatum's trust in Tanner was shattered—at the same time someone was hurting her. It is my opinion that unless something changes, Tatum is going to stay at The Lemonade Stand as long as Tanner will allow her to do so. And if he tries to force her to come home, she's going to use whatever legal means she can to get away from him. I honestly believe that in her fifteen-year-old mind, her shattered trust in Tanner is far worse than a bruised arm."

"She told you that?"

"Not outright. But she's been asking questions about making a motion to the courts about having her legal guardianship changed."

"To who?"

"Again, she hasn't specifically said, but I suspect that she's under the impression that Del Harcourt's mother would gladly take her."

Tatum hadn't told her so. But the girl mentioned Del's mother often in their casual conversations—speaking about how much the woman liked her, how kind she was, how welcoming. Tatum could very well have built up a scenario in her mind where Del's mother became her own, before she officially became her mother-in-law.

She'd asked Tatum if she had anyone in mind for guardianship and the girl had prevaricated. And after what she'd heard about Tammy today, Sedona could see how Tanner was panicking about Tammy's life replaying itself through Tatum. Rich boy, telling her he loved her with one goal in mind—to get in her pants.

"Tanner's done a great job with Tatum!" Talia's vehement defensiveness surprised her.

"Tatum seems to think you think he's too controlling."

"Well, to a sixteen-year-old he was, of course. Most parents are, aren't they? And don't get me wrong. My brother has faults. Maddening ones. But in his own way, he's the best parent any kid could hope to have. Besides, he's her flesh and blood. And no one adores her more than he does."

"You seem pretty fond of her yourself."

"I am." Talia's voice softened. "Tatum's birth was like this little piece of heaven in our lives. I was nine going on ten when she was born and it was like I'd just outgrown my baby dolls and then had one in real life. Tanner let me help with her from the very beginning. And then I grew up and started wanting a baby of my own. Almost as much as I wanted away from Tammy. I didn't understand how Tanner could put up with her. With the constant tension of not knowing when she'd show up, who'd she have with her or what state she'd be in. I get it now, of course. He couldn't leave without us and Tammy wouldn't let him take us with him. Until…suddenly when I was sixteen, she did. Just like that."

"You don't know why?"

"Tanner said something about her having met someone who wanted her to go on the road with him, and with Tatum no longer being a baby she thought Tanner could handle us kids, but I knew at the time he was lying to me. He wouldn't look me in the eye the whole time he was giving Thomas and me his story. But I also knew he wasn't going to tell us the real reason.

"Besides, I wasn't sure I wanted to know. For sure, I didn't care. I was just glad to know that she was going to be gone forever."

That had been when he'd overheard Tammy offering up Talia in the shower for a hundred bucks. He'd said it would be his word against Tammy's if he pressed charges, but he'd probably have won. He'd also have had to let Talia know what had nearly happened. She'd have found out how little her mother valued her. He'd threatened Tammy with court. And he'd won.

"But then, a few weeks later I met Rex and everything fell apart."

And now Tatum had Del, and Tanner's life was being obliterated again.

It wasn't Sedona's job to care about that.

But she did care. A lot. Which meant that her time was up.

She had some decisions to make.

Or other people did.

She couldn't go on representing Tatum without letting the Malones know that she wasn't impartial anymore.

CHAPTER TWENTY-ONE

TANNER GOT THE painting done. The white trim took a couple of hours and looked good. Tatum's paint-color call had been a good one.

Standing out in the yard, just left of the driveway, he turned around and surveyed his work, trying to see it through his sister's eyes the next time she rounded the corner and pulled up to her home.

She was going to love it. And he should have done it a long time ago. Years ago. When she'd first asked.

The porch was the first thing you saw when you came onto the property. The first thing that had greeted her every day when she got home from school.

But it wasn't too late. Tatum was fifteen. They still had three more years of homecomings. At least.

It wasn't like he was kicking her out on her eighteenth birthday. She could live at home for the rest of her life if she wanted to.

After college, that was. He couldn't back down on his insistence that Tatum have the means to support herself if and when the need ever arose. And not just support herself, but to be able to do so in a field she'd chosen, that the aptitude tests said she'd be good at, so that she didn't ever need to think about reverting to Tammy's means of support.

He stood there alone and, for a moment, felt completely lost. No one was there, needing him.

And for the first time since he'd bought the place, the old farm didn't feel like home to him. It felt like a prison.

Where had he gone wrong?

Pulling his phone out of his pocket, he called Talia. But not before he'd done enough of a self-check to know that he could handle the conversation in a manner that wouldn't upset her. He wasn't going to fail her again.

"Tanner? What's wrong?" Talia picked up on his first ring. Almost as though she'd been holding the phone. It was early yet—just past five.

Pacing in the big yard that he mowed regularly, but had never manicured, he had a thought about sod. About how the green would look against the yellow and white that now graced the front of the house.

"Why does something have to be wrong every time I call?"

"I don't know." The comeback was quick, but held none of its usual sharpness. "Why is it that you only call when something's wrong?"

She had him there.

Until now.

"Well, nothing's wrong." That wasn't entirely true. It felt as if pretty much everything was wrong. But that wasn't why he'd phoned.

"I want to make a suggestion," he said, watching the blades of crabgrass mix with dirt as he crushed them with his shoes. "An offer, if you will, but I don't want to piss you off."

"You don't piss me off, Tanner, and that's no way to talk, anyway. You make me angry sometimes, but today, you're pretty much off the hook, so shoot."

That worried him. With a frown he asked, "Why am I off the hook today?"

"Because I'm in a good mood."

Could life really be that simple?

Steeling himself for her anger, he said, "I'd like to pay for you to go to college," he said. "You can study wherever you want, whatever you want. I just…I'd like to give you that."

He'd offered before. She'd told him to quit trying to live her life for her.

"You don't have to do that, Tanner."

"I'm not asking you to quit your job." He said the words quickly before he choked on them. Because while he knew full well now that he had no convincing powers left where she was concerned, he wanted, more than just about anything other than for Tatum to come home, for Talia to quit that job.

"Glad to hear it."

Was the sarcasm back? If so, she was managing to rein it in a bit.

"I just want you to have other options in the wings if you ever want them."

"What options do you have?"

Why was everything coming back on him today? First Sedona, now Talia. He was fine. Always had been.

"I have the winery," he said, very clearly. And with all the confidence in the world. Because he knew the words to be true. "The grapes are coming in better than ever. I have more customers than I can supply. And my own wine is…not bad." He finished the last with a bit of a smile. Remembering Sedona's first sip—the look on her face.

And then he heard Talia's question again. *What options do you have?* And he said, "I have the option to ask you to accept my gift, or to spend the next ten years worrying about your future." He gave her the honest answer, and he wasn't even sure why. Perhaps it was because Sedona had been asking him too many questions. Making him think too much. And he wasn't sure he'd made all the right choices in the past.

"I don't need your help, Tanner."

"I understand that you don't think so now, but—"

"No, big brother, what I'm telling you is that I don't need your help because I've been going to college since you… Well, for a year now. It turns out I got some funds from my divorce from Donald…I know, I owe you a huge chunk since you bought him off to begin with, but I'm in my sophomore year at UNLV.

"I wasn't going to tell you about it until I graduated and could start paying you back, but I'm actually thinking about making a change and I have to run it by you first."

Tanner stopped in his tracks. He glanced at his phone screen, as though he needed to see Talia's name and number there to convince himself that he was really speaking with her.

She'd been planning to speak with him? When? Talia's calls in his direction, other than lately regarding Tatum, were pretty much...nonexistent.

As the questions toppled over themselves in his mind, not the least of which was what she was studying, he said, "So run it by me."

"I've been attending class part-time because, with working full-time, I wanted to have enough time to get the 4.0 I'm capable of...."

As if from above, looking down on himself, Tanner saw himself glance at his phone again. And half expected to wake from a dream. How many times in the past ten years had he willed Talia to...just call him even. And now she was telling him she was in school with a 4.0?

Feeling as though he was in the twilight zone, he tuned back in to what she was saying. Just in case it was real. "So I was thinking, if I cut my living expenses down to, say, nil, then I could work part-time, at something that made a bit less money, like maybe a salesclerk in a high-end department store, which would not only provide me with some income, but also fulfill some of my internship hours required to graduate."

Tanner made it to a tree, slid down and let it prop his back.

"What's your major?"

"Fashion design. I can work as a buyer for any high-end chain, or, if I'm lucky, get on with a designer, until I can sell some designs of my own. I've already got a guy here in Vegas who likes some of my stuff and…"

The enthusiasm in her voice filled places that had been empty for so long. After a bit, she asked, "You still there?"

"Of course. I'm listening to every word," he said, surprised to hear his voice sounding so strong. So sure. Talia had always loved clothes. Makeup. Jewelry. All things girlie. And it had scared the shit out of him. Because all of those things made her beauty stand out more—which made her prey to creeps like Donald, her ex-husband. And too much temptation to resist for weak men like Rex Chelshire.

"The only problem is, there's only one place I can think of where I could live rent-free…."

Here it came. She was going to move in with some creep. Be his sugar baby, or whatever the hell they called young girls who shacked up with old guys these days. Again. First Rex, then Donald and now…

"Where is that?" he asked, because he'd told her he'd listen and he would. He'd accept her choice, too. Because he wanted her in his life and understood now that the only way that was going to happen was if he accepted who she was.

God knew, he loved her, no matter who or what she was. "Seriously?" Her chuckle was odd. He couldn't tell if she was insulted, or making fun of him.

"I was thinking I could move home, Tanner. I've

already checked and I can transfer to UC without losing any credits. I could start the summer semester. It would be a commute, but nothing I can't handle." Her voice was dry.

His reaction was not.

For the second time in a week he felt tears pushing at his eyelids.

If he wasn't careful, tough guy Tanner Malone was going to go to hell in a handbasket.

SEDONA HAD DINNER with her folks Saturday night. When she'd called, after her talk with Talia, they'd been getting ready to go to their regular Saturday night spot that overlooked the water, and she'd invited herself along. Over taco salad, she'd talked to them about Grady. About her concern that her brother was settling for less in his quest to have the most. She'd told her parents, in no uncertain terms, what she thought of Brooke.

And her mother, in her usual calm way, smiled and said nothing.

Her father, on the other hand, suggested that she might want to try to be a little more forgiving. By allowing mistakes in others and in herself, he'd said, she became human. And without the ability to allow them, she'd never be able to fully love someone.

It was the most philosophical he'd ever been with her.

And the look in his eye told her he hadn't been kidding.

Sedona had left them in the parking lot feeling more

like a recalcitrant kid who'd been called to task than a successful lawyer with her own private practice, and she wasn't even sure what she'd done wrong.

At home, she changed into silk lounge pants and the softest T-shirt she owned, poured herself a glass of wine and settled on the deck with Ellie. She was physically tired. But she was mentally exhausted.

It should have surprised her when she heard a truck in her driveway. But it didn't. Nor did she bother getting up to greet her visitor. He'd find his way back to her.

What did surprise her was the way Ellie jumped down from her lap and moseyed her way over to the top step, peering around the corner of the porch to the side yard, wagging her tail.

It was good to know that she wasn't the only one who was under Tanner Malone's spell.

"It's not anything to write home about, but the bottle's in the fridge, and you know where the glasses are," she said as he stepped up onto the deck. With her head against the back of her chair, she stared out at the pinks and oranges rimming the ocean. The sun would be setting soon.

"I brought a bottle," he offered, and she finally turned to look at him. In black jeans and a white short-sleeved button-down shirt, he looked as though he was heading out on the town.

And he was holding one of his prized private-collection bottles. She'd told her dad about his wine over dinner that night—in between conversational manslaughter. As enthusiastic as the older man had been she really should call him now. Invite him over to share.

She didn't.

Nor did she demur when Tanner returned a few minutes later, removing her mostly full wineglass to replace it with another one filled with his pinot grigio.

The man had a knack for knowing what she most wanted. And seemed willing to give it to her, too.

"I offer this in apology," he said, holding up his own glass for a toast before he sipped. Her gaze met his as their glasses clinked, and continued to hold his as they sipped.

He broke the contact when he sat beside her. Ellie jumped into his lap, turned once and lay down. Tanner stroked the dog gently, with his free hand, but stared out at the beach beyond.

It was as though he knew, as she did, that life's toughest answers lay out there, tumbling in the waves, just waiting to be discovered.

"I don't like you knowing that I didn't finish high school."

"Labels are for people who are too stupid to see reality."

"It's not the label. It's...just always been something only I knew," he said. "I'm not ashamed. I know I'm not less of a person because I missed the last six months of high school. I'm proud of my choice. It was the right one. But it was also something I consciously chose to keep to myself. It wasn't a big deal. And I didn't want it to become one."

She knew before she opened her mouth that by doing so she was becoming more than a friend to him.

"It was something that you hoarded, but that belonged to those who care about you," she said quite deliberately. "Because it defines you. Not in terms of education or knowledge, or potential for success, but in terms of determination and loyalty, of hard choices and reliability. And it's a pretty amazing example, too, of the old adage that you can do whatever you want to do if you put your mind to it."

It looked as if philosophizing ran in the family that evening.

"Talia's coming home, but then you already know that, don't you?"

His intent look was almost too much for her. But she held on, meeting him eye to eye. "She told you I called?"

His raised brow did crazy things inside of her. "She told me she spoke to you. She didn't say who initiated the conversation."

Did she also tell Tanner how she'd interfered in their lives? Talia had told her about her plans to move home later in their conversation, after Sedona had already stuck her nose in the family's business. "What else did she say?"

"Only to tell you hello and that she was looking forward to meeting you in person."

His look held a question she wasn't ready to answer.

CHAPTER TWENTY-TWO

SITTING WITH SEDONA wasn't wise. Tanner knew he was in danger. There were too many emotions simmering just beneath his surface. He had them tamed, wasn't really feeling them, but he knew they were there.

And if he wasn't careful, they'd erupt into a mass of confusion and fear and desire and want and hope and need and not anything he could share with her.

But he'd had to come. To try to explain why he'd behaved so childishly that afternoon. Walking off and leaving her standing there as if she was little more than the hired help.

He'd had to come because she'd spoken with Talia. His sister was coming home and Tanner couldn't sit quietly with the news. It was bursting through him. Tangling with everything else in there that he couldn't control.

Like the fact that he'd lost Tatum's trust at the most critical point of her life.

No. He studied the waves. Tried to become a part of their rhythm. He couldn't deal with Tatum's disillusion tonight. Tomorrow he'd go to her. Sit outside The Lemonade Stand and call her cell phone until she answered if he had to. Somehow he'd make this right.

Just not tonight. He wasn't at his best. And Tatum didn't deserve to be on the receiving end of his own vulnerability.

For that matter, neither did Sedona.

"She's given me a second chance and I'm afraid I'm going to mess it up," he said now. He was asking for help.

From the only person he could think of to ask.

"Just be yourself, Tanner. She knows you. Probably better than you do sometimes. She's coming home to you."

"She knew me before, too."

"She was also a teenager, your ward and feeling powerless. She's not powerless anymore."

He wasn't stupid; he knew where this was going.

"She'll stand up to me, you mean."

"Yeah."

And as a bit of the pressure eased, he was glad he'd come.

FROM THE MOMENT Ellie had jumped in Tanner's lap he'd been quietly stroking the little dog. Sedona watched that strong, gentle hand and couldn't imagine it hurting anyone, ever.

"She told me about the time you slapped her." It wasn't her place to tell Tanner what else Talia had told him about that incident—about how Talia had used his guilt to manipulate him. But she was fairly certain the other woman would do so. When the time was right.

His hand clenched and, as the poochin raised her

head, settled back on Ellie's fur. Moving slowly along her spine and then repeating the action.

"I don't think what you did was appalling." She didn't have her case planned. Was standing before the jury without knowing what to say. It was her worst nightmare.

Shaking his head, Tanner seemed to be studying the tips of his loafers. "To this day I don't know what came over me," he said. "I heard those words coming from that sweet little mouth and it was like my mother had taken control of Talia's body. Did you ever see the movie *The Exorcist?*" he asked.

"Yeah."

"That's how I felt. As though this demon had possessed my sister and I had to get it out of there. It was a split second. Ruled by fear. And I will never, ever forgive myself."

"My mother slapped my face once." She'd forgotten all about it until Talia had talked about the sting of fingers against her skin. "I was fourteen and had just found out that my father had been unfaithful to her, several years before. It only happened once. They'd been separated for a week and that's when he did it and I guess that's all it took for him to come home begging. And to solidify their love and loyalty to each other for a lifetime. But at fourteen, as a girl who idolized my father, it was hard to take. I made a comment to my mother about him, having to do with his parentage. I was telling her she could do better. And she slapped me."

He was looking at her now. She could feel his gaze like a physical touch. And she turned, letting him see the moisture in her eyes.

"I told her I hated them both and ran to my room." She'd never told anyone about that day. Not even Grady. "An hour later they came to my room, knocked on my door and asked if they could come in. I almost said no, I was so ashamed. But I loved them so much and was scared to death of what I'd done, or what I'd do if they quit loving me." She smiled, remembering, for a second, how it felt to be fourteen. Hormonal. Emotional.

And realized that she hadn't changed nearly as much as she thought she had.

"Before I could say a word my mother apologized for slapping me. She said there was no excuse for having done so and that I was not to accept that kind of behavior from anyone. Ever. No matter what I'd done. While I was still sitting there with my mouth hanging open, my father apologized for the insecurity in him that had had him believing he wasn't good enough for a woman as accomplished as my mother. He swore to her, in front of me, that it would never, ever happen again."

Tanner didn't blink. He didn't move at all. It was as though he was there in the room with the three of them, in that long-ago memory. Living it with her.

"I started to cry and told them I hadn't meant a word of what I'd said but was afraid they'd never forget my words. I was so afraid I'd put words out there that would live forever. They told me that sometimes that happened with words, but that this time wasn't one of them. We made a pact that day that those sins would die the second we walked out of my room together, and we've never spoken of them since."

Until that moment. She'd broken her sacred pact with her parents for Tanner.

And that's when she knew that her time wasn't only up. Life as she'd known it before was over.

MILLIE CAMPBELL HAD been moved to slap her daughter. Tanner let the information wash over him. And while he felt no less shame for the one time he'd lost complete control of himself, he felt somehow cleaner.

"It occurs to me that I couldn't have made up a story that fit this moment more perfectly," Sedona said, breaking the silence that had fallen over them. She'd been sipping wine.

He'd been watching the ocean fading in the distance beneath a falling dusk, and trying to make sense of everything coming at him.

Too many changes.

Too much to contemplate.

To know.

To understand.

He'd told Sedona something he'd never told anyone else. She'd just done the same. It felt as if they'd had sex. Only it was so much more.

And not nearly enough. Never had he needed to sink

his body into a woman as badly as he needed to make love to Sedona Campbell in that moment.

The night before, at his table, they'd kissed. More than once. Just lips touching lips. Like it was a part of everyday normal conversation. He'd leaned over and kissed her. She'd kissed him back, and they'd gone on talking. Not about kissing.

Whatever was happening between them meant something.

He had to know what it was.

"I told you about what happened with my parents, in part, to excuse myself from not being horrified that you hit Talia. My mother was a grown woman when she disciplined me. You were what, sixteen, seventeen? Carrying the weight of the world on your shoulders?"

"There's no excuse for what I did."

"Maybe not. But sometimes an explanation is all that it takes to sway a jury from a guilty to an innocent verdict."

What he'd done was wrong. He wouldn't do it again. End of story.

"Tatum's fifteen. I was fourteen. And felt horribly betrayed by my father." Her voice gathered momentum as she sat forward, facing him. "And all it took was an explanation, Tanner. Tell Tatum why you didn't tell her about quitting school. Maybe, instead of protecting your loved ones, you'd serve them better by sharing some of the ugliness. Not all of it, but some of it." As she spoke, her eyes lit up and he had to listen.

"It's just a thought," she said, sitting back.

God, she was lovely. And so…there.

More real than anything he could ever remember. "I'll think about it," he said. And he would. But not tonight.

He couldn't let the maelstrom out tonight.

So he sipped wine. Watched the ocean. And sat next to the woman who turned him on more than any other.

"YOU SHOULD GET a dog," Sedona told Tanner. Tatum had said they'd had one once. That it had been hit by a car and Tanner had refused to buy another.

The hand on Ellie's back stilled, as though Tanner had just realized that he'd been petting the little poochin.

"I don't have time to house-train a dog," he said. "And it wouldn't be fair to the creature to leave it alone all day every day."

"Ellie's alone all day." A lot of pets were. "And Talia will be around now, too, to help."

She wanted him to tell her about the dog that died. Wanted him to open up to her about all of the pain he stored in that heart of his.

He looked over at her. "I'll tell you what," he said. "You get Tatum to come home and I'll let her pick out any dog she wants."

It wasn't what she'd been looking for, exactly. But it was more than she'd expected. Tanner was changing, little by little. Opening up, lightening up. He might not know it, but Sedona, who was far too tuned in to him for anyone's good, could feel the difference.

And…

"We have a…situation," she said. She'd been waiting for the closing argument to present itself, but it wasn't happening. And her day in court was ending.

"What?" He watched her, but she figured he couldn't see much. Maybe the glint of her eyes in the darkening night. The private beach had no lights, other than the moon that was rising over the water.

They were each still on their first glass of wine. She took a sip of hers and wanted more. A lot more.

He seemed relaxed now.

"I've crossed a line, a professional line." She could lose her license to practice law if an ethics complaint was filed against her. She probably wouldn't. But she could. Which meant that what she was doing was wrong.

His hand, those fingers that handled fragile grapes with precision and care, stroked Ellie's head. The little dog lay contentedly with her chin on Tanner's leg. And Sedona was jealous.

"I can't be impartial where you're concerned. And so I'm doing your sister a disservice. I can't guarantee that the decisions I make will be in her best interest."

Still, he watched her. And she couldn't figure him out.

"Why can't you be impartial?"

She had a feeling that hadn't been his first question. And it was the one she most didn't want to answer.

"You're… I care as much about you as I do about

her." No. That wasn't even true. "I care more about you than I do about her."

It didn't matter how softly she said the words, or how active the waves were in the distance, her voice still sounded too loud.

"I don't trust myself to put my client's needs first. I'm too aware of your needs and how I can help and—"

"I don't have any needs."

"Of course you do, Tanner. Everyone does."

"I can take care of myself."

To an extent, sure. And for a man who'd never had anyone looking out for him—even as a young boy—she could understand him not realizing what he was missing.

"You need Tatum home with you."

"And I'll get her home." He really believed that.

Maybe she was worrying about nothing. Maybe it didn't matter that she cared, because he wasn't going to let her in.

Maybe he wouldn't let her choose him over Tatum.

"And if she decides to go to the police, after all? If she asks me to petition to have her guardianship changed?"

"That's the second time you've mentioned that. Is that her plan?"

"See, you're already doing it—asking me to give you something you need that, in Tatum's best interests, I shouldn't tell you. In this case, it doesn't matter because she hasn't asked. But she could."

"She won't."

"I think she will. If she's pushed hard enough."

"And I trust you to do the right thing if it comes to that."

He wasn't making this easy. Rather, he was making it downright impossible. So maybe he was right. Maybe the man really was an island unto himself—the exception that proved the rule. Maybe he was strong enough, determined enough, something enough, to make certain that she did her job where his sister was concerned.

By not letting her put him first.

Maybe she just wanted to be off the hook. Because she didn't want to be off the case.

Tatum trusted her. And she cared about the girl. More than she'd cared about any other client she'd had during her four years of practice.

She took another sip of wine. A recklessly big sip.

Ellie, who must have sensed something amiss in her mistress, jumped off Tanner's lap, looked up at Sedona and lay down at her feet.

"So you can sit there and honestly tell me that you have no needs that I can fill," she said, just to clarify.

"Honestly?"

Breathing was a little hard. "Yeah."

"Then, to be completely honest, there is one need that I have that you can definitely fill."

She knew what was coming. His low sexy tone told her. But knowing didn't stop her. "And that is?"

"I need to strip you naked, take you to bed and sink

myself so deeply inside you that neither of us will ever be the same."

Her wine was gone.

"I need that, too."

CHAPTER TWENTY-THREE

TANNER WAS ROCK-HARD as he stood and reached for Sedona's hand. Some things weren't about right and wrong. About perfect or imperfect.

Some things just were.

"I have a condom in my wallet." And whether she was on the pill or not, he'd wear it. As he'd lectured all three of his siblings, safe sex wasn't just about pregnancy prevention.

"I have some in my bedroom, too." There could have been some awkwardness in the exchange. If there was any, he wasn't feeling it.

He led her through the door into her house. She led him down the hall and into a small bedroom suite with white walls and a large bed with a rose-covered comforter and more pillows than a bed needed.

As if on cue, they stopped a couple of feet from the bed. He wasn't hesitating. There was no thought of turning back. He was savoring this.

Like the finest wine, Sedona melted all of his senses, making him heady and excited.

The lion's mane of blond hair, so thick and untamable.

He ran his fingers through it—claiming the right. Claiming her. Her head lolled backward, resting in his palm, and he pulled her gently forward. Slowly. Until her thighs were touching his and his penis pressed against her pelvis. Her breasts, large enough to fill his hand, touched his chest and only then did he bend his head toward hers.

As he touched his lips to hers, taking tonight's first tentative taste, the sensation was exquisite. Light, with a hint of fruitiness. His wine on Sedona's lips.

"I've wanted women before." Her perfection seemed to pull honesty from him. Demanded it. "I've never needed one."

The only light in the room came from the hallway behind them, a soft glow from a sconce on the wall, but he could see the tilt at her lips—a sexy, knowing tilt—as she looked up at him and said, "You need me."

A simple statement. And life-changing.

"Yes."

"I need you, too."

While still holding his gaze, she undid the buttons on his shirt, and as the backs of her knuckles brushed against the hair on his chest, his ribs, his belly, he sucked in what air he could. Held it as though it was his last.

And didn't care if it was.

There came a time in a man's life when he had to face reality. When he wasn't a god, or strong enough to fight. This was Tanner's time.

Sedona Campbell had captivated him.

And he succumbed.

THE MAN WAS EVERYTHING. Everywhere. Lying on her bed in her panties and shirt, she watched as Tanner shrugged off the shirt she'd undone, unbuttoned the fly of his jeans and pulled them off. His black briefs followed and before she'd had nearly enough of the visual feast he presented, he was over her, coming down to settle half on top of her, with one naked leg in between hers. Propping his elbows on either side of her he held his face inches from hers. Studying her.

His brown eyes were a drug, and their effect instantaneous. She was hypnotized, aware only of him. And her need to have sex with him.

His chest was smooth with a scattering of hair between the nipples; the muscles, clearly defined and hardened with strength, fit his somewhat slender frame perfectly. They didn't bulge. Weren't overgrown. But, like his wine, honed to perfection.

He was an artist. A piece of art.

And she'd never been given to fanciful moments.

HE WAS COMMITTING her to memory. The women in Tanner's life were just moments. Sedona could be no different.

And yet she was completely different.

He kissed her, and kissed her again, lowering his mouth to hers, pressing her head into the pillow, touching his tongue to hers, and wasn't satisfied. There was more of her to know, more ways to know her.

His penis ached with the need for release. He rubbed it against her thigh and almost came when she drew in a ragged breath and stuck her tongue farther into his mouth, mimicking the act of love.

Undoing her bra, Tanner covered Sedona's breast with his hand, and while he'd never touched her there before, the size and shape of her fit his grip so perfectly she felt familiar.

Her nipples were hard and he broke from their wet kiss to suckle them. He was more animal than man and knew that in a different moment he was going to regret behaving with such an uncharacteristic lack of control.

His reaction to Sedona would scare him. In a different moment.

In this one, he was unfettered from the chains of life. Freed from his self-imposed prison.

And when the moment came, when she spread her legs and urged him between them, when he finally pushed himself to her core, he knew he wasn't going to be able to go back to what he'd been.

THE COUPLE OF lovers Sedona had taken had usually fallen asleep seconds after orgasm. She'd expected the same of Tanner—and she needed the time alone to recover physically before she could tend to the emotional avalanche assaulting her.

Who was this man? Why did he affect her so? And what had she done?

Disentangling himself from on top of her, he rolled over and sat up, picking up his briefs and sliding them on, condom and all, before heading toward her adjoining bathroom.

When he came back into the room, she was sitting on the end of the bed, wearing her robe. Waiting for him.

"I have to recuse myself as Tatum's legal counsel."

Stepping into his jeans, he didn't even hesitate. "No, you don't."

"I can't be impartial." More than ever. His lovemaking had been... She wasn't ever going to find another man who turned her on like that.

She wasn't sure she'd have known her own name if someone had asked while he'd been moving inside her.

Or that she'd even have noticed if someone else walked into the room. During those moments he'd obliterated everything else.

"I want you on the case."

"Of course you do. You know I couldn't help but look out for your interests as well as hers."

"And that's bad? To have someone on our side as a family?"

"It is if, ultimately, it's best for Tatum to live somewhere else."

The words were harsh—a kind of sacrilege in that room where things had been perfect just minutes ago—and yet he showed no reaction to them at all.

With his shoulders straight, he buttoned up his shirt slowly, without a fumble. She was afraid if she stood, her knees would give out on her.

"I need you there for Tatum's sake," he said. "You see the possibility that she needs to be saved from herself. I know my sister, Sedona. I love her. If I thought, for one second, that she'd be better off someplace besides her home, I would be petitioning the courts myself to have her removed from my guardianship."

She believed him.

"If I've proven nothing else in my lifetime, certainly my choices show that I put the well-being of my brother and sisters above my own happiness."

She had to give him that.

He stepped closer, but still kept enough distance between them that he wasn't invading her space. "Any pressure I put on them to do as I would have them do is with their own good in mind, not my own. If I wanted to keep Tatum home, why would I be pushing so hard for her to go to college? It's because I want her to be independent, free, equipped to provide for herself and make her own choices, and to not ever be beholden to anyone else to provide a roof over her head. Not even me."

"Like your mother was."

"Like Tammy was, yes."

And, she knew, like Talia had been, too. He wasn't pacing. Or gesturing. He wasn't opposing counsel delivering a closing argument. He sat on the end of the bed with her, keeping a couple of feet between them and his hands folded in his lap, and looked over at her.

"If you abandon her, Tatum is at risk of someone else taking her at face value, believing the surface of her words and not hearing the truth that is hiding someplace inside of her."

"What is that truth?" She had to ask. What if she was prey to him?

For the first time in her life, Sedona was doubting herself. Tanner made her vulnerable somehow.

It frightened her.

"I know what I believe it is," he said.

"What's that?"

She was fairly certain what he was going to say. But she needed to hear it again. To mentally record every statement he made from now on, and play it back for her inner judge. To see if there was a nuance, a clue, to something she might have missed.

"Harcourt is the one who is controlling her," he said, his voice tinged with anger, but with sadness, as well. "Somehow he's convinced her that her happiness rests with him and because she believes that, she's either not seeing the truth about him, or she thinks she can do something about it. She clearly doesn't see the anger issues, or if she does, she excuses them and must be convinced he can't help it and will get over it. For her, of course."

Tanner Malone was speaking from experience. His words rang with conviction, not rehearsal.

And she realized something else. Having had sex with Tanner might have the opposite effect on her ability to do her job. Rather than making her more prone to do as he wanted, she was doubting him. Not because of him, but because she no longer trusted herself to be able to tell the difference between his truth and anything she might want to believe to show him in the most advantageous light. And that made her look at everything more closely.

To test each and every thing he said.

"If you turn her over to someone else—who decides it's time to do something with her one way or the other—chances are she'll end up petitioning to have her guardianship changed, or we're back to the possibility that she'd be put into the system. Which would most likely leave her open to see Harcourt anytime she pleases. I'm begging you not to take that chance. Tatum will be the one to pay," he said. "I will have failed her by this...." He pointed between the two of them. And motioned with a thumb to the bed behind them.

"As far as I'm concerned, tonight changes nothing. Tatum trusts you. And she comes first. If, in the end, you press forward with some kind of motion on her behalf, then you do."

"That's just it." She clasped her hands so tightly together her nails bit into her palms. And she welcomed the diversion from the other sensations that were overwhelming her. "It's not you I'm worried about."

His head was even with hers as he looked her straight in the eye and let her see a glimpse of the emotion that had to be eating him up inside.

"Don't let my sister pay for my indiscretion."

The rawness in his voice ate at her.

As did hearing him put into words the very thoughts she'd been having about their sex.

It had been an indiscretion.

Not lovemaking.

"I have to talk to Tatum," she said. "I have to tell her that you and I have developed a friendship...."

"I'd prefer you not tell her we had sex. It's not something she needs to be thinking about."

"I have no intention of telling anyone about tonight," Sedona told him, her private parts still tingling from his invasion. "My sex life is no one's business but mine."

She had no idea how she'd ever describe the incident, or be able to help anyone understand what had driven her to get naked with the older brother of a vulnerable client.

Most particularly since she couldn't understand it herself.

She stood, walked toward the front of the house, aware of every single step Tanner took behind her. As they stood by her back door—the door he'd entered from and the one he'd leave from, too—she said, "As long as Tatum is okay with the fact that I care about what happens to you, and if she decides she still wants me to represent her, I will continue to do so. The choice has to be hers."

"Okay." He didn't look completely happy with the decision.

"And I'm going to ask you to hold off phoning her, about the hypnotism or anything else, until I have a chance to speak with her."

"I'll agree, of course," he told her, his back to the door. "You've got me over a barrel here. But I'd like to know why."

"Because I need to be sure that you don't get to her first and convince her to keep me on."

She'd as much as admitted that she didn't trust him. The news didn't seem to faze Tanner a bit.

CHAPTER TWENTY-FOUR

SEDONA WAITED UNTIL midmorning on Sunday before pulling into The Stand. She didn't know if Tatum attended the nondenominational church service offered in the multipurpose hall, but she knew Lila did and she didn't want to conduct business with a minor in Lila's care without the other woman available for consultation.

If Tatum got upset and chose to dismiss Sedona from her case, Lila would have to be notified immediately. The other woman would then have to decide whether to call in another attorney, or call child protective services and turn the situation over to them.

Of course, she could just let Tatum remain at The Stand on her own behalf for as long as Tanner would agree to the arrangement. She already had his permission to that effect. But it was based on Sedona's involvement.

Sedona had dressed in work clothes—a pair of navy pants and pumps with a white tailored silk blouse. She'd tied back her thick hair with a blue scarf.

Her appearance was impeccable as she moved forward to face her own personal jury. An emotionally fragile fifteen-year-old who'd only known her for a month.

It seemed like a lifetime.

She was on her way across campus, taking the most direct route from the main building through the grass, rehearsing in her mind what she was going to say.

And changing her mind as she went.

Just as she'd been doing all morning.

Was she trying to present herself in such a way that Tatum would agree to keep her on? Because she agreed with Tanner that Tatum was best served by Sedona? Or because she'd allowed Tanner to convince her that his sister needed her?

Or was she trying to convince Tatum that she could no longer trust her?

"Sedona!"

Recognizing Lila's voice behind her, Sedona turned guiltily. And remembered that Lila had no idea what Sedona had done.

And wouldn't know if Tatum decided it wasn't an issue.

"I was just getting ready to call you," the older woman said as she caught up with Sedona. Lila was dressed, as usual, in grays and browns. Her hair was in its usual bun on the back of her head.

"What's up?" Sedona asked, wondering if Lila had another new client that needed help.

"It's Tatum Malone," the woman said, frowning. They walked farther into the grass, away from hearing distance of anyone passing by on the sidewalk.

Sedona missed a step.

"Tatum?" The Stand's grounds were busier on Sunday than any other day of the week as many of the women who worked, and all those who were in school, were free for the day.

"Maddie called Lynn early this morning," the managing director said, naming Tatum's roommate and The Stand's on-site medical professional. "She found a pair of Tatum's panties in the laundry room. They had blood on them. Maddie knew it wasn't time for Tatum's period because…Maddie pays attention to things like that. She got concerned because the blood was something she didn't understand, so she called Lynn."

Lynn, who'd taken Maddie under her wing from the moment the two women met a couple of years before.

"Apparently when Lynn stopped by the bungalow, Tatum wouldn't let her see the panties. She said Maddie was mistaken. That she must have seen a tomato stain on the blouse that was in the laundry with the panties."

Starting to feel sick, Sedona looked toward the middle of the walk in the distance, knowing that Maddie's bungalow was off to the right of there. She didn't like where this was going.

"When Lynn pushed Tatum, Tatum said she'd only talk to you."

Tanner had said his sister trusted her. So maybe he'd been right that Tatum needed her.

At the moment, her own conscience didn't matter a whit.

"Where is she?" she asked Lila, picking up her pace as they headed back toward the more populated part of campus.

"In her bungalow."

"Is Maddie there?"

"No, she's with Lynn and Kara." Lynn's three-year-old daughter. "They're working on wedding stuff today." Sedona had her invitation to the wedding hanging on her refrigerator at home. She wouldn't miss it for anything.

"I'll go talk to her," she told Lila, speaking of Tatum. And fearing what she was going to find out.

If she'd been asked last night, she'd have said things couldn't get any worse.

She feared now that she'd have been wrong.

LATE SUNDAY MORNING, because he couldn't stand to be with his own thoughts any longer, Tanner speed-dialed a number he rarely called.

He was out in the vineyard, checking pH balances and irrigation systems, when he stopped to make the call.

"Hey, bro, what's up?" Thomas's voice answered—a minor miracle in itself—his tone friendly and familiar, as though the two were as close now as they'd been growing up.

"You got a couple of minutes?"

"Yeah, not much going on in the financial district on Sunday morning."

That hadn't stopped Thomas from ignoring other Sunday calls over the years.

"Talia called you, didn't she?"

"She might have left a voice mail, sure."

"What did she tell you?"

"That I should get my ass in gear and give you a call."

"When?"

"Yesterday, actually. It was on my agenda for today. I just hadn't worked myself up to it yet."

Tanner's spirits sank, in spite of the sweet smell of grapes enveloping him. His crop he got right. Even he couldn't deny that.

"So what's up? You're not sick, are you?"

"Of course not. I'd have called if I was." Because, in that case, he'd expect Thomas to step into his shoes, at least until Tatum turned eighteen. Wall Street be damned.

And he knew his brother would, too, if it came down to it.

"Thank God," Thomas said. Shading his eyes from the sun, Tanner looked up to the perfectly blue sky above him, forcing his emotions under control. "Whew." His brother chuckled. "I was dreading the call for nothing. So what's going on? Why's Talia calling?"

"She's moving home." Tanner said the first thing that came to mind. The easy thing.

Because he wanted Thomas to know that his family, strange as it was, was still intact.

Because he needed his brother's support.

"No kidding!" Thomas said. "How's that going to work? She's still dancing, isn't she?"

Tanner hadn't said what kind of dancing Talia did when he'd called his brother after having located Talia. But he'd told Thomas where she was, and figured his brother had figured it out for himself.

"She's been putting herself through college," Tanner said now, a grin rising to the surface. "She's got enough money put aside that she can get a part-time salesclerk position and go to school full-time if she doesn't have to worry about rent and utilities. She's going to be starting at UC in the summer."

The idea still unnerved him. In a good way. Talia was turning her life around. After all of his years of hoping and praying.

He'd just had to hold on.

It had been the same with getting his mother to grant him custody of the kids. He'd just had to wait. To hang on. Hang around. It had all worked out in the end.

He listened as Thomas expressed sincere relief at Talia's most recent life choices.

And then, switching his phone from one ear to the other, he took a deep breath and filled his younger brother in on Tatum's situation.

"What in the hell...?" Thomas let fly with a series of questions and Tanner answered them as best as he could. He told his brother about Harcourt. His suspicions of abuse and control and manipulation.

"Because she was vulnerable to them," Thomas

said, clearly struggling to find some way to understand. "If she's still as sweet and naive as I remember, she'd fall for the lines."

If Thomas had come home, even periodically over the past ten years, he'd know Tatum. And yet, oddly enough, he'd pinned her accurately.

"One of her options is to petition the courts to have me removed as her guardian," Tanner said. If that happened, Thomas might be called to testify. Talia, too. He'd raised all of them.

And in their own ways, they were all dysfunctional.

"You are the one solid in that girl's life, and there is no place on this earth she could go to get more selfless loving or responsible care," Thomas said. All excitability had left Thomas's voice. His tone was calm, assured.

Tanner was walking among his grapes. Up and down the carefully laid rows. He'd been using the grapes as a diversion, to keep himself from worrying about the situation with Tatum, but suddenly they were a distraction. Because Thomas didn't bullshit him.

Which was why he'd chosen then to call. He'd needed to know what the courts would hear if Thomas was called. Because he didn't intend to wait much longer to bring his sister home. With Sedona ready to fly the coop, he couldn't wait for someone else to take over Tatum's case. Couldn't risk the chance that child services would be called in.

They might still be, if Tatum continued to balk at the idea of moving home—if she chose to pursue other actions once he brought her back there. He'd just have to hope that once she was home, sleeping in her own bed, with her big sister in residence and her phone and internet access restored, she'd settle down and want to stay.

He wasn't backing down from his ban on Tatum's seeing Del Harcourt, though. The punk wasn't getting anywhere near his little sister again. Ever.

Tatum was fifteen. She'd meet another boy soon enough.

"The courts would probably want to know why you left here the second you could and have never been back, not even for a visit. I know Tatum's attorney has already asked her about her relationship with you." They couldn't play nice here. They had to face the facts. Because if the court got involved that's how it would be. Thomas knew that as well as he did.

"And if it comes to keeping Tatum at home with you, I'll tell them why," Thomas said. "If I never do another thing worth a damn in my life, I'll do this," the twenty-eight-year-old Wall Street genius continued. "Without you, I would never have made it to adulthood, Tanner. If it wasn't for you, I'd likely have ended up in prison or something. Everything good in my life I owe to you. Everything."

Tanner felt he should say something. Interject. But his brother wouldn't let him get a word in. His tone was impassioned, adamant.

"My work ethic, the fact that I even have an education at all and, most importantly, my ability to love, all start with you."

Tanner had to ask. "Then why, if that's true, haven't I seen you in ten long years?"

Silence hung on the line. Tanner walked up a row and down the next. He couldn't take the question back. It was out there, hanging between them.

"Remember when my old man took me that time? I was gone for a few days, and you were frantic when I got back. You wouldn't let me out of your sight after that. Even slept between me and the door. For years."

Of course he remembered. "Yeah."

"He was using me to get Tammy to do what he wanted, Tanner. Kept me locked up in a closet for three days." Thomas choked up and fell silent. And Tanner felt like puking.

"It's okay, bro," Tanner said now. Maybe Thomas would tell him the details someday. Maybe not. It didn't change anything. "I'm here. I've always been here."

"I felt helpless, like an animal, or something. Powerless. He let me go, and I came home, but the feeling stayed with me. Until I left California," Thomas said, his voice back in control. "A strange thing happened when I got on the plane to go to college. That feeling slipped off my shoulders. The memory, that will always be there, but knowing that it happened doesn't hold me back here. It's like I'm a different person in a different life. I left the bad parts of the past behind because I had to. And I couldn't leave the bad without leaving all of it, I guess."

"When you talk to me, you get that feeling again."
He could understand. Completely.

"Yeah. But, more than just you, California reminds me of that time."

"So…we'll talk on the phone now and then…keep in touch." And if the courts called, Thomas would come home. That was enough for Tanner. More than enough.

"Actually, I was thinking… I've…I've met a woman, Tanner. Courtney Matthews. She's a schoolteacher and I did some work for her after she inherited a bit of money from her grandmother. I'm…thinking about asking her to marry me. And…I'd like you to meet her first. I was hoping…maybe you all could come out to New York for a vacation this summer. I thought it would be nice for Tatum to see the city. She'd love the museums and the Empire State Building and the Statue of Liberty…."

Tanner left the vineyard, heading toward the barn. So much was happening, so fast. Feeling overwhelmed, grateful and scared, too, he made it to an antique stool Tatum had set aside as a keeper, and dropped onto it.

"I think a trip to New York sounds wonderful," he managed to put together from all of the thoughts and words rambling around in his brain. "And congratulations, bro," he added. "I very much want to meet your Courtney."

"Not half as much as she wants to meet you," Thomas said with an easier chuckle. "The woman's been after me for six months to arrange something."

Six months. Thomas had been seriously involved that long and hadn't said anything.

"Does she know about—"

"She knows everything," Thomas interrupted.

So she *was* the one. She'd freed his little brother from hell.

With his lips firmly pressed together, Tanner laid his head back against the wall of the barn and waited for emotion to pass.

CHAPTER TWENTY-FIVE

TATUM ANSWERED THE door looking like any of a million other California blonde teenaged girls, in short shorts, a spaghetti-strap tank top that rested far enough above her waistband for her belly button ring to show and sandals. With her long silky hair, she could have walked off the set of any one of the major Hollywood networks.

"Can I come in?" Sedona asked.

I'm guessing that's not an outfit your brother's seen you in. She bit off the first words that came to her mouth. Tanner would have seen the clothes. She'd seen Tatum take them from her drawer. But she'd bet that when Tatum's brother was around, that tank was an undershirt.

"Sure." Tatum stepped back and Sedona followed the girl to a spotlessly clean and quiet living room.

"I was in my room, studying," the girl said, sitting on the edge of the sofa. "I've got finals this coming week."

Tatum was still carrying a 4.0. Tanner had been keeping her up to date on that end.

Sitting down next to Tatum, Sedona jumped right in. "Tell me about the panties."

Picking at her fingernails, short now with no polish, Tatum faced the floor, her expression pained.

"I can't help you if you aren't up front with me," she reminded in her sternest voice. Her heart ached for the girl, but they were running out of time.

When Tatum glanced up, Sedona knew it was bad. "I had sex with Del," she said, looking more afraid than anything else. "I made him use protection and I took the morning-after pill," she added in a rush. "I had a friend of mine bring me one. I was responsible."

She'd been afraid Del Harcourt had been involved. And her heart sank.

"There was blood in your panties."

"I know. It... Del told me that happens to girls on their first time."

Oh, God. Please help us.

"Lila said it was a lot of blood. That you told her it was spaghetti sauce."

Nodding, Tatum sat still, meeting Sedona's gaze head-on.

And that's when Sedona knew things were really bad.

"Did it hurt?" she asked, scrambling for the right way to handle this. The best way. She'd had some training in family counseling, but...

Tatum nodded again. And this time her gray-blue eyes filled with tears. "A lot more than I was expecting."

She covered Tatum's hand with her own and the

girl turned her hand over, weaving her fingers through Sedona's.

"Has there been any blood since?" How bad was the situation?

"No."

Thank you, God. "I'm going to take you to see Lynn Duncan," she said next, leaving no room for argument. "A girl's first time does cause a little bleeding sometimes, but only a little. There might be something else going on with you and we're going to have to let Lynn take a look. Or I can call your doctor."

Harcourt could have caused some tearing.

Tatum surprised her when she said, "No, Lynn would be fine."

Something else occurred to her. "Does it still hurt?" she asked.

"Yes."

"Then let's go."

Tatum stood, still holding on to Sedona's hand. "Aren't you going to ask how I had sex while I'm living here?"

Sedona had already figured that out. And at the moment it was the least of her worries. "I'm assuming it happened one of those times you missed class because you were sick."

"Twice, actually. I thought the second time would hurt less, but it didn't. Del, he… Anyway, that second time, he was in a hurry and so he got kind of…rough… and it hurt more. A lot more," Tatum said, still not moving toward the door. "I don't want you to think I'm a liar or anything, Sedona," she said. "I really was sick all the other times. But Del's been sending me messages through our friends and we saw each other when he drove over to the school. And he's been at my locker after school, too. We really miss each other. He understands about me being here and he's so sweet about it. He wants me to figure out what to do so we can be together. He really loves me, Sedona."

Sedona believed that Tatum believed it. But she didn't. Not anymore.

"A boy doesn't usually hurt a girl so much." Not enough to cause a substantial amount of blood.

"It was his first time, too. He told me that after the second time because I was crying. I couldn't help it. It was awful. And he swore to me he'd never done it before, either, and that he'd get better at it. He said I could do things to help it go better, too. I was really surprised about him not doing it before because he's a couple of years older than me and he's got every girl in the county after him. But he picked me. He really loves me," she said again.

If it was Del's first time, Sedona would sell her house.

Tanner was going to be heartbroken.

"Usually when a guy loves a girl, he makes sure her first time is special."

"I know. And he wanted to. But with me being here…he said he could wait for me to make up my mind about where I was going to live as long as he knew we were going to be together forever. He said that was the way we could both know. If we did that together and with no one else. So we met in his car during English class and—"

"In the school parking lot?"

"On the road behind it. He found a private spot. And made sure both times that I got back inside without being caught before class was over."

Sedona needed to speak with Sara.

"He thanked me for giving him my virginity. He knew how important it was."

The kid pulled out all the stops....

"So this just happened?"

"Thursday was the second time. It was our last day of regular class. Friday we had an end-of-the-year assembly and shorter classes, and I can't miss out on finals next week. Then who knows when we'll get to see each other again. He had a blanket on the seat and brought me a rose and a card, too."

Sedona focused on one thing. For a girl who was so in love, Tatum didn't seem all that upset about not seeing Harcourt for a while.

But she wouldn't go home because she couldn't see him?

Nothing was making sense.

And in a frightening way, everything was.

Maybe Del Harcourt was a creep, just like Tanner said. Maybe he was controlling and manipulative and was taking advantage of a sweet girl's innocence. Bringing her roses, cards. Saying all the right things.

Maybe Tatum was prey to him, vulnerable to his

manipulation, and maybe she was being hit by him, too. If the sexual violence—or at least his complete disregard for her feelings, her physical comfort—was anything to judge by...

The idea was horrifying.

And made a sickening kind of sense, as well.

AFTER A SUNDAY lunch meeting with a couple of board members from the local vintners' association—who were pressuring him to run, uncontested, for a board position—Tanner headed to the nursery just outside of Santa Raquel. He'd bought his first grape plants from the place.

That day he wasn't thinking about grapes.

He wanted sod. Not grass seed, as the salesperson was trying to convince him. Yes, he understood it would be much more cost effective, but this job wasn't about money.

It was about creating a home Tatum would be proud to come home to. And creating it now.

Within the next couple of days.

Before Sedona turned his little sister over to one of her peers and they ended up in court.

If he could just get Tatum home, he felt confident that he and Thomas and Talia would be able to help her—and keep her there. Just until she was old enough and equipped with the appropriate life tools to fend for herself.

Then she'd be free to fly as far away as she needed to go.

Who knew there were so many different types of grass for front yards? He chose the softest. Tatum liked to go barefoot.

Ordering enough to cover the ground all the way out to the road and arranging for it to be laid the middle of that week, he then picked out everything he was going to need to get the in-ground irrigation system in. That he could do himself, over the next few days, and be ready for the grass when it arrived.

On his way out the door, he saw a couple of big clay pots with butterflies painted in dramatic colors. He bought those, too. And enough geraniums to fill them. They could sit on either side of the cracked porch steps for now. Until he could arrange to get new steps poured.

Talia was coming home. And, maybe, after they all visited Thomas in New York and met Courtney, the two of them would be able to make it out to California for a visit. Maybe even for Christmas.

Or he and Tatum and Talia could fly to New York and spend Christmas in the Big Apple. Experience their first white Christmas ever.

With thoughts of sugar plums dancing in his head, Tanner turned into his driveway and saw Sedona's Thunderbird sitting in front of his house.

He hadn't known if she'd call or show up. But he'd been waiting to hear from her. To know how her talk went with Tatum.

To kiss her again. Just one kiss.

She got out when he did, meeting him at his truck as he reached in the bed for the first clay pot.

The store clerk had insisted that he should plant the geraniums immediately so they wouldn't go into shock and lose their blossoms. If he wanted them to be in full bloom on Wednesday, the day he'd told them his yard had to be done.

He had to know. "Did you talk to her?" he asked as he placed the pot on the ground to the left of the steps and went back for the second one.

"Yes." Bending, she positioned the pot a little in front of the stoop, in line with the corner. Far enough away not to intrude on the space people would need to climb the steps, but close enough that the eye focused on the pot rather than the cracked cement.

At least that was how Tanner saw it when he went back with the second pot in hand.

"What did she say?" he asked, leaving the pot on the ground in close proximity to where it would probably end up.

"She still wants me to represent her."

Holy hell. He let out a huge breath as he lifted a forty-pound bag of potting soil. Maybe they *were* on some god's radar.

Dropping the bag by the pots, he said, "You told her about us?" and headed back to the tailgate for the tray of geraniums.

"I told her that we've become friends over the past several weeks. She knew of your condition to let her stay there, of course."

Tatum had had to sign their agreement, as well. While, as a minor, her signature hadn't been legally binding, as Sedona had pointed out, Tanner had insisted that his sister take on ownership of their plan.

"What did she say?"

"Nothing."

"Nothing?" He stood there, holding the tray of flowers, staring at her.

"Nothing."

"She didn't ask any questions?"

"I told her I care about both of you and that she had to understand that my perceptions where her case were concerned might be skewed by that fact. She said she understood."

"And that she still wants you to represent her."

He hadn't expected it to be so easy. Setting the tray down, Tanner ripped into the bag of potting soil, filling each pot three-quarters of the way with the dirt, just like the woman at the store had instructed.

"She said she trusts me to do what's right by her."

So why wasn't Sedona smiling? Why were there clouds in her eyes? Peering up at her, Tanner decided that maybe the sun was just in his eyes.

He wanted to kiss her.

More than once.

Placing the flowers in the pot, he waited for the moment of intense desire to pass.

"Here, let me help you with that."

"You're dressed too nice. You'll get dirty."

He still wanted her.

Not that she seemed to notice. Or seemed to be having any trouble keeping her hands off him.

"My clothes are washable," she said. "And unless you plan to smear dirt all over them, all that's likely to get dirty are my hands." By the time she'd finished talking, she had flowers in both hands and was placing them in what appeared to him to be haphazard fashion.

Reaching behind her, he straightened a couple of them.

And she put them back where she'd placed them.

"You don't plant flowers in neat, even rows in a pot," she said calmly. "They grow out more than up and will fill whole areas. The idea here is to make certain that when they do, you've filled up the entire pot with blooms."

Conceding that she knew more about planting flowers than he did, Tanner took half a step back, loosening each dirt pod from the tray and handing it to her when she was ready.

When they were done, he lifted the bag of soil and poured as she directed.

Then he stood back with her and they surveyed the results.

The pots looked good. Nice. Great.

She wasn't smiling yet.

Bending down, Tanner kissed her. Just mouth to mouth, not body to body. When her lips responded to his, he lingered, careful to keep his dirty hands off her clean clothes.

She kept her hands to herself, too, until she reached up to Tanner's shoulders and pushed him away.

She shook her head.

And he wasn't smiling anymore, either.

CHAPTER TWENTY-SIX

SEDONA LONGED FOR ELLIE. For a ship on the ocean, with waves surrounding her, cosseting her, buffering her and taking her away.

She longed for a moment of childhood so she could creep up on her mother's lap and feel those loving arms around her as Millie kissed her boo-boo better.

There was no kiss, no Band-Aid or any salve that was going to make this go away.

"What's wrong?" Tanner's frown put a cramp in her stomach.

"I took Tatum to see Lynn Duncan this morning."

"The nurse? Why, is her throat bad again? I thought they did a culture. Have they checked for tonsillitis?"

With a heart that cried for him, she searched for a way to soften the blow.

"She's got some vaginal tearing." She stuck with the facts. "It's nothing to be concerned about long-term. It's relatively minor and she's already healing. There's no internal or other damage."

His face went white. And as still as stone.

"Tell me how one gets vaginal tearing in a women's shelter." The softness of his words didn't fool her. Tanner was angry. Bone-deep angry.

She'd known he would be. The loss his precious sister had suffered at the hands of a boy who was, at the very least, unduly selfish in his eagerness had to be devastating for him.

"It didn't happen at The Stand."

"You swore to me that she wouldn't leave there without my permission." There wasn't accusation in his tone. Yet.

"She didn't."

"You're telling me this happened at school?" Both hands by his sides, he watched her as though she was a fly and he had the swatter.

"During school hours, yes." She'd do this his way. Answer his questions as he asked them. Feed him what he determined he could handle, when he was ready for it. She'd have done anything to ease the burden from this man who'd lain so tenderly in her bed the night before.

"She was raped at school?"

Sedona bit her lip. "It wasn't rape. The tearing indicates roughness, but not rape."

"Who was it?"

"Del Harcourt."

He turned his back to her and faced the house.

"He's been seeing her at lunch, sneaking over to her school."

She waited for a response that didn't come.

"Someone had told Del that she hadn't been feeling well, that she'd missed class a few times. He talked her into missing class again."

"When?"

"A week ago Monday and then again Thursday."

There was no way any of them could have known. Nothing he could have done differently if Tatum had been at home with him. They'd thought they had all their bases covered.

"How is she?"

"Okay. She was scared, I think, but we talked. She asked me to stay with her while Lynn examined her, so I did. She was better when I dropped her off."

His silence was what she'd dreaded most.

"I'm going to ask you to promise me that you'll leave her at The Stand, Tanner. At least for a little bit longer."

He didn't respond. Or turn. So she walked around to face him. "She's not going to be able to see Harcourt next week because of finals. And after that she'll be at The Stand full-time. She knows she won't be able to see him at all then. She seemed truly okay with that, Tanner. I don't know what to make of that, but I think it's good. Maybe having sex with him has made her think twice about how much she loves him. Clearly the experience wasn't a good one for her. But what I do know is that as long as she's with us, he's not going to get near her."

And if the creep *was* the one abusing Tatum, which Sedona strongly suspected at this point, she'd do whatever it took to be able to prove that.

Rough consensual sex among minors over fourteen wasn't a crime. But it could very easily be a factor in one.

"Please? Give me a chance to get something solid on this guy? In the meantime, Sara will be having daily sessions with her."

He looked down at her and she had no idea what he was thinking.

"Fine."

His concession was a shock.

A huge one.

For the first time all day, Sedona felt a surge of hope.

SEDONA STAYED A bit longer. They'd done something he'd sworn to himself they weren't going to do again. At least not until Tatum was home and well.

He wasn't proud of himself.

She hadn't seemed all that happy about their love-making, either.

She'd dressed quietly, left without a word.

And Tanner set to work cleaning the house. From top to bottom. He hauled the sheets off Tatum's bed, and washed them, putting extra softener in. When they were dry, he made it again.

He did the same for Talia's bed.

And his own.

He vacuumed and dusted and scoured the upstairs bathroom. Then repeated the process for the half bath downstairs.

Giving Tatum a chance to call him, he watched the clock. And when dinner hour at the shelter had passed, when it was nearly time for his little sister to turn in so she'd be rested for exams the next day, he dialed her number.

She'd promised Sedona she'd pick up when he called. But that had been in another lifetime.

"Hello?"

"Hi, sweetie, how are you doing?" He wanted to be angry with her. But couldn't find it in him. She thought she was in love. Believed this guy loved her. And so many girls her age were having sex these days.

He didn't like it. Didn't approve. Didn't want it for her.

"Okay."

"Good. I just wanted to tell you you'll do fine tomorrow and to get some rest." He'd see her again in the morning.

"Thanks."

It was the first actual conversation they'd had in weeks. And he could hardly think of a thing to say.

But he knew what he was going to do.

"You're sure you're okay?"

"Yeah."

He just couldn't leave it at that. Tatum was hurting and needed to know she was loved.

"I talked to Sedona."

"She told you?"

"Yeah."

"I know you're pissed."

"Not at you."

"I'm sorry…" Tatum's voice broke and so did a part of Tanner's heart.

"I know, sweetie. I just want you to know that I love you."

"I love you, too."

"'Kay, get some sleep now, promise?"

"Yeah."

She hung up and Tanner sat on the stairs, elbows on his knees, and stared into the darkness.

THINGS DIDN'T GO so well the next day. It started with a letter from the detective he'd hired to find Tammy.

The woman had passed away the year before of a drug overdose. He wanted to feel something. A sense of loss. Or maybe even relief. He felt nothing. He asked about her burial and was told she'd been cremated.

He didn't feel much about that, either. The woman had been dead to them for so long that any mourning he might have done had already happened. Back when he'd still been naive enough to hope she'd change, only to have her disappoint him again and again.

He called Thomas and left a message, telling him what he'd found out. And only afterward did it even occur to him that leaving a voice mail message might have been a little cold. Thomas might still feel something where Tammy was concerned. So he called back and left a second message. And when he called Talia, he was more mindful that she might have some feelings regarding their mother's passing.

"I'm actually glad," she said, her voice soft, but not the least bit upset. "We don't have to look over our shoulders anymore, you know? Fearing she might show up."

"I tried to shield you from that."

"You did shield us. But that doesn't mean I didn't worry about it."

There was silence for a minute while Tanner tried to figure out what to say.

"At least she's at peace," Talia said. And something inside Tanner settled. Living with Tammy was over. She was at peace. And somehow her peace became his.

TATUM NOTICED THE box of things in Tanner's truck when he picked her up after her last exam of the day.

"What's that?" she asked, her face twisted with horror.

He'd already experienced the disapproval of Lila, Lynn and Sara. And was sure Sedona would have her say, too, when she had her chance with him.

"Your things. I stopped by the shelter to pick them up before coming here."

Standing with one foot in the truck and the other still on the ground, she looked from the backseat to him. "So they know?"

"Yes."

Someone called out to her and Tatum turned, gave a weak wave and then got in the truck, yanking the door closed behind her.

"Go," she said through gritted teeth.

Understanding that she didn't want to cause a scene

in front of her classmates, Tanner pulled away from the curb and slid into traffic.

"Sedona's a part of this, then?"

He regretted the disappointment he heard in Tatum's tone but couldn't do anything about it at that point.

"No, she's not. I haven't spoken with her. But I suspect someone at the shelter has called her by now. If you look at your phone you've probably got a missed call from her."

He'd had three. In the past fifteen minutes.

Pulling out her little flip phone, Tatum clicked it on and waited for it to boot up.

"I can't believe you're doing this." Her disgust was evident.

"It's something I should've done weeks ago," he said. "It's been weeks and we're no closer to solving our problems. Because we aren't even working on them. All we've done is let you run away from the whole situation. And that's creating more problems. It's time to fix them. Before you get hurt any more."

"You're the only one who's hurt me."

It was on the tip of his tongue to remind her of the trip to the clinic she'd had the day before. But he didn't.

"We're going to talk about that, sweetie. And this time, I give you my word, I'm going to listen. Really listen. I'm bringing you home, because it's your space, too. But things are going to change from here on in."

"I'll bet they are."

"I give you my word, Tatum."

He'd spoken sternly. And she looked over at him.

"I've made mistakes," he said. "If you'll work with me here, I'll do my best to correct them."

"Right. Like giving me my phone back?"

"It's in the glove box. Charged and ready to go."

Her fingers shot out so fast he would have smiled if smiling had been appropriate. Within seconds she had the phone on and was typing in her secret passcode to access her private information.

And the rest of the ride home her thumbs flew over the on-screen keyboard.

He hoped to God she hadn't been texting Del Harcourt, but he was fairly certain she had been.

It was all in the plan. He was going to help the guy hang himself. While he figured out how to give Tatum more freedom and keep her safe at the same time.

"I DON'T UNDERSTAND." Sitting in Sara's little office with Lila and the counselor, Sedona shook her head. "He agreed to leave her here. Did he say anything?"

Had he given any indication that something had changed since she'd left the man's bed the afternoon before? She hadn't planned to sleep with him again. But after they'd planted the flowers she hadn't been able to just leave him there alone. She'd put her arms around him, intending to offer comfort.

And somehow they'd ended up in his room.

"He called me," Lila said. "Asked me to gather her things and have them ready. I did so. What choice did I have? He's her guardian and our agreement stated that he could take her anytime he deemed it necessary."

It had. But that was not the agreement he'd made with her, just the day before.

"I called Sara and she was with me when he arrived. We both tried to talk to him, but he wasn't having any of it."

"It was odd," Sara spoke up. "If I hadn't known differently, I'd have thought we were doing a normal move out. He was pleasant. Polite. But uninterested in conversation of any kind."

Looking from one woman to the other, Sedona's heart sank. She'd trusted him.

He hadn't trusted her.

Because Tanner Malone didn't trust anyone.

She'd had plenty of warning. Knew that the chances of him changing hadn't been good. Tanner's developmental environment had taught him not to trust people as a safety measure. A survival tool.

She understood the psychology of it all.

And she'd listened to her heart, anyway.

"I offered to continue to see Tatum on an outpatient basis," Sara added.

She latched on to the news with a last ray of hope. "What did he say?"

"Thank you."

"Was it an acceptance thank-you or…"

"It was just a thank-you. I have no idea what it meant."

With a request to be kept informed if anything else transpired, Sedona left The Stand.

When Lila had first called to let her know what had

happened, she'd thought that the managing director had misunderstood. She'd tried contacting Tanner repeatedly, hoped to be able to change his mind. And after Lila had phoned to say he'd been there and gone, she'd tried again, repeatedly, in between court sessions.

She didn't know what he was going to do about Harcourt. Or if she was expected to continue to try to prove that the boy had been abusive toward Tatum.

She didn't know anything other than the fact that he wasn't speaking to her.

And that when he'd given her his word the day before, he'd lied.

CHAPTER TWENTY-SEVEN

TATUM WENT STRAIGHT UP to her room when they got home. He'd planned for them to sit down over the brownies he'd made that morning—her favorite— and a glass of milk and make a new plan for the next three years.

To set ground rules. Hers, that he was going to have to follow to keep her happy.

And his, the ones he would expect her to respect.

Thomas was who he was, at least in part, because of Tanner's expectations. They had been in touch several times over the past twenty-four hours, and his little brother had reminded him of that fact every chance he got.

He'd do Tatum as much disservice by spoiling her and giving her everything she wanted, as he would by being too strict and hardheaded. His job was to find the right balance.

He'd kind of been hoping she was going to help with that.

He also had to tell her that Tammy was gone.

He ordered pizza for dinner. It was easy and she liked it. When it arrived, he climbed the stairs and tapped on her door.

"What?"

"Dinner's here."

She didn't respond. Turning, Tanner descended the stairs as quietly as he'd climbed them, set the table with paper plates and napkins, poured two glasses of tea and sat down to eat.

Five minutes into the meal, Tatum slid into her chair. She asked what kind of pizza he'd ordered.

The same kind they'd always ordered, ham with onion and tomato.

Taking a big gulp of tea, the sun-brewed kind she liked best, Tatum helped herself to a couple of pieces of pizza and, napkin on her lap, started to eat.

Like she'd always done.

Almost as if she'd never left.

"Talia's coming home."

Tatum swallowed and held her slice of pizza aloft. "Why?"

"To live."

"You're kidding."

"Nope."

"What did you do to her?"

What had he done to her?

"I didn't do anything to her," he said calmly, when he felt like hollering. "She's been going to college parttime. She did some checking and found out that she could graduate in half the time if she didn't have to pay living expenses," he explained. "She found out that she could transfer to UC without losing any credits and asked me if she could live here free of charge. So, she's coming home."

Tatum took a bite of her pizza.

"I thought you'd be glad."

"Why'd you think that?"

She was being a bit of a brat. But she was home, at the dinner table, eating with him. That miracle would carry him through.

"Because I thought you loved talking to her."

"That was before she was in cahoots with you. Now she'll just spout out whatever you tell her to."

"Tatum! That's not fair. To your sister or to me."

"It's true, though," she said softly, lowering her chin. Like someone who was afraid of retribution.

"If she's coming home it's because you bought her off."

This bratty girl wasn't his sister. What the hell had happened to the sweet young woman he'd raised?

And that's when he remembered the GED application. With everything that had gone on that weekend, he'd forgotten that Tatum didn't trust him to be straight up with her about anything.

He forgot that not only were they dealing with rough sex and a potentially abusive boyfriend, his sister felt as though he'd betrayed her, too.

"I am not buying your sister off nor is she in my pocket," he said, choosing to deal with one thing at a time. "You of all people should know that Talia has a mind of her own where I'm concerned."

"Then why did she change her number and stop talking to me when you told her to?"

"I did not tell her to, exactly. When she found out that I was unaware that you two were talking, she realized that you were putting more trust in her than you were in me. And she didn't want to be the example you followed. Not until she'd made her life right. Her words, not mine."

Tatum's frown wasn't reassuring.

"You're there for people until they make a choice you don't like and then you're done."

Where was all this coming from? He wasn't hungry, but he kept eating. Chewing. At least she was home. Even better, she was talking to him.

"Why do you say that?" he asked. He couldn't help until he understood the problem. Or so he told himself.

In reality, he had no idea what to say. How to handle the situation.

"Thomas left and hasn't been back once. I don't even know what he looks like anymore. And when you call, he hardly ever answers and doesn't call you back."

"Thomas had some issues of his own to deal with," he said. "I think it would be best if he told you about them."

"Yeah, right. Like we ever have a conversation."

"He wants us to come to New York this summer. We'll be staying with him. He wants to take you to the museums and the Empire State Building and the Statue of Liberty."

Tatum had always wanted to travel. To take vacations. There just hadn't been any money.

Or rather, he'd been too focused on her future to spend the money he'd put aside for her. Like he'd said, he'd made some mistakes.

"I'm not a little kid anymore. I don't need to be carted around to museums."

She'd come around. Once she talked to Thomas. And Talia. And…

"You cut Talia out of the family when you found out what she was doing with her life."

"I—" He'd been about to tell her how he'd spent thirty thousand dollars to get Talia away from Donald, a rich john who'd married her one night at a Vegas all-night chapel. Donald had seen her as an investment, intending to share her with his friends. For profit. Tanner stopped himself. Tatum already thought he'd bought Talia off.

"Even before that, you had her boyfriend sent to prison so that he couldn't get to her."

"He'd committed a crime." He didn't know how much Talia had told Tatum about Rex.

"Statutory rape. When she was sixteen. That's stretching it."

"I told you I made some mistakes." He almost choked on his pizza.

"Maybe you should tell her."

"I think you'll find, when you speak with your sister, that she and I are good."

"Because you bought her off."

Good God, he'd raised a girl who could hold her own, exactly like he'd set out to do. He'd just never considered, for one second, that she'd be using it against him.

"And what about Melissa Winchell?"

Talia's best friend who'd come by the farm for a while after Talia had run away.

"What about her?"

"You ran her off, too."

He'd had no idea Tatum even remembered Melissa. Or cared.

"She wanted there to be more between us than was there, Tatum. She said she was in love with me. I wasn't in love with her. She went off to college, fell in love and she's married with a little girl now."

"How do you know that? Did Talia tell you?"

"No, Melissa told me. We were invited to her wedding but it was the weekend you were in the state spelling bee."

"You could have told me."

Which reminded him of another thing they had to talk about.

"Sedona told me you know about my GED application. She said she told you why I quit school."

"Yeah, so what."

Sedona had told him about the conversation she'd had with Tatum, just before they'd ended up in bed together. She'd said when they were on their way back from Lynn's office, Tatum had asked her if she'd told him about Tatum's snooping in his desk. And when

Tatum found out that he knew, she'd wanted to know what he said.

Sedona had apologized for giving her client information that hadn't technically been hers to give. And had used the incident as proof that the two of them could not make love again.

Right before she'd hugged him.

And then they'd had sex.

"I should have told you myself," he said now. "I'm sorry. I didn't want any of you—Thomas or Talia or you—to feel like you were responsible. Or feel guilty. The choice to leave school was mine and I was good with it." He could leave it there. He considered doing so. But coddling hadn't served any of his siblings. "I also didn't want any of you to know because I didn't want to set an example of how someone could quit high school and still be a success in life."

He was going to end there. But Tatum was chewing slowly. Drinking her tea. And listening. So he told her about Tammy. About how she'd had plans to go to college, to be different from her mother, until Tanner came along and she was dumped by Tanner's father and had to quit school.

And he told her that their mother had passed away.

She shrugged. "I didn't really know her. But I'm glad that she's off the streets and not having to do drugs anymore."

Poor Tammy. Four children and not one of them mourned her death.

Tatum helped herself to another bite of pizza.

When that was gone, she wiped her mouth and put her napkin on her plate.

"Did you get it?"

"What?"

"The GED?"

"Yes."

"I really couldn't care less."

All in all, Tanner figured the dinner went pretty well.

SEDONA DIDN'T SLEEP Monday night. She tried. And then she gave up and sat out on her balcony, listening to waves she couldn't see, feeling emotions she didn't understand. She'd slept with Tanner twice.

There was no reason to feel as though his betrayal had sucked the life out of her.

And she knew other clients better than she knew Tatum. Had lost a case even more heart-wrenching than Tatum's. But it had been work. A job. She'd mourned. And she'd been able to move on.

By Tuesday morning, her head felt twice its normal size and encased in thick cotton. When she should have been in the shower and then on the way to her office, she was in bed, having taken an aspirin, sleeping off the night before.

She had no idea what time it was when her phone rang. Shooting straight up in a room flooded with sunshine, she grabbed the cell phone off her nightstand, not remembering when she'd put it there.

"Hello?"

"Sedona?"

She recognized the voice immediately. Throwing off the covers, Sedona stood, forcing her weary mind awake. "Tatum? Where are you?"

"I'm at school. I finished my exam early. Tanner's going to be here soon so I don't have long."

"How are you?"

"Fine."

Okay. Good. She'd known Tanner wouldn't hurt her, but she hadn't expected him to take Tatum, either, and, oh, God, she loved them. Loved them both.

Through the fog in her mind, Sedona stood in her room, wearing a nightgown in the middle of the day, completely poleaxed. How was it possible? She'd only known them a matter of weeks and…

"I just need to know…now that I'm not at The Lemonade Stand, does that mean you're not my lawyer anymore? Since I got you free because of them and—"

"No! I'm your lawyer as long as you want me," she said. Unless her brother expressly told her she couldn't be. And if he did, she'd figure out another way to help them.

"Okay, good." Tatum sounded rushed.

"Did you need something today?"

"No. I just…I'm glad you're still on my case. I have to go. Tanner's going to be here and I don't want him to see me on the phone and ask who I'm talking to."

"Call if you need me."

"I will."

"Doesn't matter what time it is."

"Okay, Sedona. Thank you." The sweet voice told her goodbye.

And Sedona started to shake.

She was in love with Tanner Malone. A man who trusted no one but himself. A man who could never give her the once-in-a-lifetime, all-consuming relationship she'd been waiting her whole life to find.

Wanting to climb back into bed, Sedona got in the shower instead.

Her entire world had shattered.

And the only thing she could think of to do was get back to work.

TANNER SPENT ALL day Tuesday working on the in-ground irrigation system for the sod that was going to be delivered the next day. Tatum hadn't said a word about the porch or the flowers—either the previous afternoon when he'd brought her home or that morning when they'd left for school.

But she had to have noticed.

And he figured she'd liked them because she sure as hell wouldn't have missed the opportunity to tell him that she didn't.

He had pruning to do. And would get to that, too. But the sod came first. Then he was going to have to return Sedona's calls and texts. He just wasn't sure what he was going to say.

"You're fired. Stay away from us," might be the best option.

He took a deep breath. Waiting for the emotion to pass.

It was the longest breath he'd ever taken. Forty-eight hours and counting. Hard to believe it had been that long since he'd spoken to her. Touched her.

His skin still burned from her tenderness.

His tongue still tasted her.

But she stood between him and Tatum—keeping Tatum locked up in that shelter where he couldn't help her. Where they couldn't work on repairing the damage between them.

One thing was for certain. Tatum held a load of misconceptions where he was concerned.

And they hadn't been built in just the two months since she'd met Harcourt. Apparently they'd been festering for years. Because his silences had left her to draw her own conclusions. About so many things.

Apparently he should have been a hell of a lot more open than he'd been. With all three of his siblings.

But silence protected them. From all of the things he'd known and seen and dealt with so they didn't have to. He'd spent his life shielding them from the ugly things in life as much as he could. When he hadn't been able to get them away from Tammy's home, he'd at least been able to block them from seeing much of what went on there.

He'd been the wall between his younger sisters and brother and the hell their mother had borne them into.

That was his purpose.

As he dug thin trenches in the hard dirt, sweat dripping down his body and into the earth, and laid the thin black tubing, Tanner had to accept the fact that he'd driven his baby sister away.

And Sedona…was he driving her away, too? The woman was different. The feelings she roused in him—he didn't recognize them. Didn't understand them.

They made him uncomfortable.

She made him soar.

He dug. He sweat. Why in the hell was he thinking about love?

Or the idea that he had one chance at it?

Tanner finished laying his tubes. He did the final leak checks. Turned on the water and walked the entire yard, looking for leaks. He fixed a couple.

And knew that the hard day's work was nothing compared to what lay ahead of him. He had half an hour before he was due to collect Tatum from school.

Pulling out his cell phone, he got in the truck, parked half a block from the school and dialed Talia's number.

"I have something to tell you," he said the second his sister picked up.

"She's home, right?" He'd told her the day before, when he'd called to tell her about Tammy, that he was going to get Tatum.

"Yes, but this isn't about Tatum."

"What, then?" Her voice changing, she added, "What's wrong, Tanner? You don't sound good."

He heard real fear in her voice. As though he mattered to her.

And he wondered how long it had been since she'd expressed that caring so freely. Or even allowed herself to acknowledge that the feeling was there.

Allowed herself to feel.

Like he allowed himself to feel?

Thoughts attacked him with swift force. He couldn't feel. He had to be the strong one. The one in control.

God knew, Tammy hadn't been.

He had to tell her the whole truth.

"The way I reacted about Rex Chelshire." He came close to blurting out the words.

"What about him?" Her voice dropped.

"He was your teacher, Tal. It didn't matter if I pressed charges or not, the school was going to. I told you that."

"I didn't believe you then. But even when I got a little older and realized you were right on that score, I still blamed you. Think about it, Tanner. After Mom left, you watched me like a hawk. With all your questions, and the way you warned off anyone who dared to come near me. You drove away every boy I knew, every boy my own age, or even close to my own age. You were crazy, Tanner. If you'd let me date like a normal teenager I wouldn't have had to…" Her voice drifted off. And he didn't want to remember.

"I know." Would it have made a difference to her if he'd told her why he'd done so? Would she have understood? "You're right. I was crazy."

"Why, Tanner? Because you knew that I was like Tammy? Did you see something in me? Some sign?"

That was what she thought?

If ever Tanner had needed a lesson in understanding why keeping secrets was sometimes as harmful as lying, he'd just had it. As it occurred to him that sometimes secrets were only safe when they were shared, he told his sister why their mother had left their home and never come back.

He told her about the man outside the bathroom door while Talia had been in the shower, a man who, after getting out of bed with Tammy, had handed their mother a hundred-dollar bill to get in the shower with her daughter.

He told her about beating the guy to a pulp before throwing him out of their home. About how that incident had opened his eyes to the danger Talia's beauty was to her. And how he'd spent every single second of every day after that worrying that someone else was going to take advantage of the beautiful sister he'd sworn to protect.

He'd panicked. Hadn't known how to protect her. And when Talia started to cry, he hung on to the phone and wished he could change so many things.

CHAPTER TWENTY-EIGHT

TANNER'S PHONE CALLS weren't done. Still fifteen minutes from exams being over, he sat in his truck on a lonely stretch of tree-lined road. He knew the ocean was on the other side of the trees. He just couldn't see it.

Branches overhead shaded him from the hot sun. With his windows rolled up, there was no breeze in the car.

He dialed his last missed call.

"Hello?" She knew who it was. She was using her courtroom voice.

She'd judged him.

Probably sentenced him, too.

"I need your help."

"What can I do for you?" Her tone had softened. Not a lot, but he noticed.

"I'm on my way to pick Tatum up from school. I'd like you to call and make arrangements for her readmittance to The Lemonade Stand."

"What?" No doubting the change now.

He didn't kid himself that her warmth was directed at him. He'd lied to her, telling her that he'd leave Tatum at The Stand when he had no intention of doing so. He'd betrayed her even as he was making love to her.

"I'll take her home and let her pack up whatever she wants. I could have her there within the next couple of hours. If you can make that work…" She was Tatum's attorney. He'd send her a check even if she didn't bill him.

"Wait." The word was spoken as a command, not a favor. "What happened?"

He wasn't sure if he heard a "what have you done" in there, or not.

"I've come to my senses," he said. Living with Tammy had taught him to hide. And by doing so, he'd hurt everyone he loved. She was gone now and he wasn't going to be the one to keep her alive. "I've made a lot of mistakes, but I love my sister. I want what's best for her. She wants to be at the shelter. You and Lila and Sara think it's best for her."

"I think that Tatum needs help, Tanner. I have no idea what's best for her or I'd be doing what I could to make it happen."

"I've never hit her."

"I know that."

"But she doesn't trust me at all anymore. And I can't believe it's just the GED. I can see where it was a shock to her. I can understand her feeling betrayed. But the things coming out of her mouth last night at dinner…there's something more going on. I don't know what it is. But I'm fairly certain that as long as she feels trapped in that house with me, we aren't going to find out."

"Maybe with Talia coming home…"

"I don't think so."

"When is she due?"

"Next week. She's just finishing her final exams."

"Maybe when she gets here Tatum will talk to her."

"She thinks I've bought Talia off."

"She said that to you?"

"Yes."

"That doesn't sound like Tatum. She's clearly upset with you, I'll admit that, but from what I understood, she wanted you to lift her ban on talking to Talia."

"I told her we'd take a new look at the house rules, choose them together. She wasn't interested. Right now, nothing I do is going to be right."

It was incredibly painful to admit. And deep breaths weren't taking the pain away.

"If it was just Harcourt manipulating her, I'd think that your concessions would weaken his hold on her. She's still a kid in so many ways and it was pretty clear to me and to my parents and Sara that she loves you very much."

He'd never doubted Tatum's love. Until the night before. "I hope you're right," he said now, looking toward where he knew the ocean to be. "I have to go pick her up. Do you think you can take her back in this afternoon?"

"I'm certain I can."

He told her briefly about Tammy's passing, about Tatum's reaction to the news.

"How do you feel about it?" she asked. "You were the one who knew her best."

"I'm glad she's at peace," he said, stealing Talia's words. *Peace*. His goal for what Tammy had left inside of him was peace.

And maybe, as the news of her death settled more clearly upon him, he was a little sad, too. For the girl she'd been before he'd been conceived. For the mother she'd wanted to be.

"Do you want me to meet you at The Lemonade Stand?" Sedona's question brought him back to the present. He had business here to take of. The most important business of his life.

"I was hoping you would," he admitted. It would be easier to let Tatum walk away with Sedona there, taking her in. And he had to make certain that this move was as easy as possible. For his sister's sake. "She told you about having sex with Harcourt when she wouldn't talk to anyone else. Maybe she'll talk to you."

Sedona made a sound and then seemed to hesitate, as though she might say more. "I'll do my best," she said, and he wondered what she'd held back.

But knew he had no right to ask.

FIVE MINUTES AFTER she got off the phone with Tanner, Sedona had made arrangements for Tatum to return to The Stand. Maddie's spare bed was still available, so Tatum could slide right back into the life she'd left the day before.

In the end, Tanner's move the previous day might just have helped them all. Maybe it had shown him something he'd needed to see to help his sister. Maybe, when he took Tatum back to the shelter, Tatum would see that Tanner really did support her and want what was best for her. Maybe his actions could start to rebuild her trust in him.

Her phone rang as she was pulling a green pantsuit out of her closet. She'd just stepped out of the shower when Tanner had phoned before. And now he was calling again.

"Hello?"

"She's not here."

Something dawned on her. Tatum had called half an hour earlier, to ask if she was still her lawyer. She'd been in a rush, saying Tanner was going to be there in what had sounded like seconds.

Tanner had called fifteen minutes later with fifteen minutes left before he was due to pick her up....

She held on to the closet door as her thoughts flew. And screeched to a halt.

Del. He had a car. Visited Tatum at school.

"Oh, God, Tanner, I'm afraid she's with Harcourt," she blurted, telling him about the call she'd had from Tatum.

"I'm going to kill him."

"No, you aren't." Thinking quickly, she spat out the first thing that sounded good to her—because it would keep Tanner safe while they figured out what to do. "Come over here. I'm just out of the shower, but I'll call Tatum and see if she'll pick up. By the time you get here, I'll be ready to go and maybe I'll have some answers for you."

"Shouldn't we call the police?"

"I don't think she's missing, Tanner. She was clearly expecting someone to get her from school half an hour ago. Let me make some calls. If I don't find out anything solid, I'll call you back and we can call the police together. Just come here, okay?"

She didn't want him to do anything foolish. She'd just figured out she loved the man. She couldn't have him ruining his life because his heart was in pieces and he was scared to death.

Even if she couldn't have him, she could help him.

And in that instant, she understood, on a very minute scale, how Tanner must have felt with three younger siblings needing help and him being the only one there to give it. He'd still been a kid himself—and he'd been man enough, even then, to know that it was up to him to look out for them.

Even though, ultimately, there wasn't anything in it for him.

He'd done it because he loved them. Period.

It didn't get any better than that.

TANNER DROVE STRAIGHT to Sedona's. If he'd been in his right mind, he'd have been pounding on Harcourt's front door with the police on the line. But his right mind hadn't been serving him so well lately.

Sedona seemed so sure that he had to be at her place. And so, breaking the speed limit the entire way, he was at her back door in less than twenty minutes.

Dressed in a green suit, with her mane of hair tied back and makeup on her face, she was at the door waiting for him.

"Thank God," she said as she looked him over from head to toe. His breathing faltered as he feared what she'd found out when she'd phoned his sister.

"I was afraid you'd go to the Harcourts' and get yourself arrested for trespassing, or, at the very least, make Tatum so angry with you she'd never speak to you again."

She'd been afraid for him? He shook his head. "Did you get ahold of her?"

"Not exactly."

He studied her face, trying to read what she was withholding from him, needing to know whatever she knew. "What does that mean?"

"I spoke with Del's mother, Callie. She answered the phone."

"Why does Callie Harcourt have my sister's phone?" He just needed her to tell him Tatum was okay. That she was safe and that no harm had come to her.

"Tatum called her and said she needed a ride home from school. Del was already home when they got there and the two of them went out to get some ice cream. Tatum forgot her phone on the counter when she left."

Relief flooded him.

He thought about calling the police. Having Callie Harcourt brought up on charges of kidnapping for taking his underage sister without his permission.

"She said she'd have Tatum call me the second she gets back."

"Does she know who you are?"

Sedona stepped back, pulling him into the small dining area just inside the door. "Yes," she said. "Tatum told her."

"Does she know that Tatum lied to her about not having a ride home from school?"

"I don't think so. She didn't seem to think anything was wrong and I didn't want to alert her and have her warn Tatum before we got to her."

Good thinking.

So, all was not lost. Tatum had gone home from school with a friend without permission. That was all.

They could still fix this....

"Tatum doesn't like ice cream," he said, telling himself again that everything was going to be just fine. He wasn't alone anymore. Tatum had other people who cared and were looking out for her.

"But she likes Del and if he wanted ice cream…"

"It's also not like her to leave her phone anywhere. Especially since she just got it back. That damn thing is more friend to her than any human I know of." He couldn't let it go. Couldn't just sit back and calmly wait for the phone to ring.

Something wasn't right.

Sedona's hand on his got his attention. He looked down to see her slender fingers threading through his. "Relax," she said. "Callie's not going to let anything happen to Tatum. Let's give them half an hour more and then I'll call back."

What was he going to do for half an hour? Did she have any idea what could happen in half an hour?

"Let's go sit outside," she said. "I'll pour some tea." Like the child he'd never been, Tanner let Sedona lead him out to the chair he'd occupied a couple of times before. She left him then, but only long enough to pour their tea.

It was too long.

He didn't want tea. Or to sit. Hands clenched on the arms of the chair, he was on the verge of springing up and getting the hell out of there, heading over to see Callie Harcourt for himself and find out where Del would have taken Tatum for ice cream.

The ringing of Sedona's phone stopped him from trying to make his break.

"It's not her," she said, joining him on the porch without tea, her phone in her hand.

"Hello?"

Her eyes widened and she looked over at Tanner, putting the phone on speaker.

"Tatum? Where are you?"

"I'm at a friend of Del's." Tatum's voice wasn't right. Tanner tensed, shaking his head at Sedona.

"Where's your phone?" It wasn't the question he'd have asked.

Frustrated, Tanner sat powerlessly and listened as a strange-sounding Tatum said, "Del thought I should leave it at his house in case Tanner put a trace on it."

His sudden intake of breath was so sharp his chest hurt. Sedona's hand came down on his and she said, "Why would Tanner put a trace out on your phone?"

"Because I wasn't at school when he went to pick me up. I had Del's mom come get me. He told me to. He said she'd agree to be my guardian and I was going to ask her tonight, but Del said I should wait until after his father goes to bed tonight because that's the best time to talk to her. When she's not distracted by dinner and Del's dad and things."

"Does that sound right to you? That Del's dad goes to bed and then family business is discussed?"

Tanner stared at Tatum's attorney as a strange sense of calm momentarily eased his panic.

"No."

"So why did you accept him telling you so?"

"Because Del's dad is mean."

"And you want to live where the man of the house is mean?"

"No, and Del doesn't, either. That's the point. We're going to make our own life, have our own home, so Del can get away from his dad. His dad hits him, Sedona."

Tanner raised his brows at Sedona.

"Did Mr. Harcourt hit you, too?"

That thought hadn't occurred to him.

Tatum's "No" came before he could process the idea and he gladly let it go.

"So it was Del?"

Tatum's hesitation had Tanner up and out of his chair. He'd *known* it.

"Tatum, where is Del right now?"

"He's outside in the garage with his friend. They had something to do with the car."

"Are you alone?"

"Yeah, but a couple of friends are going to stop by. Some other girls and all. We're going to get ice cream."

"Where?"

"I'm not sure. Someplace they all hang out. I couldn't ever go before because Tanner wouldn't let me."

Hands in his pockets, he paced the small deck. Ellie, who'd been left inside, stood on the other side of the sliding glass door, watching him.

He should have let Tatum have a dog. Something to love that was all her own.

"Whose phone are you using?"

"Del's. I told him I was going to call you to find out what we have to do to get his mom set as my guardian."

Find out where she is. He mouthed the words to Sedona.

"You didn't answer my earlier question," Sedona said into the phone. "Is Del the one who hit you?"

Silence hung on the line again.

"Tatum? Remember, I can't help you if you aren't completely honest with me."

"I mean, he's been mad a couple of times and when he loses it he sometimes does things he doesn't want to do. He can't really help it. His dad's, like, abusive with him. I've been telling him the things that Sara's said to me, and he totally gets it. He's going to talk to his mom about going to counseling and try to get her to go, too. It's like I told you, Sedona. He really loves me and…" Tatum's voice drifted off.

"Tatum?"

"Yeah?"

"You still there?"

"Yeah. I just…I don't know, I felt a little sick for a second, but I'm fine."

She didn't sound fine. She sounded tired. Or something he couldn't put his finger on. When Sedona glanced up at him, he shook his head. And again mouthed the words to find out where Tatum was.

"Have you been feeling sick before just now?"

"No."

"Tatum, was it Del who caused your bruises, who hit you before you came to the shelter?"

He waited.

"I need the complete truth, Tatum."

"Yes."

Tanner breathed.

CHAPTER TWENTY-NINE

Seeing Tanner go white, Sedona almost dropped the phone. Keeping an eye on him, she knew that while he deserved to have her arms around him, deserved to have someone looking out for him, he needed her tending to Tatum.

"So why did you tell me that it was Tanner who hit you?"

"He ruined Talia's life as soon as she fell in love. He was going to do the same to me. Like he thinks, because of Tammy, we couldn't have good relationships with men."

"But why say he hit you?"

Tanner sat down, watching her, his gaze avid, alert.

And his ability to focus somehow kicked hers into full gear. She was in court, doing her job. At her best. And trying to think like a fifteen-year-old.

"Was it because he threw Del out of your house?" Forcing Del to go back to an abusive situation?

"He didn't throw Del out of the house. He told him he had to leave and Del did."

Frowning, her lawyer's ear hearing something important, but unable to pull it out and put everything together, Sedona said, "I wasn't being literal. And you didn't answer my questions. Is that why you blamed Tanner for something he didn't do?"

"Tanner didn't hit me, but I saw him."

"You saw him?"

"He nearly killed a man. With his bare fists. In our house." Tatum's voice faded in and out a bit, as if she were exhausted, as if she didn't have the energy to keep her secrets any longer. "He took me to the neighbors' to get a ride to school, but I had to go to the bathroom and didn't want to go over there so I ran back home to go and when I walked in the back door, Tanner was pummeling this guy in our living room. He just kept hitting him, Sedona. Over and over. The guy was bleeding and stumbling, and Tanner hit him some more and then he opened the front door and picked him up and threw him down the front steps. I was so scared I ran out the back door and back to the neighbors' before he found me...."

She had to turn her back on the look of horror on Tanner's face. She couldn't feel his pain and do her job.

"Did you tell anyone what you saw?"

"No! Tanner was... We couldn't make it without him. I was afraid to get him in trouble."

Tatum had been five the day that Tammy had finally brought her young family to the ground. The woman's actions that day had inspired consequences that had irrevocably changed all of their lives.

And had driven all of them ever since.

"Did you ask him about it?"

"No. When I got home from school, everything was

normal and I just… I guess I pretended it didn't happen. I didn't think about it anymore and Tanner was always so nice and never yelled. And then, when Del… That first time he hit me…I remembered it all. Like, it made me sick. And then Del said he didn't mean to hit me. And he was so sorry and he was usually always so nice and sweet, and he was always telling me how much he loved me…."

Her voice faded off.

"Tatum?" The girl seemed to have fallen asleep. "Are you feeling okay?" It was an inane question considering that they'd just relived a ten-year-old nightmare.

"Not really," she groaned sleepily. "I'm kind of sick to my stomach."

Tanner had said the girl reacted that way to stress. She heard him move behind her but didn't turn around. Tatum could be her only concern at the moment.

"I need you to tell me where you are," she said. "If Del is as good a guy as you say, he wouldn't want you to hide from your attorney, would he? I mean there'd be no reason, right?"

"I guess not." She was starting to sound more confused. Alarm shot through Sedona.

"Where are you?"

"I'm not sure of the address, but…" Tatum went on to describe the neighborhood, the turns they'd made at the end. Enough so that, with Del's car out front, someone who knew the area should be able to find the house quickly.

"I have a police friend, a woman, who I'm going to call," Sedona said with a calm she absolutely did not feel. "I want you to stay where you are, no matter what Del says, until my friend gets there, okay?"

"Okay. I'm really not feeling well."

Tanner moved again. A chair fell over.

"I can hear that, sweetie. Just go out front and wait. Can you do that for me?"

"Yeah."

"I'm going to call my friend now, but I'll keep you on the line, okay?"

"Okay."

Tanner's phone appeared in front of Sedona and without looking at anything but the hand that held it out to her, she took the phone, dialed a friend of hers— Donna Brady, a beat cop on the Santa Raquel police force—and described to her where she'd find Tatum Malone. Telling her to hurry.

Donna didn't hang up as she expected, but rather kept Sedona on the phone while she drove, and at Donna's instruction, Sedona asked Tatum if she'd had anything to eat or drink lately.

"Only the lemonade Del gave me before he went outside with his friend."

"Who poured it?" Donna asked. So Sedona asked Tatum.

"Del did. I had to use the restroom and when I came back to the living room he told me he was going out to the garage for a few and gave me the lemonade. He knew I was thirsty…." The words fell off.

"Hurry." Sedona told Donna what was going on.

"Sounds like a derivative of 'X,'" Donna said. "We've had four busts in area schools in the past six months. Just small amounts, though. Shouldn't be anything serious."

"Tell her to take her straight to the hospital," Tanner said, loudly enough for everyone on both phones to hear. "I'll meet her there."

With both phones still at her ears, Sedona hurried after him, making it inside the opened passenger door of his truck before he burned rubber down her driveway.

"TAMMY WAS A user part of the time she was pregnant with Tatum." Tanner was talking as quickly as he drove through the streets of Santa Raquel to reach the small county hospital just outside of town. "By some miracle Tatum was born clean, but she could be more susceptible to stimulation."

Sedona told Donna, who called for a paramedic backup and then, apparently sighting Tatum, said, "We've got her, I'm hanging up now."

"Tatum?" Sedona said into her other phone. "You still there, hon?"

"Uh-huh. I think your friend's here."

"Son of a bitch. What's going on?" The voice, young and male and clearly angry, came from the background of Tatum's phone. "Give me that..." was the last thing Sedona heard before the line went dead.

Tanner's stonelike expression told her that he'd heard the muffled words, as well.

"Donna's there," she said. "She'll make sure Tatum's safe."

For the moment. But until they knew what Del might have put in her drink, or how much of it, she couldn't make any other promises.

"DID TATUM KNOW she could be particularly sensitive to illegal substances?" Sedona's question was soft as she came up beside Tanner in the hallway outside the hospital examining room where a team of medical personnel were doing various things to his sister.

No, of course she hadn't known. He'd opted not to tell her. "I didn't want her to label herself. Tammy used some when she was carrying Talia and Thomas, too, but not as much."

Yet, the courts had still given Tammy's babies to her.

And once they were home, those babies became his.

"Do they know?"

"Yes. I told them both when they turned sixteen. I figured they were old enough by then to have formed a healthy self-concept, and they were also entering the age when they'd be tempted to try drugs."

"Kids are experimenting at twelve and thirteen these days."

"None of the three was automatically going to be affected by Tammy's addiction. It was just that they *could* be." Sedona's hand slid into his and he held on. For a moment, he knew a strange moment of calm.

Looking over at her, he wanted to smile but couldn't yet. Not until he knew Tatum was going to be fine.

"Thank you for being here," he said instead.

"You don't need to thank me, Tanner. You should be thanking yourself."

"What for?"

"Because you are the most honorable man I've ever met. And that honor, that integrity, saved the lives of three very endangered children."

He needed to believe that.

"When push came to shove, Tatum called, didn't she?"

"You, not me."

"You set me up as your go-between. You approved of me. She knows you're my friend and that I wasn't going to be able to be impartial. And when she was in trouble, or even sensed she might be, she called me." Sedona kept her voice low, in deference to the others around them, he was sure. "Clearly, after Del's hitting her triggered the trauma from the past and she needed to tell someone, she couldn't go to you, especially since she'd just found that GED application. She couldn't trust you and she had no one else." She paused and saw that she had his complete attention.

"She had what it took to get help, Tanner. And that is certainly a tribute to you. To her upbringing."

"I lied to you."

"You made a difficult choice for the best reasons."

Tatum had seen him beating the crap out of the last

creep Tammy had brought to their home. "I can't believe she saw me beating that guy and I didn't know." He and Sedona walked up and down the small hallway, passing an empty gurney, an unused IV pole.

"All this time she's never said a word."

"I don't think she remembered, Tanner. Not until Harcourt hit her. Kids suppress things all the time. Particularly when it's something they can't handle. It probably would have come up in hypnosis, though."

"Mr. Malone?"

He shot over to the curtain where the doctor was standing. "Yes?"

"You can go in now. I'd let her rest about another hour or so and then you can take her home."

"She's okay?"

"She's going to be fine. A little nauseous probably, but fine."

"Was she drugged?"

"We found a trace of a drug similar to 'X' in her blood work." He gave an official name Tanner didn't recognize. "There wasn't enough of it in her system to do much more than make her sleepy. Either there wasn't enough of it in the drink, or she didn't consume the whole glass—either way, she's lucky."

Lucky? He'd never thought of any of them in that light.

Stepping around the curtain, he sought his sister's gaze. He had to see her face, to look in her eyes, and then he'd breathe again.

THE FIRST THING he saw when he entered the small cubicle was her lips. They were cracked and dry. And then he noticed the tears on her cheeks.

"Hey, Baby Tay, it's okay." His nickname for her slipped out. When had he stopped using it?

"Tanner?"

"I'm right here, sweetie."

"I saw you, Tanner. I saw you beat that guy and I was afraid you were going to kill him."

Tatum wasn't feeling well. She didn't need any more trauma.

"I'm glad you finally told us." Sedona came up behind him. On the same side of the bed as him. Standing just to the left of his elbow.

Her arm slid around him.

And something hit home. In an emergency hospital room. With his sister crying in the bed.

Someone had his back.

Sedona had his back.

"That day you're talking about, I'd come back from dropping you off next door and I heard Tammy take money from that man in exchange for letting him get in the shower with Talia." Bile rose in his throat as he exposed his baby sister to the dirtiness, but he knew now that he couldn't keep his secrets anymore. He couldn't wipe Tammy away. "The guy was her supplier and she needed a fix."

Tanner told his sister the sordid details, his instincts bucking him the whole way.

"That's why you beat him up?" Tatum stared at him, her cloudy eyes clearing.

"Yes."

"She told me about Rex," Tatum said then, staring at Tanner openly, as if she was seeing him for the first time. Or maybe finding the man she recognized within the stranger he'd become. Whatever, it felt good having that look directed at him again. "About him being a teacher and it being against the law for them to be together, since she was a student," she said slowly. "Even if you didn't press charges, he'd have been charged."

Talia told him that she and Tatum had talked briefly. She'd never said what about.

"That's right."

"She also told me that she's thinking about looking for her baby. Just to know that he's okay."

Tatum's eyes narrowed as she watched him.

"I think it's a good idea," he said, meaning it.

"If she wants your help, you'll help her?"

"Of course."

She nodded. "I thought so."

Then she smiled, and it hit him that she was really going to be okay. *They* were going to be okay. He could feel the prick of tears behind his eyes and needed a moment to find the calm.

Instincts ingrained from childhood drove him to turn away. "I love you, big brother." Tatum's voice was groggy, but called him back to her.

"I love you, too, Baby Tay."

It would take some getting used to—this sharing

of secrets—but he figured he'd best get the hang of it. The women in his life weren't going to let him slide away from their piercing gazes again.

LATER THAT EVENING Sedona found herself watching a movie at the Malone farm with Tanner and Tatum.

Tatum had picked the film: a classic Sedona had seen at least a dozen times. One to do with old-fashioned family summer vacations and dancing and falling in love.

There'd been more tears that evening as Tatum's ordeal with Del Harcourt had come more completely to light—to the girl as much as to anyone else. Sara had made an impromptu house call, and as Tatum revealed all of the things Del had told her, it had become clear that the boy had been using his father's tactics to keep Tatum right where he wanted her.

To his credit, he probably did love her. He just didn't know how to love.

Tatum knew, however, after what she'd learned at The Stand coupled with the latest events in her life, that she didn't love Del. She'd been afraid of so many things. And Del had played into her fears.

"I was lonely," she'd told Tanner at dinner. "You were in the vineyard or the winery so much and when you came in you were always tired."

Pretending to be watching the movie, Sedona replayed the past few hours in her mind, figuring that Tanner must be doing the same. Since they'd found Tatum, he hadn't given her any indication whether she was more than a friend to him or just Tatum's attorney, other than inviting her to stay for dinner and watch the movie with them.

He hadn't had a personal word, or even shared an intimate glance with her since they'd helped Tatum into the backseat of the truck to bring her home.

"When you got Talia to quit talking to me I didn't know what to do," Tatum had said during dinner.

Tanner had listened—so patient and full of love for his sister—and Sedona had almost been jealous. Would he ever care for her as much as he cared for his siblings?

Was he capable of caring for anyone else that much?

"Then when I met Del and found that GED application…and Del hit me, I started remembering more and more about that day when I was little and I didn't have anyone to talk to and…I just got so confused."

Tanner had decided not to press charges against Del Harcourt for lacing Tatum's drink after he agreed, at Tatum's request, never to contact her or in any way bother her again. There was still the possibility that the police would file their own charges against him, however.

And with the little bug Sedona had placed in Donna's ear, they were going to be looking at the boy's father, too.

"I'd never felt like Del made me feel. It was like he looked up to me. But then I tried to get him to stop smoking pot and he hit me when I threw his joint away. He was so sorry and so sweet and swore it wouldn't happen again, and it didn't, but then…later…I wouldn't stand up to you and he hit me again. I wanted to tell you, but then, like, out of nowhere, I remembered that day I'd seen you beat up that guy and it all just got so messed up."

Sedona had asked if she'd told Del about that day so long ago.

She would probably never forget the humble expression on Tanner's face when the girl said she couldn't do that to her brother.

She'd just set out to prove to Del that she didn't put Tanner first.

Which was when the manipulation had really started to get dangerous.

Now, sitting in the Malone living room, looking from one sibling to the other, Sedona felt like the unlucky one.

She'd had a blessed childhood. Wonderful parents who loved her still. How could she possibly be envious of the life the Malones had endured?

But she knew. The love she'd known she'd taken for granted. She hadn't realized the worth of it. She'd just always imagined that someday she'd meet a man she loved like her mother loved her father, and all would be well.

She hadn't understood—as the Malones did, as her parents did, as Grady did, even—that love grew in the face of adversity.

Love conquered adversity.

She'd never personally experienced that kind of love.

Until now, sitting in that living room, feeling the love that had seen four children through more adversity than anyone should ever have to endure.

Tatum was going to be fine.

Because of the foundation Tanner—and in a smaller way, Talia and Thomas—had given her.

"Nobody puts Baby in a corner." Sedona heard the famous line coming from the stereo system Tanner had hooked up to his television. The movie was ending.

"So, what's up with you two just sitting there?" Tatum sat up on the sofa, a furry blanket spread across her lap, as she addressed her brother. "You need me to head up to bed so you can do, you know, whatever?"

"No!" Tanner sat forward. "You're fine."

"And you're in love," Tatum said in a saucy voice, and then looked to Sedona. "Since my brother has now shown that his greatest fault is an inability to tell people things that are important for them to know, and because I'm the luckiest girl on earth to have him, I'm going to do him a favor and just say it for him. Tanner loves you."

He coughed. "You do," Tatum insisted. "You've never, ever, let anyone step in for you. Not the police. Not child services. Not anyone. But you let her. You could only do that if you loved her."

Taking her cue from her fifteen-year-old ex-client, Sedona looked at Tanner. "Do you?" she asked. "Because I have to tell you, I'm head over heels in love with you, and you know how determined I am to get married and stay that way forever."

"Like your parents," Tatum said.

"That's right."

"Okay." Tanner stood, holding up both hands in a gesture of surrender. "I can't take it from two of you at once. Yes, Baby Tay, since you offered, please go to bed. Make some noise when you get up in the morning. And I'm going to tell you right now, you'll probably see Sedona's car still here."

"Cool!" Tatum stood up, her long slender legs seeming to be steady and strong. "So it's gone that far? Like, when we go see Thomas this summer, we'll be, like, legal and all?"

"If Sedona will have me."

"You have to ask her, big brother."

Sedona had dreamed of her once-in-a-lifetime proposal her entire life. She and the guy would be having a candlelit dinner on the beach. He'd pass her a rose and there'd be a diamond attached. It didn't have to be big. It just had to be accompanied by the right words.

Tatum turned to leave, her blanket trailing on the ground behind her, and Sedona said, "Wait."

The girl turned back, her gray-blue eyes looking expectantly at Sedona.

"I need a witness," Sedona said, the words becoming clear to her as she spoke them. "Tanner Malone, will you marry me?"

The man coughed again.

"I think that was a 'yes,'" Tatum said.

"Scram, brat." Tanner got those words out quite clearly.

And spent the rest of the night giving Sedona his answer.

"SEDONA?"

She'd been dozing. After hours of lovemaking and talking about the innocuous things that most people discuss when they first meet. Like favorite movies and colors.

"Yeah?"

"Will you marry me?"

"Of course. I thought we'd already covered that."

"Soon?"

"We can fly to Vegas tomorrow and get married with Talia as a witness if you want." Now that she knew what really mattered, dreams of her huge wedding flew right out the window. She couldn't wait that long. Tatum was home. Talia was coming home. The family was flying to New York to see Thomas and meet his fiancée. She couldn't miss any of it.

"Tatum has finals."

"Then Saturday is fine."

"What will your parents say?"

"Bring Dad a bottle of your wine when we tell them and they'll be on the plane with us."

She said the words. But knew that her parents would be on that plane without any kind of bribe at all.

Because they loved her.
And she loved Tanner.
It really was that simple.

* * * * *

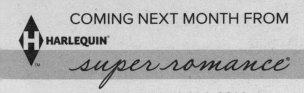
#1932 COP BY HER SIDE
The Mysteries of Angel Butte • by Janice Kay Johnson

No way is Lieutenant Jane Vahalik giving Sergeant Clay Renner a second chance. Their brief romance is history! But when her niece is kidnapped, suddenly Clay is the only cop Jane trusts to solve the case. And being this close to him shows Jane another side of the man....

#1933 CHALLENGING MATT
Those Hollister Boys • by Julianna Morris

For Layne McGraw, clearing her late uncle's name is all-important. Proving he wasn't an embezzler isn't easy. Especially when Matt Hollister gets involved. The former playboy has his own reasons for helping her—and the attraction between them could derail everything.

#1934 HEARTS IN VEGAS • by Colleen Collins

When former jewel thief turned investigator Frances Jefferies is sent to retrieve a stolen diamond, one thing stands in her way: bodyguard Braxton Morgan. She has to succeed to clear her record, which makes him a sexy distraction she doesn't need.

#1935 A SINCLAIR HOMECOMING
The Sinclairs of Alaska • by Kimberly Van Meter

Wade Sinclair has finally come home to Alaska after his sister's murder eight years ago. His family is struggling. When psychiatrist Morgan O'Hare is called in, Wade and Morgan can't fight the attraction between them. With Morgan's help, Wade can finally move on and embrace the future—with Morgan.

#1936 A PERFECT TRADE
by Anna Sugden

Should she make a deal with a man she no longer trusts? With her life in shambles, Jenny Martin doesn't have much choice. Professional hockey player Tru Jelinek has the money she needs and he owes her. It's a good trade as long as their attraction doesn't interfere!

#1937 DATING A SINGLE DAD
by Kris Fletcher

Brynn Catalano is everyone's rock. She doesn't think twice about taking a temp job to help her cousin in crisis. Before she knows it, though, gorgeous Hank North and his sweet little daughter make her feel like staying...and putting her own happiness first, for once.

Cop by Her Side

By **Janice Kay Johnson**

When Lieutenant Jane Vahalik met
Seargent Clay Renner she thought she'd
finally found the one man who could accept that
she was a cop. Too bad he proved that wrong.
So why does she get a thrill when he calls out
of the blue? Read on for an exciting excerpt of
the upcoming book **COP BY HER SIDE**
by Janice Kay Johnson, the latest in
The Mysteries of Angel Butte series.

Jane felt a weird twist in her chest when she saw the displayed
name on her cell phone. Clay Renner. Somehow, despite the
disastrous end to their brief relationship, she'd never deleted
his phone number from her address book. Why would *he* be
calling in the middle of the afternoon?

"Vahalik."

"Jane, Clay Renner here."

As always, she reacted to his voice in a way that aggravated
her. It was so blasted *male*.

"Sergeant," she said stiffly.

"This is about your sister." He hesitated. "We've found
Melissa's vehicle located in a ditch. She suffered a head injury,
Jane. She's in ICU. But I'm focusing on another problem.

The girl, Brianna, is missing."

Of all the things she'd expected him to say, this didn't even come close.

"*What?*" she whispered. "Did anyone see the accident?"

"Unfortunately, no. Some hikers came along afterward."

"If another car caused the accident and the driver freaked…?" Even in shock, she knew that was stupid.

"A logical assumption, except that we've been unable to locate Brianna. We still haven't given up hope that your sister dropped her off somewhere, but at this point—"

"You have no idea where she is." Ouch. She sounded so harsh.

"Thanks for the vote of confidence, Lieutenant."

She closed her eyes. As angry as she still was at him, she knew he was a smart cop and a strong man. He didn't need her attitude. "I'm sorry. I didn't mean…"

"We're organizing a search."

She swallowed, trying to think past her panic. "I'll come help search."

"All right," Clay said. He told her where the SUV had gone off the road. "You okay to drive?"

"Of course I am!"

"Then I'll look for you."

Those were the most reassuring words he'd said during the entire conversation. And as Jane disconnected, she didn't want to think about how much she wanted *his* reassurance.

**Will this case bring Clay and Jane together?
Find out what happens in COP BY HER SIDE
by Janice Kay Johnson, available July 2014 from
Harlequin® Superromance®.
And look for the other books in
The Mysteries of Angel Butte series.**

HSRLP13R